W9-BKR-912

A Town Called Ruby Prairie

Center Point
Large Print

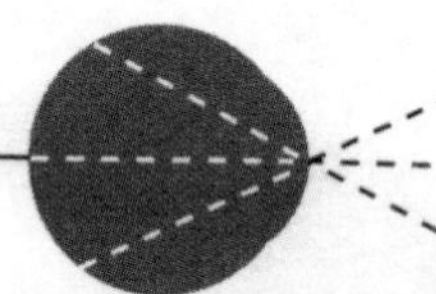

A Town Called Ruby Prairie

ANNETTE SMITH

CENTER POINT PUBLISHING
THORNDIKE, MAINE

This Center Point Large Print edition
is published in the year 2006 by arrangement with
Moody Publishers.

The text of this Large Print edition is unabridged. In other aspects, this book may vary from the original edition. Printed in Thailand. Set in 16-point Times New Roman type.

ISBN 1-58547-847-4

Library of Congress Cataloging-in-Publication Data

Smith, Annette Gail, 1959-
A town called Ruby Prairie / Annette Smith.--Center Point large print ed.
p. cm.
Originally published: Chicago : Moody Publishers, 2004, in series:
Smith, Annette Gail, 1959- . Coming home to Ruby Prairie series.
ISBN 1-58547-847-4 (lib. bdg. : alk. paper)
1. Foster home care--Fiction. 2. Problem youth--Fiction. 3. Widows--Fiction.
4. Girls--Fiction. 5. Large type books. I. Title.

PS3619.M55T69 2006
813'.6--dc22

2006011973

To the memory of
my grandma,
Ruby Woodall

Chapter One

The little cat lay heavy, warm, and limp in Charlotte Carter's lap—bleeding right onto her new white pants. She stroked the animal with one hand and struggled to hold the phone and punch numbers with the other. After four long rings, an answer.

"Hello?"

Her words tumbled out in a hyperventilated rush. "Have I reached Dr. Ross? the veterinarian?"

"You have. Who's calling?"

"It's Snowball . . . I mean, it's Charlotte. Charlotte Carter. We met last Sunday. At church."

There was a thoughtful pause. "Mrs. Carter. Yes, I remember. You were sitting by yourself, toward the back. Do you wear glasses?"

"Yes. Sometimes. I need them for reading. About my—"

"Of course. I remember now, Mrs. Carter. I'm a deacon at Lighted Way, and I read your visitor card. You bought Tanglewood, didn't you? A great old house. I'm sure you'll fit right in at Lighted Way. You do realize that wasn't our regular preacher. Pastor Jock was out of town. But we were glad to have you anyway. Hope you'll come back. Nice of you to call, Mrs. Carter."

"Thank you. Yes. I will. I mean I'll try to. Uh, Dr. Ross, what I'm calling about is my cat. I know it's late, and I am so sorry to bother you at home; but I didn't know who to call, and I'm afraid she just got hit by a car. I—I found her in the middle of the street, a good quarter mile from my house—which doesn't make any sense because Snowball has never been one to wander."

"Cats tend to roam when they're in a new place," said Dr. Ross. "You did just move here?"

"Yes. Two weeks ago tomorrow."

"Mrs. Carter, have you ever taught Sunday school?"

"Yes, but Snow—"

"Wonderful. Now you know cats will roam till they get settled in. You might want to keep her inside till she gets used to the new place. An old wives' tale says that if you put butter between a cat's toes it won't try to go back to its old home. Never put much stock in the procedure myself, though." Dr. Ross chuckled. "I'm trying to remember now. Is it the third graders or the fifth graders who need someone to fill in?"

"Yes, sir. About my cat—I planned on keeping her inside for a while, but it's sort of too late. You see, at first I thought she was just an empty sack or some trash or something, but when I got closer . . ."

This time Charlotte's words got through.

"You say she got hit? Your cat? How's her breathing?"

"Kind of funny."

"She trying to fight you?"

"No." Stroking the limp cat, Charlotte tried not to cry.

"We best take a look. Have you got a cat carrier? No? Well, then, wrap her up in a towel and put her in a box. I'll meet you at the clinic. You know where it is?"

"Just down from the post office?"

"That's right. Four Paws Pet Clinic. Sign's out front."

Charlotte wiped her eyes on the tail of her shirt.

"Don't get in any hurry. Be careful. Are you okay to drive?"

"I think so. Yes. I am." She had to be.

"Okay. See you in ten minutes."

Charlotte eased the injured cat out of her lap and onto a kitchen chair and raced through the house looking for a box. A shoe box, a packing box, any kind of box. But as she'd unpacked her things, she had carted all the boxes to the curb, and the garbage truck had come yesterday.

Think, Charlotte. Think. She made herself take a deep breath. Pantry.

Crackers. They came in a box.

Charlotte grabbed the cracker box and emptied it out onto the kitchen counter.

"Mew," came a weak sound.

"Hold on," Charlotte called to the cat. The way the cracker box was shaped, she'd need to tape up the end and cut an opening in the side. Masking tape? Duct tape? Did she even have any? Charlotte scrambled through drawer after drawer but did not find a thing. Drat! What was she thinking? Snowball was not going to fit in a cracker box! What now?

She dashed to her bedroom. Yes! She pulled out her lingerie drawer and dumped all her underwear out onto the bed. This would do. Once she'd wrapped Snowball in a pink bath towel and set her in the drawer, off they went.

Or at least, off they went once Charlotte found her keys.

Dr. Ross, short, squat, and dressed in his everyday uniform of blue work pants and a loose-fitting embroidered Mexican shirt, was waiting when they arrived. It was almost eleven.

"Let's see here." He lifted Snowball out of the drawer and laid her on the exam table. Matted with blood and mud, the little thing was so injured that she didn't even try to get away.

The vet snapped on a pair of latex gloves and flipped on a bright overhead light. After giving the cat a shot to ease her pain, he proceeded to look her over from head to tail.

"How bad is she?" asked Charlotte.

"Not good. See how her hip's positioned? Got some broken bones in that back leg, probably in both back legs. I'll X-ray her. Probably has other injuries, too. Belly's hard as a rock."

"That's not good?"

"Internal bleeding."

"What can you do for her?"

Dr. Ross sighed. "Mrs. Carter, after thirty-seven years of practice, I still hate this part. We've got a couple of options."

Charlotte stroked the cat's chin. She thought she detected a weak little purr.

"I can do surgery on her and maybe fix her up. But nothing's for sure."

"Surgery?"

He nodded. "Cats are tricky. Patching her up will be expensive. Could run close to a thousand dollars, and there's no guarantee that she'll be all right when we're done. It might be better to think about putting her to—"

"Can I pay it out?" Charlotte cut him off.

Dr. Ross looked up.

Charlotte bit her lip. "I'm not one to fuss over animals. I understand there comes a time when it's best to put them down. But Snowball belonged to my late husband, J.D. He was a fool over her. Kept one hook baited on his trotline down at our little pond just so she could have her fresh fish. So many times I've watched him sit and pick the bones out of a catfish and feed it to Snowball right out of his hand."

Dr. Ross peeled off his gloves and took a seat on a stool. "How long has your husband been gone, Mrs. Carter?"

"It's Charlotte. Six months."

"I see. I'm sorry to hear of your loss. I can't help but wonder what's brought a new widow like you to Ruby Prairie. We've not exactly got a booming metropolis here. There aren't many jobs for a person unless you're a schoolteacher or a nurse or you own some kind of business. I don't recall any Carters in Ruby

Prairie. Are your people from around here?"

"No. Just me." Charlotte wasn't inclined to share more.

The short-acting shot began to wear off. Snowball raised her head, looked at Charlotte, then lay back down.

"I don't think I can let her go just yet," said Charlotte, her voice tight.

"Okay then." Dr. Ross stood up and patted Charlotte's hand. "I'll do my best to fix the little gal up. Let me call Lindy, my granddaughter. She assists me when I do surgery. Soon as she can get up here, I'll take Snowball back and we'll get started. In the meantime, you go on home and get some rest. Jot down your number, and we'll call you when we're finished. It may take several hours."

Charlotte hesitated. "May I stay with her till you're ready to start?"

"Sure." Dr. Ross went to make coffee.

"Poor baby." Charlotte stroked Snowball's bloody, matted fur. "You're going be all right. Yes, you are." Tears fell. "Doctor's gonna take good care of you. You'll be out catching a mouse before you know it."

How in the world am I going pay for all this? She hadn't budgeted for such an expense. And until she got the money from . . .

The kitty looked up with adoring blue eyes.

Within fifteen minutes a teenaged girl—apparently the granddaughter—popped her head into the exam room where Charlotte waited with Snowball. She had dressed for surgery in snowman-print pajama bottoms, pink flip-flops, and a Camp Red Oak T-shirt, size extra small.

"Hi. I'm Lindy. Sorry about your cat," she said as she pulled her hair back into a ponytail. "Granddad says she got hit."

"She did. I appreciate you coming up here in the middle of the night."

"No problem." Lindy yawned as she headed toward the back. "I'll see if he's ready for her." A moment later she was back: "Time to take her on back."

Charlotte gave the white cat one final rub behind the ears. "You be a sweet kitty. I'll be back."

"Don't worry," said Lindy. "We'll call you."

The night J.D. brought Snowball home, he had found her wet and mad, weaned but missing her mother. She was out alone in the rain, yowling her head off in the parking lot of a gas station where J.D. had stopped to fill up on his way home. When nobody claimed her, he scooped up the kitten and tucked her inside his sweatshirt jacket.

He'd come in the front door empty-handed, feigning ignorance of the little white head sticking out of his coat. "Cat? What cat?" he had teased.

How she missed that man. Only six months since he died, a year since he was first diagnosed.

"*The bad news is that just as we suspected, the tumor was malignant. The good news is we think we got it all.*"

Nervous smiles all around.

Final bill in the mail.

Then weight loss.

Pain.

Loss of balance.

And optimism that quickly wore thin.

The doctors were wrong. Like a hidden hot ember left smoldering in the attic of a once-burned house, J.D.'s cancer came back with a fury, tongues of it infiltrating lymph nodes, lungs, liver, and brain.

Turning down offer after offer of assistance from friends and extended family, Charlotte did everything for her husband. Bathed him, turned him, cleaned him up. She slept on a camp cot inches from his hospital bed in their living room. It was when she left him for ten minutes to sit alone on the front stoop of their house, to rest her back against the cold concrete steps and inhale her first whiff of outside air in three days, that J.D. chose to take his leave.

"Where is everybody?" he'd asked her the day before.

"Who, sweetheart? It's just you and me."

"Mother and Daddy. Grandma and little Jackson. They were just here. Standing right there."

Gone to glory. All four of them.

Seems they had come to bear her husband away.

For the first time since her move, weary and worried, Charlotte allowed doubts to enter her mind. Well-meaning friends and family had implored her not to make any major decisions or changes until at least a year after J.D.'s death. She'd politely listened to all their advice, then, true to her lone-ranger nature, gone against every word of it. What was the point of waiting some arbitrary length of time? Charlotte knew exactly what she wanted to do with the rest of her life.

Would things work out according to plan? She hoped so. She'd prayed so. As soon as the money came in and all the legal stuff was settled, she could get on with her dream. And, as far as she could tell, Ruby Prairie was the perfect location for what she had in mind. Good schools. Good churches. Low cost of living. Small-town values.

She'd done her research, but one could never be sure.

The drive home took ten minutes. In her haste to get Snowball to the vet she had neglected to turn on the porch light, and the night was dark and moonless. Not yet adjusted to the worrisome bifocals her forty-year-old eyes had only recently begun to require, Charlotte carefully picked her way across the yard, avoiding gopher holes. Had she locked the house? She couldn't remember but paused to dig in her purse for her keys just in case.

"Meow."

Charlotte jumped.

"Meow. Meow."

She felt soft fur against her ankles.

What was this? Charlotte only had one cat. A white one. Which was the color of the cat at her feet.

A small one.

Which was the size of the one at her feet.

Doing her best to avoid tripping over the strange cat, Charlotte made her way to the porch and turned on the light. It couldn't be.

"Snowball?"

"Meow."

"Snowball?"

"Meow. Meow." The cat's message was clear: *Where have you been? I'm hungry. And what* is *that strange cat smell that's all over you?*

Charlotte sat down hard in the rocking chair next to her front door. Snowball jumped up on her lap. The cat's erect tail grazed her face as the she padded back and forth across Charlotte's knees.

"Oh my."

She didn't know whether to laugh or cry. So she did a little of both.

At ten past eight the next morning, Charlotte heard the phone ring.

"Dr. Ross here. Mrs. Carter, we're done, and I've got good news. Only one leg's broken, and the internal injuries weren't as bad as I first thought. You should be able to pick up your cat by the end of the week. Uh, can you hold on just a sec?"

He held his hand over the mouthpiece of the phone.

"Sorry 'bout that," said Dr. Ross. "Lindy's filling out the records on your cat right now. What did you say her name was?"

"Visa," said Charlotte. "Just put down Visa."

Lord, prayed Charlotte later that day, *I told You I was ready to take in a few extras, ready to take care* of *them, love them, provide them with what they need. I've got to be honest, Lord. A stray cat was not what I had in mind.*

She held Snowball in her lap and let her mind drift. If things went according to plan, Visa—the lucky kitty of mistaken identity—would not be the last stray to come to live at her new Ruby Prairie home.

Chapter Two

Kerilynn Bell, mayor of Ruby Prairie and owner of the 'Round the Clock Cafe, came up behind Chilly Reed and nudged his arm. "You boys planning on ordering or paying rent on this booth?" Chilly jumped. "Why you always sneaking up like that?" he asked.

"Not sneaking up on nobody. You're just goosey 'cause you're feeling guilty. If you hadn't been gossiping you'd of known I was here." She poured them coffee without being asked. "What're y'all having?"

As if she didn't know. Chilly and his sidekick, Gabe Eden, would have the Thursday Morning Special—two eggs over easy, coffee, and a side of hash browns for $2.29—just as they did every week.

"I'll have the special," said Chilly.

"Me too," said Gabe.

Kerilynn didn't bother to write it down. She went to the kitchen and returned in a few minutes with their food.

"Single gal?" Chilly was asking.

"What I hear," said Gabe.

Gabe looked up at Kerilynn. "Sugar, you gonna bring us some extra biscuits?"

"More biscuits!" fussed Kerilynn, refilling their coffee cups. "You boys 'bout run me ragged. No wonder I can't keep any meat on these bones. Speaking of which, Gabe Eden, the way your gut's swelled up, looks like you've got a case of biscuit poisoning already. You sure you don't want dry toast instead?"

"Yeah. Bring him dry toast. Make it whole wheat." Chilly winked at Kerilynn as she headed back to the kitchen.

Gabe ignored them both.

"Come on. What you figure a woman by herself is doing buying a big place like Tanglewood? That house has got five bedrooms at least. And what does it sit on—an acre and a half?"

"Six," corrected Chilly, who dabbled in real estate on the side. "Little better'n an acre. She ain't bought it yet, though. Got a lease with an option."

"That right? Still, seems to me that's an awful big place for a single gal."

"She's not single. She's a widow. Could be she's putting in one of them bed-and-breakfast joints. Or a beauty parlor. Might be a gift shop. Maybe she sells Amway. Place is big enough she could live upstairs and have a business down below."

"I reckon." Gabe sipped from his cup. "You seen her?"

"Yep. She was at church last Sunday. Got out before I could meet her, though."

"Nice looking?"

"Better'n average."

"Pretty as me?" Bottle-blonde Kerilynn, grandmother of three, was back with hot biscuits—which she held just out of the reach of both men.

"Nowhere near, darlin'," said Gabe.

"Good answer." She plopped the biscuit basket down dead center in front of his plate and sashayed her skinny self back to the kitchen.

"Come in, girls," said Sassy Clyde to the arriving members of the Ruby Prairie Women's Culture Club. "Make yourselves at home."

Ginger Collins, fearful of dogs all her life, lingered on the front stoop.

"Ginger, you're clear. I've got the dogs put up in the guest bedroom."

Nomie Jenkins, this year's Culture Club president, called the meeting to order. "We've got lots to discuss tonight, ladies. Let's get started. Lucky?"

Lucky Jamison, at eighty-four the club's oldest member, led the group in prayer as she'd done every month for the past forty-odd years. When she was finished, Sassy began serving refreshments, with Kerilynn's help.

"Everybody having spiced tea? I've got cream cheese pound cake for the regulars and sugar-free angel food for the diabetics."

"As I said," continued Nomie, once everyone had cake, "we've lots to discuss. First on the agenda is a possible new member. Charlotte Carter's her name, and she's just moved to Ruby Prairie."

"Carter," said Lucky. "Don't believe I know any Carters. Her people from around here?"

"Don't believe so," said Nomie. "Ginger, can you hand me another packet of Sweet 'N Low? I need another smidgen of pound cake too, please."

"Where'd she come from?" asked Sassy.

"Somewhere up North," said Alice Buck.

"Oklahoma City," said Kerilynn.

"Les and I called upon her the night she moved in," said Ginger. "We didn't go inside, just stood out on the porch."

"She didn't ask you in?" said Alice.

"No. Said she'd been painting her bathroom. That's probably why. I took her some honey whole-wheat oatmeal bread I made from scratch in the machine Les gave me for Valentine's Day. She seemed like a sweet person."

"Did you mention the club to her?" asked Lucky.

"I did. She said it sounded like a good organization, but I got the impression she needed some time to get settled before she made any big decisions."

"What's her husband do?" asked Lucky.

"Poor thing doesn't have one. She's a widow," said

Ginger. "I got the impression she was a young woman," said Nomie. "She is. About forty would be my best guess."

"Children?" asked Sassy.

"Doesn't have any."

"Bless her heart," chorused the others in the room.

"Why'd she move to Ruby Prairie?" asked Sassy.

"I didn't ask. It didn't seem right to get too personal standing on her porch. Besides, Les was in a hurry to get back to the house. Remember? That was the night *Home and Garden* ran their special on compost."

The ladies of the Ruby Prairie Women's Culture Club took their tea sipping seriously—so much so that if an uninformed visitor to the community chose to listen to the good-natured complaints of the men gathered at the 'Round the Clock Cafe on meeting night, that person would be led to believe that every bit of what the club ladies did was sit around and drink tea.

As if any of them would know.

Most any day of the week, beneath the manicured fingernails of the ladies' properly curled pinkies could be found traces of flour, sugar, peat moss, and potting mix. Established in 1912, the Women's Culture Club was Ruby Prairie's most active civic organization.

Despite their preference for tea in china cups, fancy desserts, and getting dressed up on a weeknight, the ladies made important contributions to the community. From the funds raised at their monthly bake sales—cunningly held on the sidewalk in front of city hall on the exact day of the month the residents' water and sewer bills were due—the club ladies made a sizable annual donation to the Shining Stars Scholarship fund. They were the ones to thank for the half dozen benches surrounding the water fountain in the middle of the downtown square, not to mention the perennial beds flanking the *Welcome to Ruby Prairie* sign that greeted folks upon their arrival to town.

Not only that, but every fall the ladies purchased school supplies, even backpacks if necessary, for children whose parents were down on their luck. During the holiday season, residents of the New Energy Rest Home were the grateful recipients of fruit and nut baskets, courtesy of the club.

According to the club's charter, no more than twenty-five names could be listed on the membership roster at any given time. Some years back, prospective members were forced to wait anxiously, sometimes for half a decade or more, for a member to move off or pass away so that they could apply to get in.

Unfortunately, that was no longer the case. In the past six months, four active club members had moved, two had died, and three were put by their kids into the rest home. Five open spots were currently going begging. No one spoke of it, but some members feared the beginning of a trend. After all, the average age of the membership was creeping its way near sixty.

The doorbell rang.

"Come in! You must be Charlotte. So glad you made

it," Nomie greeted her at the door.

Charlotte Carter stood framed in front of the open front door while the western sun beat down on the porch. Her stance caused an unfortunate fact to be made painfully plain. Charlotte wasn't wearing a slip.

Neither Nomie nor any other club member would dream of being rude to an invited guest—taken aback though they might be by Charlotte's bare legs, breezy gauze dress, and naturally curly, flyaway hair.

"Ladies, I'd like you to meet Mrs. Carter. Charlotte's her given name. She's only recently moved to our town."

"Thank you for inviting me. What a pretty house."

Charlotte wore barefoot sandals. Her toenails were painted with pink polish.

"Honey, have you a seat," said Nomie real quick. "I'll bring you a cup of tea. It's that Russian tea that's so good—secret club recipe." She winked, then bent close to whisper in Charlotte's ear. "Made with Lipton instant, sugar, and orange-flavored Tang."

"Dear, you are truly blessed tonight. Nomie's made her famous Neiman Marcus cake," said Ginger Collins. "Have you had it before? She'll cut you a piece."

"Thank you, I'd love some cake, but no tea for me," said Charlotte. "I'm a soda drinker."

She had brought her own. Diet A&W Cream. In a can. Nomie sprang into action. "I'll get you a glass, dear."

"Don't go to any trouble. I'm fine."

Why, of course, she was.

The club waited until Charlotte had left to go home before they got down to the night's sticky business. Since she was president, Nomie opened the floor. What did the ladies think of asking Mrs. Carter to become a member of the club?

Not surprisingly, reactions were mixed.

"She never did say why she moved here. And I asked her pointblank," said Sassy.

"I noticed that," said Alice. "She changed the subject. Started talking about where in town could she buy beige mini blinds to put in her dining room window."

"Nice enough woman, I guess, but no doubt, she wasn't raised. You could see right through that dress. And what was it? Rayon?"

"Some kind of blend."

"I, for one, think she seems nice enough." Ginger Collins, all four feet ten inches of her, took up for Charlotte. "And I don't see why a person should be called to share all her personal business with a bunch of strangers the first time she meets them. I don't blame her for keeping some things to herself." Ginger got up to go to the bathroom.

Alice went and cut herself some more cake.

For a long minute, no one said anything.

"Ladies, there's something that we haven't thought of," said Lucky.

"What's that?"

"Mrs. Carter is still young enough to drive at night."

Yes.

She was.

The women fell silent again. Not only could she drive at night, but Charlotte Carter owned some kind of a four-door Ford. Nomie had seen it when she drove up. A member like that would be a real help. Many members of the Culture Club had to be picked up, especially for winter meetings when the sun was nearly all the way down by five o'clock.

"No rule says a woman of the club *has* to drink tea," said Lucky, one of those who always needed a ride.

"Wonder where she got that dress. Looked real comfortable," said Alice.

"Carter. Wasn't there a teacher by the name of Carter lived here some time back?" said Sassy.

It was Nomie who called to tell Charlotte the great news. "Honey, the Ruby Prairie Women's Culture Club has voted you in. Congratulations! You are our newest member."

Well.

Yes.

That sure was news.

Charlotte had not even known she'd applied.

Chapter Three

From her seat outside the door of the Ruby Prairie school principal's office, Charlotte squinted over her glasses to read the weekly cafeteria lunch menu posted on the bulletin board. *Tuesday. Fish sticks, macaroni and cheese, applesauce, chocolate sandwich cookies, choice of orange juice or milk.* Not bad.

The board was covered with notices and memos. *Free Flu Shots Available in Nurse Medford's Office. Mandatory faculty meeting, 4:00 Friday, September 12. No one excused!!!!*

Wasn't that last week? Charlotte looked at her watch.

"Miz Carter?"

"Yes."

"Mr. Jackson's expecting you. Go right on in."

"Thank you." Charlotte wondered if a person ever outgrew that nervous feeling associated with being called into the principal's office. She stood up, then realized she had cat hair all over her pants. She brushed it off as best she could.

When Mr. Jackson spotted her in the doorway, he waved her on in. At least six feet tall, he loomed over his desk, his ear to the phone.

The man couldn't be more than thirty years old. And since when did they allow principals to wear goatees?

"Have a seat," the principal mouthed, hand over the

receiver. "I'm on hold. Be right with you."

Four heavy wooden chairs sat in a row across from Mr. Jackson's desk. Charlotte took a seat next to a boy who looked about six. He sat motionless, silent, head down, hands on his knees, feet not even nearly touching the floor.

Odd, thought Charlotte, that she would be called in while the principal was making a phone call. Odder still that she be present while he was in the midst of dealing with a child. Feeling out of place, she studied her shoes.

"Yes! Thank you for taking my call," Mr. Jackson's voice boomed. The little boy's head popped up.

Charlotte's did too.

Mr. Jackson ran his free hand through his wavy black hair. "Mr. Claus, I hate to bother you, but we've got a little problem down here in Ruby Prairie. I'm calling about Forest Freeman.

"Yes, sir. That's the one . . . six and a half. Two brothers. One sister. Red hair. Lives on Melody Lane, near the old skating rink."

The child next to Charlotte began to chew on his lip.

"Right . . . uh-huh . . . You see, Santa, I'm afraid that Forest here has not been doing his work. . . . No, not his math or his reading. Not only that, sir, but he said some bad words on the playground yesterday. And this morning his teacher sent him to my office because he told Marcie Parker that she had the cooties. Made her cry.

"What's that? Oh no, sir. Believe it's just dry scalp."

Mr. Jackson was silent a long moment, but his face went grave. Forest and Charlotte watched him shift from one foot to the other. Finally he sat down.

Forest clutched at the arms of his chair.

Charlotte didn't dare breathe.

"To tell you the truth, I'm hoping that won't be necessary. You see, Forest and I have had a little talk. He's promised me that he will do better, and I believe he means it.

"Less than three months? Why, I didn't realize Christmas was that close! I'll tell him. Santa, Forest really is a good boy. He's just gotten a bit off track, is what I think. Now don't take offense; I'm not telling you how to run your business, but I'd keep him on the list a while longer if I were you. I expect that Forest is going to behave from now on."

Pale-faced Forest nodded his head.

Oh yes.

Charlotte was sure Forest would be good.

"Why, certainly. That's a great idea. I'd be happy to call you next week and give you a report. Thanks again for your time. By the way, will you make it to our school Christmas party this year? That's great. We'll look forward to seeing you. Bye now."

With a huge sigh of relief, Forest slid out of his chair. "I will be good, Mr. Jackson. I'll be really good."

"I believe you will, son. I expect to be calling in a good report next week."

"You will! I promise!"

"Mrs. Jones, could you take Forest back to class for me, please?"

"Sure will," said the secretary who had directed Charlotte in.

Once Forest was gone, Mr. Jackson closed the door and slipped Charlotte a grin. "When teachers get to the end of their ropes with rowdy students," he explained, "they send them down here for me to paddle."

Corporal punishment? Charlotte didn't like the sound of that. "District policy says I can give three swats, but I hate to do it. Fact is, I'll do about anything not to have to. A quick call to the North Pole generally does just as much good—at least till they get past the second grade."

He extended his hand. "Ben Jackson."

Charlotte hoped hers wasn't too damp. "Nice to meet you. Charlotte Carter. I've recently moved to town—into Tanglewood—the old Pete Joslin place, according to my Realtor." She rose from her chair, met Mr. Jackson's eyes, and matched his firm grip with one of her own.

"So you're the one who bought Tanglewood. Well, good for you. Welcome to Ruby Prairie. How can I help you? I'd venture to guess you've got some children you plan to enroll in our school. Junior high age?"

"You're partly right. I don't have any children of my own, but I am planning on enrolling some students in your school."

They sat down, and Charlotte laid out her plan. Surely a man who preferred calls to Santa over three swats with a paddle would look upon her with favor.

"Troubled children?" Mr. Jackson fiddled with a paper clip.

"Yes. But just girls. Girls who for a variety of reasons cannot live at home. Some of them will be with me for a few months while their families get back on their feet. Other girls, whose families have greater difficulties, may be with me for a year or longer."

"Sounds like foster care."

"Much the same. Like a foster home, I'm licensed by the state. However, most of the girls who come to me will have been placed by a judge or a social service agency with their parents' full consent. They'll come from parents and guardians who are in such crises that they cannot care for their children, but who have not yet lost custody or parental rights. While I'm caring for the girls, social workers will be working with their families in hopes that the girls will eventually return to stable, safe environments."

"I see." Mr. Jackson took notes on a legal pad. "Does your home have a name?"

"Just Tanglewood. I saw no reason to change it."

"It's been a long time since there were children playing in that yard. Is your home affiliated with a church, Mrs. Carter?"

"The girls and I will be worshipping in Ruby Prairie. Probably at Lighted Way. But Tanglewood's not connected to any denomination."

“So this is a project you and your husband are doing all on your own.”

“No husband,” said Charlotte. “Just me.”

“Really.” He looked up. “Mighty big undertaking for one person.”

Rankled by his innocent statement, Charlotte shifted in her chair. Mr. Jackson was not the first person to insinuate she should have help getting Tanglewood off the ground. Why did folks seem to think it their business to speculate on what she could or could not do? If she’d learned one thing in her life, it was that a person could only count on herself. She held her tongue.

“I’ve put a lot of thought and planning into this. I’m sure I’ll be just fine.”

Mr. Jackson leaned back in his chair. “I’m surprised I haven’t already heard mention of your plans. News travels fast in a small town. And in Ruby Prairie, something like this qualifies as big news. When word gets out, you’ll be the talk of the town.” He grinned. “There’s one thing you should know about Ruby Prairie, Mrs. Carter. Residents believe if they haven’t heard a rumor by 10 A.M., it’s their civic duty to make one up.”

“Is that so?” Charlotte smiled. She’d heard such things about small towns. Surely it couldn’t be as bad as that.

“Absolutely.”

“Then I suppose I’ve done a good job keeping things quiet.”

"Whatever your reasons, you certainly have."

"Here's the thing," said Charlotte. "It wasn't a big secret at all. I just thought it best to keep my plans for Tanglewood to myself until everything was settled legally and financially—and now it is. Now that it's official, I'm happy to tell people why I'm here."

"Good thing. I suspect the regulars at the 'Round the Clock have been driving themselves crazy trying to figure you out."

Charlotte jumped when a loud bell rang. Time for school lunch.

Mr. Jackson glanced at his watch, then rose to his feet.

Charlotte, on cue, stood up and eased toward the door.

Mr. Jackson stuck out his hand. "Mrs. Carter, nice to meet you. I wish you the best. One last thing—how many children are we talking about?"

"Six. All between the ages of nine and fifteen."

"Sounds fine. And when does your home open?"

"My first girl arrives early next week."

"We'll see you then."

From the school Charlotte drove the two blocks to Lighted Way Church. She found Pastor Jock Masters out front by the church's announcement sign, intent on spelling out Sunday's upcoming sermon topic. The plastic neck brace he was wearing was complicating the procedure considerably.

"Pastor?"

He jumped at her voice and dropped six letters. "Mrs. Carter! Good to see you. How are you?"

"I'm fine." She retrieved what he'd dropped. "But you—my goodness! What happened to your neck?"

"Long story. Shall we go inside?"

"Sure, but please, call me Charlotte."

Over coffee and fat-free Fig Newtons, Pastor Jock explained. "Leaky baptistry. The deacons thought we could fix it with some kind of special rubberized paint. Save us a bundle. Six of us were down in there at once. Not sure if it was the paint fumes or the onions that three of those boys had for lunch, but something got to me, and I passed clean out. I'm thirty-nine years old, and I can't remember ever fainting before in my life. Hit my head and strained my neck. No permanent damage, thanks to God. Just sore. Doc says I have to wear this brace for another few days."

"Good thing you didn't break something."

"Don't I know it." He reached for another cookie. "So what can I do for you? Seeing how you've been inside these doors every time they've been open for the last three weeks, I'm hoping you've come to tell me you plan to join our church."

"I have."

"Really? That's wonderful."

"But there's something you need to know."

"Divorce. Bankruptcy. Out-of-wedlock kids. Seventeen years of ministry, I've heard it all and then some. Mrs. Carter, there's nothing you can tell me that will keep me from welcoming you to this church." He had no difficulty meeting Charlotte's blue eyes with his own kind, brown ones.

"Oh, it's nothing like that," she said. "I've come to Ruby Prairie with a plan to open a home at Tanglewood. For girls. Girls who've had problems and who need a place to stay."

"What an awesome mission. I don't believe anything like that's been done here before."

"No, it hasn't. In fact, according to my research there's not a single foster home in this entire county. Last family quit two months ago."

"I had no idea."

"As of this week, I'm licensed by the state, with room for up to six girls. Some of them won't have spent much time in church. I'm confident they'll be fine but perhaps a bit rough around the edges at first. Pastor, before I join this church, I want to be sure we'll be welcome—all of us."

His voice was gentle. "Of course you are welcome. And those precious girls will be too. We aren't perfect here, but most of us are loving folks."

"That's my impression so far." Charlotte thought of the two loaves of banana bread, two of zucchini, and more than a dozen cards and calls she'd received since her first visit to Lighted Way.

"I'm glad. Not to pry, but since you're an Oklahoma girl, I'm curious as to what made you decide to move to Texas. And, out of all the towns in Texas, what made you choose Ruby Prairie?"

"I was born in Texas. Grew up here. Followed my husband north, is how I ended up in Oklahoma. Seemed natural to come back after he died. I wanted to settle in a small town with good schools and quiet streets. Someplace with trees. During the past six months, I've visited eighteen different towns. Lots of them would have done just fine. In the end, it was the name that made me choose to move here."

"Ruby Prairie?"

"Ruby was my grandmother's name. Her mother, who was only seventeen, died shortly after giving birth to her. People were good to my grandmother. Lots of people helped bring her up. But I'll never forget her telling me that when she was a little girl she longed for her mother and a real home. I lost my mother and father to a car accident when I was a freshman in college. Even though I was nineteen, I think I can understand what it's like to be a child in need of a home. I had no family nearby. My grandmother lived several states away at the time."

"That must have been awful for you," said Pastor Jock.

Charlotte nodded. "I was my parents' only child. They'd spoiled me. I didn't know how to do lots of things I should have, which made suddenly being on my own really difficult. I managed, though. Losing my parents taught me a lot."

"What did it teach you?" asked Pastor Jock.

Charlotte paused before answering. "I learned to depend upon no one but myself."

"Really?"

"Yes. My independent streak was hard for my husband, J.D., to accept. Caused some friction early in our marriage, but after a while I suppose he got used to my being the way that I am."

"How long ago did your husband die?" asked Pastor Jock. "Seven months ago."

"That's not long. I'm sorry for your loss."

"Thank you." Charlotte swallowed. "Anyway, as for how I'm able to be opening up Tanglewood, a year and a half ago, my grandmother died. I was her only heir." Charlotte paused. "It has taken this long to get all the legal stuff settled, but if I'm careful, what my Grandma Ruby left me will be enough to keep the home running for several years."

"What a generous way to spend that money. I can see that God has had a hand in this."

"They say that God can work good things out of bad. I believe it. My biggest regret in life is that my husband and I never had children. He and I both wanted them, expected to have three or four. We'd been married twelve years before I got pregnant. Two weeks after we found out, I had a miscarriage. I never got pregnant again."

Pastor Jock handed Charlotte a tissue, then plucked one for himself.

"As soon as I realized what my inheritance meant, I knew exactly what I wanted to do. Tanglewood is a dream."

"Charlotte, I speak for the members of this church

when I tell you that we will help you in any way we can."

"Thank you. Just so you know, I don't expect help from the church."

"Then you're in for a surprise. You don't know Ruby Prairie."

Charlotte raised her chin. "I believe God helps those who help themselves."

"My experience is God uses His people to help those who can't help themselves," said Pastor Jock.

Charlotte didn't respond to his words. "My husband was ill for a long while, and I'm used to taking care of myself. Tanglewood won't be a burden to this church. I just wanted to make sure we would all be welcome."

"Tell you what. How about I come by Friday morning and bless your new house? I'd like to pray over it, and for the girls who'll soon call it home."

"Bless—the house?"

"Not just the house. You. To His service. It would be an honor."

"I guess so," said Charlotte. "Yes. That would be nice."

"Ten o'clock?"

"Okay."

Charlotte had one more stop to make: Dallas, an hour and a half away. There she traded in her Taurus for a fire-engine red, twelve-seat van. Driving such a big vehicle would take some getting used to. She eased it into gear. After waiting until the road was clear for a good stretch, Charlotte finally pulled out of the dealership. With any luck, she'd make it home before dark.

If not—well, at least by eight.

Chapter Four

Catfish Martin, seated in his favorite booth at the 'Round the Clock Cafe, salted his eggs and put jelly on his bread. "Nobody knows a blame thing about this woman. Where'd she come from? Why's she here? And where'd she get the money to buy a place as big as Tanglewood?"

"Oklahoma City. Likes the town. Inherited from her gran'maw," snapped Kerilynn. She plunked a bowl of stewed prunes down in front of his plate.

"I didn't order these."

"You're not regular; I can tell by lookin' at you. No wonder you're in such a foul mood. Do us all a favor and eat 'em."

"Kerilynn!"

"On Gordy's grave," she said, invoking the name of her late husband, "you'll not taste another biscuit from my kitchen till you eat those prunes. Ever' one of 'em."

Catfish—known to take nothing from nobody except Kerilynn, his older-by-ten-minutes and taller-by-two-inches sister—fiddled and fumed. "Cain't I at least finish my eggs?"

"Suit yourself," said Kerilynn.

A man given to controversy, Catfish solicited favorable rulings from two cronies sitting in the next booth. "Chilly. Gabe. Y'all agree with me, don't you? All I'm saying is that we've got us a nice little town here. What do we need with somebody from out of state coming in, opening up some kind of hideaway for criminals?"

"Criminals!" said Kerilynn. "Woman's opening up a home for girls. Girls that don't have families of their own."

"Girls that will run up and down the streets doin' no tellin' what—corruptin' our boys and bringing down our schools," said Catfish. "Do you realize that the varsity football team has already lost three games? Them boys are already having enough trouble gettin' the job done without a bunch of delinquent little hussies coming in and distracting 'em. Besides that, too much riffraff will drive the good people out of town. Hurt business. Decrease revenues. Kerilynn, as mayor, I'd think that you of all people would show some concern."

"Quit your gritchin'," said Chilly. "Woman seems nice enough. She's taking in homeless children, for cryin' out loud. Don't see how one woman and a few orphans is going to cause the whole town to go south."

"Miz Carter joined the church yesterday, is what I heard," said Gabe.

"Didn't see you there," said Kerilynn.

"Had to miss," said Gabe. "My week on at the fire station. About nine o'clock, I got the call to come down to the rest home. Grease fire."

"Much damage?" asked Chilly.

"Not from the fire. Assistant administrator had it about out by the time we got there. But just as me and the boys were about to leave, one of the nurses came running and asked if we could check on some plumbing down the hall."

"Backed up?"

"I'd say. Seems Miz Myrtle Maples got mad at her new roommate because she got hold of the Milk of Magnesia Miz Myrtle keeps hid in her stocking drawer. She went and flushed all the poor woman's underpants down the toilet."

"You don't mean it!" said Kerilynn.

"Biggest mess I've ever seen." Gabe shook his head.

"Hey! Some of us are trying to eat our breakfast." Catfish stabbed at a prune.

"Wife told me pastor's gonna bless Mrs. Carter's house on Saturday," said Chilly. "Asked one or two of the members to take part. Make her feel welcome."

"I'm going." Kerilynn purposely baited her brother. "*And* I'm carrying a cake."

"Might be a nice touch if some of us went in together to send her a potted plant," said Chilly.

"Soon as I get the grease traps cleaned out, I'll fix up a donation jar. Set it by the cash register," said Kerilynn.

"Well, if that don't beat all. While you're at it, may as well make up some signs." Catfish wiped at his mouth and pushed back his plate. "Y'all can wear 'em round your necks. Invite ever' weirdo in the entire U.S. of A. to come set up housekeeping in Ruby Prairie."

He was not eating that last prune. No, he was not. Regular? Humph. From the looks of things, Catfish could see that he was the only regular person left in the entire blooming town.

"I for one aim to keep my eyes on the whole operation. That I will do. Someday ever' one of you will come to thank me. You wait and see."

Monday.

Tuesday.

Wednesday.

Thursday.

The UPS man made stops at Charlotte's house four days in a row. Sassy Clyde, whose house was just down the street, kept count.

Not a woman who enjoyed shopping, Charlotte had mail-ordered everything she could. Quilts for the girls' beds. Sheets and towels. Large cooking pots. Bulletin boards, bathrobes, and Bibles. On Thursday morning, at Hardy's Hardware in downtown Ruby Prairie, she bought a new freezer and a second washer and dryer. That afternoon, after the appliances had been delivered, installed, and tested, she drove thirty-five miles to the nearest Sam's Club to stock up on school supplies, paper goods, and groceries.

What else was there to do?

Anticipating the Monday afternoon arrival of her

first girl made Charlotte as excited as a kid on Christmas Eve. She lay in bed. Snowball and Visa snoozed at her feet, but she tossed and turned. What would the girl be like? Charlotte knew her name, age, and where she was coming from, but what would she *look* like? Would she be shy and timid or outgoing and loud? Pretty or plain? Charlotte felt as though she was getting a gift-wrapped package. She couldn't wait to see what would be on the inside.

Tomorrow Pastor Jock would come to bless the house. Tonight Charlotte took a Tylenol PM.

Only three and a half more days to wait.

Saturday morning. Twenty till ten. Five members of the Ruby Prairie Women's Culture Club stood on the sidewalk in front of Charlotte's freshly painted, white-shuttered and trimmed, pink frame house. A new metal plaque with *Tanglewood* inscribed on it hung on the porch where a weathered, hand-painted wooden sign used to hang.

"Place looks real nice," said Ginger Collins.

"Wonder how many flats of pansies she's put in," said Lucky Jamison, eyeing the beds on each side of the sidewalk that led up to the front steps.

"Ten at least," said Alice Buck.

"More like fifteen," said Nomie Jenkins.

"Didn't the porch used to be gray?"

"Think so. Looks better white."

"Especially with those wicker swings she's got hung."

"Are we early?" asked Ginger, who was always forgetting her watch.

"Look there. Sittin' in the window. She's got twin cats."

Pastor Jock parked his pickup across the street from Charlotte's house. He got out, slung his backpack over his shoulder, and joined the crowd gathering in front of the house. "Morning, ladies. Choir here yet?"

"Haven't seen them."

"What about the mayor?"

"I'm here." Kerilynn had pulled up right behind the pastor's truck. "Nomie, can you help me with this cake? Did anybody think to bring punch? What about paper plates? Lands, Pastor, how many you expect?"

It was still ten minutes before the hour when, hearing noise on her porch, Charlotte opened her door, expecting to see Pastor Jock. And she did see the pastor—and behind him twenty-two kindhearted and curious Ruby Prairie citizens, many of them bearing gifts, all of them craning their necks to get a look at her and the inside of her house.

Snowball and Visa took one look, stepped between Charlotte's feet, and flew out the front door.

"Brought along some friends." Pastor Jock smiled.

"Here's you a philodendron, ma'am." Chilly Reed presented her with the plant.

"You aren't diabetic, are you?" asked Mayor Kerilynn, showing her cake.

"Yard eggs. Laid by my hens," said Ginger Collins.

"Three cases of creamed corn. Where you want me to put 'em?" asked Gabe Eden.

"Socks and underwear. Assorted junior sizes," said Nomie Jenkins. "Provided by the Women's Culture Club. You'll go through 'em by the bunch with a house full of girls."

"Hello. Thank you. Yes. I mean no!" Charlotte stammered. "I love cake. Thank you so much. Set them down right there; that'll be fine. That was so nice." She looked at the crowd pressing toward her front door. "How kind of you all to come. I wasn't expecting anything like this. Come in. All of you. Please, come in."

"Wipe your feet," ordered Kerilynn. "Look out. Here comes the choir. Why, Junior Blevins has brought his trombone. Have you heard that boy play 'When the Saints'? Like nothing you've ever heard. Y'all let the kids through."

Everyone tried to crowd in.

"Maybe the choir should stand out on the porch," suggested Pastor Jock. "Charlotte, can we open these windows?" He parted the lace curtains. "And if we open the front door we'll be able to hear them through the screen, don't you think?"

Folks inside got quiet. They took seats where they could. Some sat on the newly covered ticking-striped sofa and love seat. Some perched in kitchen chairs. Others squeezed elbow to elbow on one of the room's three bay-window seats.

The choir on the porch warmed up. Junior did too.

Charlotte, grateful but overwhelmed and unsure how to act in her own house, took a seat in a corner. She wrapped her arms around herself, scanned the room, and tried to remember last names.

As soon as everyone was settled, Pastor Jock perched on the piano bench next to Mayor Kerilynn. "Charlotte, on behalf of Lighted Way Church, I too have brought some gifts. First, though, I want to share a couple of verses."

He began to read from Psalm 146: "Blessed is he whose help is the God of Jacob, whose hope is in the Lord his God, the Maker of heaven and earth, the sea, and everything in them—the Lord, who remains faithful forever. He upholds the cause of the oppressed and gives food to the hungry. The Lord sets prisoners free, the Lord gives sight to the blind, the Lord lifts up those who are bowed down, the Lord loves the righteous. The Lord watches over the alien and sustains the fatherless and the widow, but he frustrates the ways of the wicked. The Lord reigns forever, your God, O Zion, for all generations. Praise the Lord."

He closed the Book.

"Amen, Pastor," said Kerilynn.

"Amen," repeated the others, all around the room.

"Is it time to sing yet?" A stage whisper was heard from out on the porch. Then shuffling, stomping, and the scrambling sound of someone who had dropped sheet music off the side of the porch.

"How about let's hear from the choir now," suggested Pastor Jock. "Test week, you know." He looked at his watch. "Kids have got to be back to school by noon."

First "Jesus Loves the Little Children."

Then "He's Got the Whole World in His Hands."

Finally "Amazing Grace," followed by Junior's moving trombone solo.

Ginger Collins, real prone to cry, had wet two Kleenexes by the time the children had sung the last verse.

"Boys and girls can sure sing," said Chilly after they were done. Everyone agreed.

"Everyone," Pastor Jock began after the choir had been waved good-bye, "we've come together this morning to dedicate this house and its owner to the service of God. Some of you met Charlotte for the first time when you arrived. None of us have known her very long. However, all of us are touched by what she has set out to do. Charlotte, would you come over here, please?"

Kerilynn got up from the bench. "Here, sugar." She patted her spot.

Charlotte sat down next to Pastor Jock.

From his backpack he plucked an only slightly squashed loaf of Wonder Bread. Handing it to her, he said, "May this home never want for food. And may your girls learn while they are with you about the Bread of Life."

Charlotte took the loaf with a smile. "Thank you."

"Wait, there's more." He winked at the others in the room. From the backpack he next produced a crystal candleholder and a fat, white, gardenia-scented pillar candle. "May God be with you to light your way even on days when you feel as though you're groping around in the dark."

"Pretty," murmured a pair of club ladies.

There were three more items to be shared. First, an afghan made of crocheted granny squares. "Donated by the Craft Club at the rest home," explained Pastor Jock.

"So soft," said Charlotte. "And what pretty colors."

"Takes them forever to do one of those," Lucky Jamison informed them. She volunteered at the home once a week. "They've all got arthritis, you know."

Pastor Jock spread the afghan across her lap. "May this be a home full of warmth on even the coldest of days." Next, he produced a bag of Hershey's Kisses. "May those who live here enjoy sweetness."

"Pass that candy dish to the pastor," said Lucky. "The one on the end table. He can pour them in there."

Finally Pastor Jack topped the pile of gifts with a jumbo-sized box of sparklers left over from the Fourth. "And may you and your girls never forget to have fun."

Charlotte could not say a word. She just sat there for the longest time, eyes shining, heart full, weighted down with gifts and goodwill. Pastor Jock finally led applause all around. "Kerilynn, you cutting that cake? All right, then. Folks, let's have prayer."

Everyone in the room joined hands. Not a sound was heard, save a few sniffles and snorts.

"Father in heaven—"

"Meow."

Out on the porch, Visa and Snowball had apparently deemed it safe, in the absence of the choir, to come back inside. "—we thank You for bringing Charlotte to our town."

"Meow. Meow." They tried asking politely to come in. "We ask that You bless her and this home—"

"MEOW. MEOW."

"—and the girls who will be living under this roof. We ask that—" Someone standing nearby cracked the screen door, thinking the felines would come inside and behave.

First was heard a little "eek". Then another eek. Finally the scamper and scurry of eight—no, *twelve* critter feet.

Eyes flew open. Heads popped up. Chaos ensued.

Into the center of the prayer circle, for everyone to admire, one of the cats had brought a nice gray field mouse—the catch of the day. Only problem, the catch wasn't quite all the way dead.

Women screamed, cried, climbed, and ran. A few men did too. Someone went in search of a broom. Someone else asked if Charlotte had a baseball bat. Lucky reached for her inhaler. Chilly popped a nitro tab.

Though it took less than ten minutes to banish all three animals to the outside, Pastor Jock's prayer was a bust. "Amen," he said to himself.

Kerilynn commenced cutting cake. "If that don't

beat all. Lands, just a little mouse. Wouldn't hurt a flea. Now if it had been a snake . . . Pastor, you want a corner or an inside piece?"

It was right about then that the phone rang in the hall.

"I'm Charlotte," said Charlotte. "Yes. Yes . . . excuse me? Today? But I wasn't expecting her until—you're *where* right now? You'll be here by *when?*"

Dazed, she hung up the phone and walked into her living room. "Honey, are you all right?" asked Kerilynn. "Did you get some bad news?"

"Uh, no. Good news. I think. My first girl. She's coming today. Caseworker says they're fifteen minutes away."

"Well, I say," said Kerilynn. "Pastor, you've got good timing. Got this house blessed, we did, and in the very nick of time!"

Chapter Five

A moment of silent, frozen-in-place, slack-jawed shock passed before the news of Charlotte's change of plans sank in. Once it did, she watched her new friends spring into a dizzied flurry of helpful activity.

"People!" Kerilynn clapped her hands. "Things need to be perfect for the arrival of Tanglewood's first girl. Ruby Prairie's reputation is on the line here."

Charlotte hadn't exactly thought of it like that. Then

again, she'd never been mayor.

"Quick. Chilly, you gather up all the plates and cups," ordered Kerilynn. "Sugar"—she placed her hand on Charlotte's arm—"show him where you keep your extra garbage bags. Pastor, these chairs have got to be moved back to where they go. That little table too. Ginger, where'd you put the broom? Someone has tracked in some mud. Did you find the dustpan?"

Charlotte couldn't take a step without tripping over a Lighted Way soul.

While Ginger Collins swept, Kerilynn fluffed sofa cushions and ran over the coffee table with a dust rag she found in Charlotte's utility closet. Pastor Jock wiped cake crumbs from the counter, and Chilly poured leftover punch down the kitchen sink. In the downstairs bathroom, Nomie sprayed a cloud of Lysol, then nosed around till she found a roll of toilet paper to replace the nearly empty one on the spool.

Charlotte, her heart pounding and her stomach doing flip-flops, dashed up the stairs to put last-minute things into place in the new girl's room.

Kerilynn followed. "You just tell me what needs to be done," she said. "I'll help you."

"No telling what the social worker is going to think. I don't even have sheets on the beds," said Charlotte. She tore open a stubborn shrink-wrapped parcel with her teeth. "I can't believe she'll be here in fifteen minutes. I planned on having the room all ready—but I thought I had the whole weekend to do it. To tell the truth, I was saving these last few details so that I'd have something to do besides wait."

"Honey, get hold of yourself. We'll get it done," said Kerilynn. "Hand me that pillowcase."

"I want things to be right." Charlotte shook open the bottom sheet. "Not just for the social worker—for the girl. I imagine she'll be afraid—I would be. Just think—being away from your family in a strange house with someone you don't know. It's bound to be scary. I've read lots of books and articles and such, but I still don't know how to make it easier. Seems the least I can do is make every one of them feel as if I've fixed a special place just for her."

"And they will. There is no need to worry. You've done a wonderful job making this big old house feel like a home," said Kerilynn.

Together they dressed the room's pair of twin beds with white eyelet dust ruffles and stretchy new pink T-shirt sheets. They topped the beds off with multicolored double wedding ring-patterned quilts and fluffy pillows stuffed into shams. Kerilynn secured shades onto new bedside lamps, installed bulbs, and plugged them in while Charlotte headed down the hall to the bathroom to wipe down the sinks, put out a new towel and washcloth set, and open up a bar of Dove soap. Kerilynn parted the bedroom curtains and cracked a window to let in a bit of fresh air.

When she took a last glance around the room, Charlotte was soothed to see that everything was pretty much done.

"You did all this yourself?" Kerilynn asked. "The painting and everything?"

She had.

"Looks nice."

Truly, it did.

Charlotte had bought the home for its six bedrooms—one for herself downstairs, five for the girls upstairs. In this one the walls were painted a soft robin's egg blue with all of the woodwork done up in white. The hardwood floor shined, thanks to the hours she'd spent on her knees with a rag and a tub of polish. To make the room feel cozy, she'd put down a J.C. Penney round braided rug in shades of blue, pink, and yellow. Two desks and two dressers sat on a wall opposite a pair of floor-to-ceiling, lace-curtained windows. A corner shelf held stuffed animals, board games, and a selection of young-reader books. Some of the volumes were old childhood favorites. Good thing she'd held onto them for all of these years. Others were new titles, chosen after getting the thoughtful recommendations of Alice Buck, who taught junior high.

"Smells nice in here," said Kerilynn. "Like lemon oil and vanilla. Must be floor wax and the potpourri in that bowl. Any little girl would love this room." She straightened a pillow on one of the beds. "Looks like we're finished. Anything else you wanted done?"

In ten minutes flat, everyone gathered at the front door of Charlotte's home, chattering and laughing, some of them breathless, but all in agreement that the place looked great.

"Thank you so much," said Charlotte to the group. "You'll never know how much this afternoon has meant to me. I really appreciate all that you've done."

"You're welcome, honey."

"Our pleasure."

"Anytime."

"Okay, folks. Let's make ourselves scarce," said Pastor Jock. "There's too many people here. Crowd this big might scare a child. Let's everybody take off quick before they pull up."

"Pastor's right. Bye, dear."

"Good luck!"

"God bless."

"Let us hear if you need anything."

Charlotte had no more hugged, thanked, and waved her last guest good-bye when from her doorway she spotted a car turning the corner and heading toward her house. The white four-door Chevy she remembered as belonging to Kim Beeson—Tanglewood's assigned social worker—slowed, eased over, and finally stopped at her mailbox right next to the curb.

Charlotte reached up to arrange flyaway strands of curly hair. Smiling on the outside but trembling on the inside, she moved from the front door toward the porch steps. She gripped the railing and prayed, *I'm ready for this. I know that I am. But please, God, please, just don't let me faint.*

A wave of nausea hit.

Or throw up.

"Hello! We made it." Kim popped out of the car. "Beautiful day, isn't it?" she called up the walk. "Look at those flowers. You've put those out since I was here last. They're pretty." She moved to open the car's back door.

Charlotte managed to make it from the porch down the steps to the sidewalk. She held her breath as she walked its length to the street. This was it—the moment she'd thought of and prayed for all of these months. Charlotte remembered a story she'd read about a woman on the brink of giving birth who, delirious during transition, instructed her husband to please pull the car around. She'd changed her mind and decided instead to get her purse and go home. Like that woman, Charlotte's emotions flailed from giddy excitement to shaky apprehension to all-out terror at what she had gotten herself into.

There was no way out now.

She unlatched and opened the picket-fence gate.

"Charlotte," said Kim, "I'd like for you to meet Nikki . . . Charlotte waited.

". . . and Vikki," finished Kim.

Two girls got out of the car.

"Vikki?" Who was Vikki? Charlotte's jaw dropped.

"Goodness. Didn't I tell you?" Kim, twenty-two and only five months on the job, fumbled with her paperwork. "I thought that I did.

Two girls. Same size silhouettes against the afternoon sky. They had to be sisters. No, not just sisters. Twins. Identical twins. Even though they weren't wearing the same clothes, there was no doubt. The two little girls were a genuine nine-year-old matched set.

"Girls, this is Charlotte," said Kim.

"Hi."

"Hi."

Charlotte's eyes could not take them in fast enough. Brown hair, brown eyes, wiry, athletic builds. No different from any other new mother-of-sorts, she counted two sets of nail-bitten fingers and two sets of sandal-clad toes. In a rush of maternal emotion, right there on the sidewalk of Tanglewood, she fell instantly, unexpectedly, madly in love. Though she'd been told not to rush or to expect returned affection any time soon, it was all Charlotte could do to restrain herself from scooping the little girls up into her arms and promising them that she would forever and ever make everything always all right.

Charlotte stared so long as to make the girls giggle—which broke her out of her transfixed spell. "Welcome to my house. I mean your house." She stumbled over the words. "Actually—it's our house. How about I help you bring your things in. Maybe you'd like to look around?"

The twins brought few possessions. Backpacks, one each. The rest of their belongings were stuffed into three plastic grocery store bags.

"I gotta go to the bathroom," said Nikki.

Or was that Vikki? Charlotte wondered how she was supposed to tell them apart.

"Me too," said the other one. "Bad."

"Long drive. They've been working on 7-11 Big Gulps for the past two hours," explained Kim.

"I had Coke."

"I had Sprite."

"No problem. We'll make the bathroom our first stop." Charlotte led Nikki and Vikki and Kim back up the walk.

"You got a dog?" asked one of the girls.

"No, but I have two cats."

"How 'bout fish?"

"No. Don't have any fish."

"That's good. Cats eat fish."

"Let's set everything down right here," said Charlotte. She dropped the girls' bags on the bottom stair and showed them to the downstairs bathroom, located just across the hall from her bedroom.

"We don't need any help," said a solemn-faced Vikki—just before she closed and locked Charlotte and Kim out and the two of them in.

"Okay. Call me if you need anything."

"We will," came a muffled voice through the closed and locked door.

While the girls were in the bathroom, Charlotte and Kim sat down on the couch. Kim dug around in her satchel.

"Everything you need is in this packet," she said. "Shot records, school enrollment forms, Medicaid cards. They'll need to see a dentist soon. And here's a voucher you can use to get them some clothes."

“Anything I should know?”

“Report’s in the packet. Mom’s sick. Been unable to work or take care of them for several months. Looks like she may have cancer. Tests haven’t all come back, but that’s what the doctors are afraid of. Their grandma’s a sweet woman, but she’s not in great health herself and is worn out. Been trying to take care of the three of them, but lately the situation’s gotten to be more than she can handle. Lot of financial concerns.”

“What about their dad?”

“He’s in prison. Expects to be released in nine months.”

“How much do the girls know?”

“They know about their dad, and they’ve been told they’ll be staying with you until their mother gets well. They understand that she’s sick and needs lots of rest.”

“Will she be calling or visiting?”

“Calling. None of your girls’ families will visit here. Policy.

Though we wouldn’t expect problems, better to stay on the safe side. If family visits take place—and sometimes they will, I’ll pick up the girls and take them to a location halfway. For now, Nikki and Vikki will have phone calls and letters. Mom and Grandma both want to keep in touch. They’ll call once a week. I told them Saturday mornings. That okay with you?”

“Of course.”

“I think that’s everything. I’ll check in to see how

things are going in a week. If everything's okay, we'll begin processing your next placement. Charlotte, you've got a nice place. Lots of girls are needing a stable home. You're approved for six girls, right? I'm guessing you'll be full by Thanksgiving. You ready for that?"

Charlotte was ready for more girls next week, but suddenly she wasn't ready for Kim to go today. She attempted a stall. "Wouldn't you like something to drink before you go? Iced tea? Coke?"

"No, thanks."

"How about some cake?"

"Maybe next time. But I will take a bathroom break before I get back on the road." Kim stood.

"Those girls ought be out by now. I'd better check on them," said Charlotte. "Nikki? Vikki? Everything all right in there? Kim's ready to leave. She wants to tell you good-bye."

Charlotte heard water running, the toilet flushing, and the opening and closing of a bathroom drawer.

"We're almost through."

After waiting several more minutes, hearing yet more water running and another flush, Charlotte directed Kim to the bathroom upstairs.

Kim went up, took care of her need, made a tour of Nikki and Vikki's new room, and came back down.

Still no girls.

"Nikki, Vikki, it's time to come out now," said Charlotte.

"Open up," said Kim.

Finally the lock clicked and the door swung open. When it did, a cloud of Obsession, Charlotte's signature scent, descended upon her and Kim. The two girls emerged. Despite the pair's valiant, heads-held-high attempts to look nonchalant, there was no more wondering as to what had kept them so long. They had been busy, *very* busy—evidenced by powdered pink cheeks, brown-rimmed eyes, and frosted burgundy-rose lips.

Kim looked at Charlotte.

Charlotte struggled to keep a straight face.

Nikki sneezed. "How come you have to go already?"

"When are you coming back to get us?" asked Vikki.

"I have to get home to my dog," said Kim. "Remember how long it took us to get here? She'll be hungry for her dinner. I'll be back to see you in one week, just as we talked about. You're going to stay here with Charlotte."

The girls looked stricken.

Charlotte took each one by the hand. "Let's see if we can find a snack in the kitchen. Then we'll go upstairs to see your new room. Know what else? Both of you look so pretty, I want to put some film in my camera so I can take a picture of you."

"Can we send a picture to our mama?" asked Nikki.

"Of course you can. We'll take two."

"Bye, girls." Kim eased toward the front door. "Call me if you need anything," she whispered to Charlotte.

• • •

Ten hours later, the girls asleep upstairs, Charlotte rocked in the dark on her front porch swing. She kept the seat in motion with easy nudges of her feet against the cool plank floor, enjoying the companionable back-and-forth creak. She leaned her head back and closed her eyes.

Had this day been only twenty-four hours long?

Was it really just this morning the middle school choir stood and sang on this porch? Was it today Pastor Jock blessed her house and the cats brought in the mouse?

Charlotte smiled as she rocked.

Perhaps it was a year.

More like a lifetime.

She thought about her Grandma Ruby. Crazy about kids, she had voiced grief year after year when Charlotte conceived none of her own.

"*Maybe you should take vitamins, dear. Do you think it would help if you got more rest?*"

Grandma Ruby would think the twins grand.

I've got some children now, Grandma. Wish you could see them. They're really, really cute.

Charlotte climbed the stairs to check on the girls one last time before sleep. When she got to their room she found one bed empty. For an instant, she panicked, fearful the two had somehow gotten up and were roaming the house or had gone outside.

Then she looked at the other bed. There the twins lay, uncovered, curled on their sides, knees touching knees, holding hands while they slept.

You two have been through a lot. Such brave girls you are. They had not cried the entire afternoon, though they'd come close when it was time for bed.

"Will you be here when we wake up?" Nikki asked.

"Sometimes I wake up and I get scared in the dark. Can you leave the light on?" Vikki said.

"Yes. And yes." Charlotte had promised again and again.

She moved to cover them up. Silhouetted against the sheet, them mirror-image bodies made the shape of a heart. Charlotte tucked the quilt in around them close, kissed each of their foreheads, then slipped from the room.

It was not until she lay almost asleep in her own bed that she realized with a start—tomorrow was Sunday! How could she have forgotten? Sunday school. Church. The girls' first time at Lighted Way. Was the church ready? Was she? Were they?

Charlotte looked at the clock.

Very soon they would all find out.

Chapter Six

Beth Hollis, lying on her stomach in her bunk, stretched her bare toes and chewed on her pen. Her counselor, Anne, passed out pages of pink, lined paper torn from a pad. "Here's the deal. I've gotta run to a staff meeting that'll probably last about forty-five minutes. While I'm gone, I want you girls to make out your lists telling me why you came to camp."

From four sets of wooden bunk beds came whines and groans.

"I know. I know. We do this every year. It's important, though. When I get back, we'll see what everybody wrote. Helps me know better how to make this the best session ever. Questions? Okay. One more thing." She gave them a stern look. "No talking about boys while I'm gone."

Everybody giggled.

Beth had never been to church camp before. Never made out a list like this. She chewed her pen some more. You were probably supposed to say something about God.

Four Reasons Why I Came to Camp Crystal Lake

1. To meet new friends

2. To get closer to God

3. To learn some new songs

4. To spend time in nature

When Beth was finished she drew a squiggly border around her name, then went back and changed all the dots over her *i*'s into cute little hearts. That task completed, she drew a rainbow in each corner of the page. When she was done she tried to sneak peeks at her cabin mates' lists. She hoped what she had written was okay.

Shelly, Beth's bunkmate, propped herself up on one elbow. "Beth, is this really your first time at camp? How come you've never been here before?"

"Didn't know about it," said Beth.

"Did you just move to Texas or something?" asked Rachel. "You sound sort of like my cousins that live in Oklahoma. Maybe you know them."

"I've never been to Oklahoma. And this is my first time to go to any camp."

"Really? Didn't the kids at your church go?" asked Marty. "When I lived with my mom, we didn't go to church."

"Where do you live now?" asked Gloria.

"With my foster family." Beth scratched at a chigger bite on her leg.

The group fell silent. Though not one of them met her eyes, Beth felt the attention of every girl in the cabin.

"I'm lucky. My foster parents are really nice." She sat up and swung her legs over the side of her bunk. "Their house is out in the country. I get to ride horses at least once a week. And you wouldn't believe how much we go to church. All the time. Sunday morning. Sunday night. Even Wednesday night. We went to vacation Bible school every day for a week."

"What happened to your mom?" blurted Rachel. "Your real mom. Did she die?"

"Rachel!" shushed Ami.

Beth chewed on a fingernail. "No. My mom's not dead. I just can't stay with her. She's got some problems. I visit her in the summer and sometimes at Christmas. I try to help her out, but she has trouble with her nerves. They make her take medicine."

"That's really sad," said Gloria.

"Do you call your foster parents Mom and Dad?" asked Misty.

"Uh-uh. They told me to call them Tim and B.J. They're the ones that sent me to this camp. B.J. used to come here when she was little."

"Will you get to stay with them forever?" asked Ami.

"Caseworker says if I'm lucky, until I'm eighteen."

"Do you wish you could go back to live with your mom?" asked Lynn.

"Sometimes." Beth shrugged. "But I can't. It never works out. My mom has issues. I've been in seven foster homes since the sixth grade. Tim and B.J. are really, really nice. They like kids, but I don't think they can have any of their own. I figure that's why they got me. B.J.'s a great cook. You should eat her French toast."

"Do you have your own room?"

"Do they make you do chores and stuff?"

"Yeah. I have my own room. I have to. I think it's a rule or something. I vacuum and load the dishwasher every night. Course I make my bed and stuff too. Sometimes I forget, but B.J. doesn't get mad or anything. She just closes my door."

That night, Anne and Beth were the last two in the bathhouse. Everyone else had already finished up and gone back to the cabin.

"May I borrow your toothpaste?" asked Anne. "I forgot mine."

"Sure," said Beth. Her face and Anne's were reflected in the mirror above the sink.

Brush. Spit. Rinse. They finished at the same time.

Anne wiped her mouth on a towel. "I was thinking about what you wrote on your list," she said. "The thing you said about wanting to be close to God. How close do you want to be?"

"I don't know." Beth shrugged. It had just seemed like a good thing to write at the time.

"Do you know how a person gets close to God?" asked Anne.

That one was easy. "You have to go to church," said Beth.

"Going to church is good," said Anne. "Anything else?"

"I know you have to not do bad stuff if you want to be close to God," said Beth.

"That's sort of a problem, isn't it?" said Anne. "Since every one of us does bad stuff."

"I guess." Beth wished they could talk about something else.

"You need to know something," said Anne. "God knows everything about you."

There were some things Beth hoped God didn't know.

"And He loves you anyway," continued Anne. "You may want to be close to Him, but He wants to be close to you way more. He loves you so much he sent His Son Jesus for you."

"I know about all that," said Beth. She put the cap back on the paste and hoped Anne didn't expect her to floss. "What time do we have to get up tomorrow?"

"Seven," said Anne. "If you want, we can talk about this stuff some more tomorrow."

"Maybe."

"Got your flashlight?"

"Forgot it," said Beth.

"No problem. I've got mine.

"You've never worn eye shadow? Ever in your life? Come here, Beth; I'll show you how to put it on. You want Majestic Mauve or Luscious Lime?" Ami held a sponge-tipped applicator in her hand like a magic wand.

Anne put her hair up into a ponytail and pulled on a clean T-shirt. "Girls. Camp's not the place to worry about how you look," she chided.

"But it's church night."

"Don't you want us to look our best?"

Anne rolled her eyes.

"This shirt of mine will look really cute on you, Beth. No. Don't tuck it in. Anybody got a belt?" asked Shelly.

"Want me to blow-dry your hair straight?" offered Misty.

That night, the cutest fifteen-year-old boy at camp plopped down on the pew next to Beth. The other girls didn't get even a little bit mad.

The next morning they chanted as they skipped arm in arm down the hill to the flagpole. "We're Cabin Eight and we're really great!"

"We're the best over all the rest," they sang while

standing in line for breakfast.

"Don't be late or you'll miss Cabin Eight," the girls taunted as they raced other campers to the swimming pool.

"Pretty peppy group you've got there, Anne," said the camp director, Charlie. "Looks like everybody's getting along."

The two of them stood at the edge of the softball field watching Anne's girls practice silly cheers while waiting for their turns up to bat.

"They are," said Anne. "They're already tight, and it's just the first week. I'll tell you, this bunch of girls bonded faster than any other group I've had."

"How come?"

"Beth has a lot to do with it. She's the little blonde in the red shirt. There, on first base. She lives in a foster home. Crazy about her foster mom and dad. Talks about them all the time. Writes to them every day."

"Sad, but good she's with people who are good to her," said Charlie. "Doesn't seem to be having any trouble fitting in."

"The others have been really sweet to her. You can tell she craves affection. First I think they felt sorry for her, but not anymore. She's part of the group."

"She been in church much?" asked Charlie.

"Off and on, I think. She's a believer but a baby Christian. Still thinks being saved is about being good."

"You talking to her?"

"Much as she'll let me."

"Beth," whispered Rachel. "Beth . . . are you awake?"

"Yes."

"I'm awake too," hissed Ami. "We're all awake," said Shelly.

"Anybody got snacks?"

"I do," said Gloria. "Starbursts."

"Cookies," said Lynn.

"What kind?"

"Oreos. Double Stuff."

"Wanna sneak out? We could go sit out by the pool."

"Don't even think about it." Anne flipped on her flashlight and shined it around the cabin, illuminating eight guilty faces. "Back to sleep. All of you."

"But we're not tired."

"I'm wide awake."

"Can we at least all get into the top bunks so we can talk?"

"Okay, but keep it down."

All eight girls scrambled to crowd into two top bunks. They sat Indian style, knee to knee, and tried to eat and laugh at the same time without snorting.

"Hey. Don't put your feet on my pillow," said Shelly. "This is my bed, and it's full of sand already."

"Mine is too," said Ami.

"Everything I brought to camp is full of sand. My bed, my suitcase, even my underwear. I'm sick of sand," said Rachel. "Camp's great, but I miss my clean bed and my clean room."

"I've seen your room, and it's never clean," protested Ami.

"At least it's not covered in sand."

"I miss taking a shower in my own bathroom with nobody in there but me," said Lynn.

"I miss my mom's brownies," said Marty.

"I miss my dog," said Misty.

"I miss Tim and B.J. I wonder what they're doing while I'm gone," said Beth.

"Didn't you get some mail from them yesterday?" asked Rachel. "A card. But they didn't write anything in it."

"Are they coming to visit on Sunday?"

"I don't know. They didn't say."

"I bet they're coming. They probably didn't tell you so you'd be surprised. Everybody's parents come up on Sunday."

"Really?"

"Yeah. Your parents come in the morning so they can go to church with you. They eat lunch with you, and then you have free time until five o'clock."

"My mom and dad aren't coming because my dad had a business trip and my mom's going with him," said Ami. "My aunt Faith's coming instead."

"My mom's coming. She's bringing my grandma. And just so you know—my grandma has a 'fro," said Marty.

"I thought your grandma was white."

"She is. But she's still got a 'fro. Every two months she gets a perm. Comes out a 'fro every time."

"Guess we'll have to wait until Sunday to see," interrupted Anne from her bunk down below. "Come on, girls, back into your own beds. It's past midnight. We've got to be up in six and a half hours."

Within a few minutes all but one were enjoying sweet, sandy dreams.

Beth lay in her bunk. First on her back, then on her side. She pulled her knees up to her chest, then stretched them out.

Sunday I'll get to see Tim and B.J. I can give them the birdhouse I'm working on in crafts. I'll have to get it painted tomorrow. Hope it has time to dry. Should I write to tell them I know they're coming, or act like I'm surprised when I see them at church? I'll get Ami to help me fix my hair. I hope we sing that new song they taught us last night. Tim would really like it. After lunch I'll take B.J. up to see the horse I've been riding. I hope we clean up this cabin before all the parents come. It's a mess . . .

Sunday morning, Beth woke up before the camp director blew the rise-and-shine whistle. She was out of her bunk and into the shower before anyone else's feet had hit the gritty cabin floor.

Even for Sunday morning church, dress at camp was casual. Beth worried over whether to wear her yellow Capri pants that B.J. had bought her or the cute blue skirt Ami had offered to let her wear. She decided on the Capris.

"Want me to help you with your hair?" asked Gloria.

"I can braid it if you want."

"Sure. That'd be great."

"I've got a yellow ribbon you can borrow."

"Thanks."

At breakfast Beth only picked at her food, even though blueberry muffins were her favorite.

"Not hungry?" asked Anne.

"Guess I'm just excited about today. What time does church start?"

"Ten. But parents start getting here by nine."

It was eight forty-five.

"I'd better go brush my teeth," said Beth.

"You've got plenty of time," called Anne to Beth's back.

At nine o'clock Anne herded her girls to the camp's open-air chapel. "Everybody ready? Let's go on down. Won't hurt to be early. We can help arrange the benches."

The girls of Cabin Eight went down to the chapel and began anxiously watching for their parents' cars to pull through the camp's gate.

The first to arrive were Rachel's mom and dad in a red Suburban. Soon as her dad parked, Rachel's little brother tumbled out and ran full speed toward his sister. "Rach!" he yelled. "Are you glad to see me? Mom made you some cookies."

Rachel grinned and gave him a hug.

Next came Lynn's and Misty's moms. Because both the girls' dads were pastors who couldn't take a Sunday off, their two moms came together.

Soon after they arrived, Gloria's mom and dad pulled up.

Then Marty's mother and grandmother, who did indeed have an Afro—a rather blue one.

Ami's Aunt Faith turned lots of heads when she pulled through the gate in a baby pink convertible with the top down. "How's my favorite niece?" she called from way off. "Are you having a good week, honey?"

It was easy to see Ami was.

No Tim and B.J.

Except for them, only Shelly's mom had yet to show up.

"I'm not worried. She's always late." Shelly laughed. She was still laughing when her mom and dad parked their car in a spot close to the gate.

By then it was time for church to start.

No sign of B.J.

No sign of Tim.

Beth took a seat on the end of the pew and left some space so that when they did arrive they wouldn't have to search for her or crawl over a bunch of people's knees. Maybe they'd got lost. Had car trouble. Forgot what time they were supposed to come. What if they didn't know they were invited?

Anne came and sat next to Beth. She grasped Beth's hand during prayer.

"They're not here," Beth whispered. "I wonder what happened."

Anne held on to Beth's sweaty hand throughout the service. She sat by Beth during lunch. Finally, when lunch was done, she walked with Beth up the hill to the cabin.

"I'm pretty tired," said Beth. She crawled up on her bunk. "I'm sorry they didn't come," said Anne.

"It's okay." Beth closed her eyes.

Anne stood for a long while and stroked Beth's head, smoothing her hair back from her face.

When Anne thought Beth was asleep, she raced to Charlie's office.

"We need to call her foster parents and see if they're coming," said Anne.

"I don't think that's a good idea. They may have had other plans. It's only a suggestion that parents come up on Sunday. Certainly not a rule."

"I understand that, but her heart is broken. And she's worried. She expected them. I know they must have had a good reason. If I can just find out why they didn't come, I know it will make her feel better. Please."

Charlie made the call.

Anne stood watching him, shifting from one foot to the other, twirling her ponytail like a nervous fifth grader.

Charlie wasn't on the phone long. Something wasn't right. "What is it? An accident? Is someone sick? A death in the family?"

"Worse." He busied himself straightening some papers next to the phone. "I don't know how to say this."

"What? Tell me."

"Beth's not going back to their house. She doesn't

know it, but her foster parents had it planned all along. They don't want her back. A social worker's going to pick her up on Friday and take her to some other home."

"No," said Anne. "But why?"

"I didn't ask, and the person I spoke to—B.J., I think it was—didn't offer. She clearly did not want to talk to me. Asked me not to call again and not to let Beth call either. She kept saying that the social worker would take care of everything, and that if I had any questions I should contact her. Here's her name and number."

He held the paper in his hand. Anne touched it, as if by doing so she would somehow understand.

Kim Beeson. 982-3300.

That's all it said.

Chapter Seven

Hello?"

"Pastor? Did I wake you?"

"No. Of course not," Jock Masters fibbed. How had he overslept? What about the alarm? Without his contact lenses, Jock had to lean to within four inches of his bedside clock before he could see the illuminated numbers. Four forty-five? He eased back the covers and sat up on the side of the bed. News this early in the morning was never good.

" 'Fraid we've got us a little problem."

It was Chilly Reed on the other end. "Just got off the line with Gabe. He's on Saturday night duty this month. Hour ago, answered a call down at the schoolhouse. Lucky, though. False alarm. Bunch of junior high kids trying to pull some kind of prank. You know how they do."

Pastor Jock tried to quietly blow his nose.

"Pastor," said Chilly," ever since that cold snap first of the month, ladies been carrying on about the Sunday school classrooms not being heated up enough."

Pastor Jock scratched his head. Chilly was prone to take the long way around. "Yes, I've heard their concerns." He was shivering in his shorts, his robe out of reach of the phone. "I've been thinking about getting a timer we can preset to make the heat come on ahead of time."

"Reckon RadioShack carries something like that?"

"I imagine they do."

"Well, Pastor, seems Gabe had the same idea as you. Not exactly the same idea. I don't think he knew about the timers down at RadioShack. What I mean is about the church being so cold. He told me that since he was already in the neighborhood this morning, he stopped by the church so as to cut the heat on a little early. Give the building extra time to warm up."

"Good idea," said Jock. Why was Chilly calling before five with this news?

"Anyway, when he stepped inside he got his feet wet clear up over the tops of his shoes." Chilly paused.

"Hate to tell you this, but the church house is flooded inside."

"Not again." Pastor Jock groaned.

"Worse than last time. Already got my shop vac in the truck."

"You called the deacons?"

"All on their way. Except for Catfish. He's down with the gout. Doc told him he had to stay off his feet and quit eating so much grease at the 'Round the Clock. Guess Kerilynn's gonna have to start cooking low-fat."

"Sorry to hear."

"It's not so bad. Wife went on Weight Watchers a while back. Some recipes you can't hardly tell."

"I mean about Catfish having gout." Pastor Jock tried to stifle a yawn. "Soon as I'm dressed I'll be down to the church." He hung up the phone. Then—as he did at the start of every morning—Pastor Jock dropped to his knees by the side of his bed.

"Lord, use me today. Help me to be strong in mind and in spirit. I ask for wisdom to lead this church that You've entrusted to my care. Please give me the heart of a servant. Amen."

He put on his jeans and went in search of his keys. It was time for the servant to take up a mop.

"Baptistry?"

"Not sure. Could be. Then again, might be an overflowed toilet." Armed with flashlights, Gabe Eden and Dr. Lee Ross were trying to determine the source of the flood. "Don't know yet. Got the main valve shut off."

"Don't see any busted pipe," said Ben Jackson.

"Least it's clean water."

"Baptistry's still full."

Within two hours the men had vacuumed all the water that they could. They pulled the carpet up, propped it off the floor with chairs from the toddler room, and turned on industrial fans that Chilly had borrowed from the sewing factory down the street.

"You think that carpet'll go back down?" asked Gabe. "Won't know till it dries," said Ben.

"Stuff's bad to mildew," said Chilly. "Shrink too."

"Insurance might buy us a new one this time," said Pastor Jock. The men stood in the foyer and surveyed the sanctuary's mess. "What about this morning's service?" asked Ben.

"Can't have it here," said Gabe.

"Pastor?"

He had been thinking and praying about the matter for the past half hour. It was too cold to hold services outside. Friendship Baptist would be glad to help out, but on even a regular Sunday their little building was near to bursting at the seams. They'd held revival services all last week, and reports were of a rousing success. Lots of backsliders had rededicated their lives to the Lord. With all that, attendance at Friendship would be up so much that they'd likely be putting folding chairs in the aisles just for their regular members.

"Guess we could skip," said Chilly.

"Reckon we could." Gabe yawned.

"How long you been up?" asked Chilly.

"Since two."

Pastor Jock could not see calling church off over a leak. Lord wouldn't likely be pleased. "Guys. Come on. Christians all over the world meet for worship every Sunday. Lots of places don't have buildings at all. Ben, couldn't we meet at the school?"

"Normally I'd say yes, but the custodial crew spent all day yesterday putting some new kind of finish on the floors. Salesman said for the stuff to take, we've got to stay off them at least twenty-four hours."

"Nobody I can think of has got a house big enough to hold our bunch," said Dr. Ross.

"What've we been running on Sunday morning—close to ninety?" asked Ben.

"Sixty-five in Sunday school, eighty-eight for worship last week," said Pastor Jock.

"Can't think of any place downtown," said Chilly.

"Like I said, we could just—"

"What about the skating rink?" interrupted Pastor Jock. It was owned by the city.

"That's an idea," said Chilly.

"Good one," said Dr. Ross.

"Big enough," said Ben.

"Plenty places to sit," said Gabe. "They've got all those folding seats set up around the rink."

"Got chairs and tables in the snack bar area too, don't forget."

"Let's do it." Ben looked at his watch. "Kerilynn'll

be up by now. I'll run over and get her key."

"Meet you there. Won't take us too long to get things set up," said Chilly.

"Somebody best put a sign on all the doors so folks'll know we're not meeting here," said Gabe.

"I'll take care of that," said Ben. "We got any tape?"

"Pastor, you go on back to the house. We'll take it from here," said Dr. Ross.

"You sure?" Pastor Jock was grateful for the offer. He needed to take a shower and spend a few minutes looking over his sermon notes.

"Go on. We'll see you in—" Dr. Ross looked at his watch "—an hour and a half."

"Wait, Pastor, I need to ask you one thing," Chilly called after him.

"What's that?"

He winked. "You don't reckon this'll qualify us to be holy rollers now, do you?"

The other deacons groaned.

Charlotte woke to the piercing sound of a smoke alarm. Snowball and Visa sprang from Charlotte's warm bed. Terrified of the unfamiliar sound, the cats scampered into the closet and hid behind Charlotte's shoes. She smelled smoke. What could it be? Bad wiring? Something on the stove? She stumbled first toward the kitchen, then remembered with a start.

The twins!

Evacuate. Call for help. Extinguish. That was what the fire safety instructor had said. Or was it extinguish, evacuate, then call for help? And where was it she had put the fire extinguisher? Hall closet? Under the sink? Charlotte remembered considering both places. Now she would have to hunt. Were you supposed to pull on the pin or push the other little thingy in? It had seemed clear at the time. Why hadn't she paid better attention?

Charlotte bolted up the stairs, taking them two, even three at a time. Breathe. Stay calm. Avoid panic. Didn't fire travel up?

"Nikki, Vikki!" she called. "Wake up. Hurry. We need to go outside." She burst into their room. Both beds were empty. She dashed down the hall toward the bathroom. Not there either.

The smoke alarm stopped. Then started again. Then stopped yet again.

At the top of the stairs, Charlotte stood and caught her breath. The girls must have heard the alarm and gone outside on their own. What smart girls. She bet they'd learned that in school. Now if she could just find the extinguisher. Maybe since the alarm had quit, it wasn't something so bad after all.

Charlotte headed down the stairs and toward the kitchen. She rounded the corner from the hallway so sharply her feet slipped out from under her and she nearly fell.

"What's your name again? I forgot." Nikki's matter-of-fact voice came from an elevated spot.

Charlotte looked up.

Wearing her nightgown and a mismatched pair of

fuzzy socks, the little girl was standing on tiptoe on a kitchen chair, calmly fanning the smoke detector with a dishrag every time it chirped.

"What are you doing?" The smoke inside the kitchen made Charlotte cough.

"Making toast."

Charlotte turned around to see Vikki.

"It got a little too brown," she said in a voice as calm as her sister's.

"I can see that." Sweet relief. There was no fire. Just smoke. And on the kitchen counter, bread, butter, a knife, and three plates. Not to mention toast, speared on the end of Vikki's fork, black and crisp. Charlotte turned on the over-the-stove vent and cracked the back door.

"You girls been up awhile?" She willed her voice to match their nonchalance.

"Not too long. Got any jelly?"

"Sure. Do you usually make your own breakfast?"

"Just toast."

"How about some pancakes instead?" said Charlotte.

"I never made pancakes. I can cook an egg. Any kind except fried."

"She always breaks open the yellow part."

"But I can make scrambled. Would that be all right?" asked Vikki, charred bread still in hand.

Charlotte swallowed. "No. Yes. What I mean is that scrambled eggs are great. But how about I make breakfast for you?"

Nikki and Vikki looked at each other and shrugged. "Sure."

"That sounds good," said Nikki.

"Better than burnt toast," said Vikki. "That's for sure."

Church is flooded.
Service to be held at Buffalo Memorial Skating Rink.
Regular time.
Please come. All welcome.

Alice Buck, Bible in hand and bifocals in her purse, stood on the steps and read the sign out loud. "Skating rink? Church at the skating rink? That can't be right."

"That's what it says," said Nomie Jenkins.

The two of them, Sunday school teachers with more than thirty-five years' combined experience, were among the first to arrive and find the doors of Lighted Way locked up tight.

"Flooded?"

"Not again."

"Must be the baptistry."

"If we sprinkled like the Methodists instead of dunking like the Baptists, we wouldn't keep having these problems."

"Nomie!"

"Well, we wouldn't. Water bill wouldn't be so high either. Besides that, it's a wonder no one has caught pneumonia and died from leaving the church house with a wet head."

"At least they'd have die saved," said Alice. "Come on. You and I better get over there and see what in the world those deacons have cooked up. Bet they need some help."

Three more cars pulled into the parking lot as they were leaving. Alice motioned to the drivers to roll their windows down. "Church isn't meeting here. Flooded. Had to move services to the skating rink," she explained. "So says the note on the door."

Alice and Nomie watched car after car turn around and head in the opposite direction of the rink. "Guess some folks look on a flood as a sign from God that they should turn around and go back home," said Alice.

The two of them fell in line with the faithful and curious portion of the Lighted Way church members who drove the three blocks to see how services at the skating rink would pan out.

The deacons had done a good job setting up. The building was toasty warm. Seats were in place.

"Look there," said Nomie.

Round and round the disco ball twirled, casting psychedelic shadows all around the dimly lit rink.

"Tried every switch in the place. Can't get the thing to shut down," explained Ben Jackson. "Must be wired in with the lights somehow."

"Sort of distracting."

"The teenagers think it's cool."

"Has Pastor requested a first song?"

" 'Old Rugged Cross.' "

"Maybe he could change to 'Send the Light.' "

Alice and Nomie took seats near the front.

Pastor Jock wondered how this day would turn out.

By ten o'clock, the parking lot at the skating rink held more than a dozen Lighted Way members' cars. Deacons Ben Jackson and Dr. Lee Ross stood inside the door to welcome everyone as they arrived. Folks walked in squinting at the contrast of the bright, sunny day to the dim rink.

"This way. Come right this way." Mayor Kerilynn stood guard over the entrance to the wood-floored rink. "Sorry. Got to pull those shoes off unless they've got rubber soles on them. Can't be ruining this floor, not even for church. Go on now. Slip them off. You can leave them right here. Won't nobody be worrying about anybody's smelly feet. Least they shouldn't be."

"You saying this here's holy ground?" teased Lester Collins. He struggled to pull off his boots.

Pastor Jock grinned.

Kerilynn glanced toward the door. "Here's Charlotte Carter. Has she got the little girl with her?"

"Looks like."

"I can't wait to see what she looks like."

"Hello, ladies," Pastor Jock welcomed them. "Charlotte, I see you've brought a couple of visitors along with you."

"We're not visitors."

"We're sisters."

"I can see that."

"When do we get to skate?"

"Pastor Jock, this is Nikki and this is Vikki."

"Two girls? I thought—"

"Me too." Charlotte smiled. "Big surprise. Two for the price of one." She guided Nikki and Vikki to a trio of empty seats near the back. "Girls, let's sit over here."

Pastor Jock stalled a bit. Folks trailed in. Finally, only fifteen minutes later than normal, the service commenced.

The location was a distraction for everyone, and especially challenging to the moms and dads. Pastor Jock heard parents whisper repeated explanations as to why their kids were not getting to skate. As for the disco ball—even he found it difficult not to watch it twirl. The prominently posted, professionally lettered signs admonishing patrons to avoid the triple vices of pushing, profanity, and spitting did not exactly lend reverence to this day of the Lord.

You know our hearts, Lord. Help us muddle through.

Ben led the group in singing the first verses of songs that most everyone knew. After that, a prayer; then Pastor Jock got up to preach.

He was more than halfway through his sermon when he was interrupted by the scraping sound of the heavy outside door. It opened partway, then closed, then opened up all the way wide, letting in a bright shaft of light and the honeyed sound of a female voice just outside.

Every worshipper turned to look.

Having made it inside, the woman, clad in a plus-size, strawberry-print pink patio dress, wiped her feet on the rubber mat. "Lands!" she said, obviously perplexed. "Thought I were early." She squinted. "Didn't expect this."

She surveyed the group and their mostly Caucasian-toned skin. "Y'all must be from some other side of the family. Good to see you." She carried a green, covered Tupperware bowl in one hand and two stacked aluminum-foil-wrapped casserole dishes in the other. Within seconds, the smells of home cooking wafted over the congregation, prompting a few stomachs to growl and a couple of hungry babies to cry. It was, after all, ten minutes until noon.

"May I help you?" Pastor Jock held his place in his Bible.

"Thank you. I sure could use some help carrying things in. Got the back of my minivan loaded down. It's a long way from Oklahoma. Honey, where you want me to set this food? I've got a green salad in this bowl. Peach cobbler in the one pan, sage dressing in the other."

"Deacons?" said Pastor Jock.

They sprang to her aid, while the rest of the congregation stared.

"Appreciate it. My arms felt like they were about to fall off."

Suddenly the light dawned on Kerilynn. She stood up, her face bright pink. "My word. I can't believe I forgot. Pastor, today's the day of the Evans family reunion. I am so sorry. They booked the rink a good three months ago. Supposed to have the place from twelve-thirty until late tonight. They've got folks coming in from all over."

The woman with the food looked puzzled. "You mean y'all are not on anyone's side? Then who are you?"

Pastor Jock moved from his spot and stuck out his hand. "Welcome. I'm Jock Masters. Pastor of Lighted Way Church."

"Treasure Evans. You mean you all are having *church? Here?*"

"Just today. Our building flooded, and we had to find someplace to meet."

"Pastor, I'm so sorry. I didn't know I was in the Lord's house. I've gone and set up a stir. Pardon me. You all go on ahead. This food can wait until you good folks finish with what you came to get." Treasure took a seat. "Go on. Don't mind me." She folded her hands in her lap, leaned back, and closed her eyes. "Thank You, Jesus," she said.

Pastor Jock looked out over his distracted, hungry flock and decided to take Mrs. Evans's cue. "Friends, let us bow our heads in prayer."

Soon the last amen had been said, and the Lighted Way members prepared to clear out.

"Nice to meet you." They shook the woman's hand.

"Hope you and your family enjoy your day."

"Mrs. Evans, I am so sorry about the mix-up," said Pastor Jock. "I appreciate your understanding."

"It was all my fault," said Mayor Kerilynn.

"Don't worry about it a bit," said Treasure. "Hope you get your church back in shape before next Sunday. I'll keep you in my prayers."

Across the room, Charlotte was trying to make her way to the door. Everyone wanted to meet the twins, so the going was slow. She had just gotten near the exit when Treasure Evans caught sight of her face and froze in her tracks.

"Lord, I cannot believe what I see. Honey. Tell me you are Ruby Pratter's girl."

Nikki and Vikki were out the door without her, but Charlotte stood, rooted and stunned. "Excuse me?"

Treasure took Charlotte's hands in her own. She studied her face and spoke with great hope. "Ruby Pratter. Was neighbors to me and my daddy when we lived in Durant years ago. You look just like her. Are you her kin?"

"She was my grandmother."

At Charlotte's words, Treasure encased her in a giant hug around the neck, then sat down hard and began to weep.

Chapter Eight

Turkey or tuna?" asked Kerilynn. Working at the 'Round the Clock all week had not left her in the mood for fancy cooking. She was not inclined to prepare more than her usual Sunday fare, a heated-up can of chicken noodle soup or a slapped-together sandwich. Not for herself, nor to ease the hunger of her twin brother Catfish—even if he had come down with the gout.

"Ham and Swiss. With Miracle Whip. Sliced onions too. But no lettuce," said Catfish, whose painful, swollen feet were propped up in front of him.

"Can't have ham. Too much fat."

"All right. Turkey, then. But make it on white."

"You two are twins?" Charlotte had asked Kerilynn shortly after meeting them both.

"Yep. Folks who don't know us can't hardly believe it," said Kerilynn. "We've been of a different bend ever since we were little kids. We get along most of the time—long as we're together for no more than a couple of hours at a stretch. Any longer'n that, and we start getting on each other's nerves."

Charlotte hadn't intended to be rude. "I'm sure he's a nice man. Just a little gruff, is all I meant."

"Sugar, you don't have to mince words with me. I know my brother. On any given day Catfish'll wake up steeled and ready for what's bound to go wrong. Thing is, he's so good at hunting trouble, he finds it most ever'where he looks. Don't get me wrong. We love each other. Reckon either one of us'd fight a bear for the other one if we needed to."

"You live close?" Charlotte asked.

"Next door to each other. Catfish lost his wife and I lost my husband the same year. That was ten years back. Both of us being alone all of a sudden, we went in together and bought our duplex. You've seen it, red brick, down from the school. He lives in one side, I live in the other. I stay busy at the cafe; he's got his video store and bait shop. Some days we hardly see each other. Works out pretty good."

Charlotte could see that it did.

"You picked a pretty good day to be out of commission." Kerilynn set Catfish's paper plate down on the TV tray next to his chair. "Deacons were up before daylight cleaning that awful mess at the church."

"Blame building's falling apart. Wasn't plumbed right when it was built. Roof's bad too," said Catfish. "Gonna cost us a mint to fix ever'-thing that's broke." He wiped his mouth and took a swig of iced tea. "Something don't taste right. You sure that turkey's not gone bad?"

"It's Miracle Whip Light."

"Should have known. Stuff's got a whang to it." He took another bite. "I expect Jock'll be hitting us up for a raise pretty soon too."

"When's the last time he had one—two years ago?"

"Not like the Lord's money grows on trees."

"Pretty good crowd today." Kerilynn steered him to another topic.

"Moving church to the skating rink. Who came up with that notion?"

"Pastor, I suppose. Turned out to be fine."

"Any visitors?"

"No. But Charlotte Carter was there. You know—she's the one that's opened up Tanglewood for a girls' home."

"I ain't forgot who she is," Catfish grumbled.

"She had with her two of the cutest little girls you've ever seen. Twins. Like two beans in a pot. Hate I can't remember their names. Think they were Brenda and Linda. Maybe Ann and Nan. Anyway, she told me she's expecting another girl this week. Probably have a full house by Thanksgiving."

Catfish released the foot of his La-Z-Boy, and it went down with a thump. "For the life of me, Kerilynn, I cannot understand how you think this is a good thing. I know. Everyone keeps saying she's looking after orphan children. Don't get me wrong; that's all well and good." He leaned forward, put his elbows on his knees and began cleaning his fingernails with the blade of his knife. "All I'm saying is that first off, we ought to be looking out after our own. There's enough needy kids here in Ruby Prairie what could use a leg up. Children whose mamas and daddies are hard-working, tax-paying citizens. It's not that I've anything against what this woman's doing; it just pains me to see so many of our local children doing without."

"I'm touched," Kerilynn said. "Catfish, I believe your old heart's going soft. In fact, your concern has about brought me to tears. Seeing as how you're suddenly so worried about Ruby Prairie children, I'm going to help you out. This very day you can make out a check to the Culture Club. I happen to know we came up short this year. School supply drive and scholarship fund are both hurting for cash."

Catfish waffled. "There you go, turning stuff all around. Kerilynn, I have never known of a woman so easily confused."

She picked up her brother's checkbook from the desk nearby and slapped it right down onto his knee. "Your money in place of your mouth, old man. Two hundred. Not one penny less."

Beaten at his own game, Catfish took out a pen and, in a huff, did exactly as he was told.

"Two of them look so much alike. You must have a time telling them apart," said Treasure Evans. At Charlotte's invitation, Treasure had stopped by on her way home from the reunion. "Vikki has a cowlick on her left side," said Charlotte.

"That's a good thing."

Free from the relatively quiet constraints of skating rink church and full from a Crock-Pot lunch, Nikki and Vikki had changed their clothes and escaped into Charlotte's shady yard. They'd been playing outside the entire afternoon, swinging on the tire swing, exploring the arbor.

Snowball and Visa, curious and glad for the company but a bit skittish still, kept the girls in sight but trailed just out of their reach. The cats chased each other and staged fierce pretend fights. Occasionally one of them pounced on an imaginary mouse.

In the fall air the girls' voices carried, crisp and clear. Illuminated by the late afternoon sun, from a distance they looked like impish, poorly dressed fairies, their skinny brown arms and legs free, their flying ponytails taking on shiny tones of dappled light.

"Let's go back to the secret place," one of them called, and they scampered across the yard to step inside the vine-covered arbor.

Charlotte had fallen in love with the partially hidden green nook even before deciding to buy the house. It was the perfect place for Tanglewood girls to go when they wanted to be alone or hide out. A cozy place for her to escape to as well, should the need ever arise. To enhance the hidden room, she had placed in its shade two wrought-iron chairs and a little round table gleaned from a garage sale. A fringed hammock with an attached little pillow, suspended from a metal frame, took up one end of the space. Early fall flowers bloomed around the borders; and a wind chime, hung from a bushy branch, tinkled in the breeze.

"Your grandma Ruby would be so proud of you," said Treasure, looking at Charlotte's smile of satisfaction. "You favor her so much. Same eyes. Same nose. She had a fair complexion and that one dimple on the left just like you. You're built like her too. Slim through the hips, strong shoulders. And I can see from what you've done here that you've got her same ways."

Charlotte rocked and listened.

"How that woman loved children. Didn't matter to

your grandmother if a child was white like her or black like me. Weren't any Mexicans around the neighborhood back then, but if there had been, she would have been good to them too. When I knew her she was a young bride. Twenty years old. Didn't have two nickels to rub together, but that didn't stop her from feeding and helping clothe half the neighborhood children who was worse off than her."

Charlotte took a sip of iced tea.

"I'll never forget her," said Treasure. She dabbed at her eyes with a hankie she pulled from her bodice. "I lived with my daddy a little piece down from her house. My mother died when I was five, and my daddy wasn't no account. Drank day and night. Didn't know what to do with me, so he left me alone."

"That must have been hard." Charlotte stopped rocking.

"It was. Didn't have proper food and never good clothes. That was bad, but the worst was being so lonesome. My daddy didn't talk to me none. I mean days would go by, and he would just not say a word. But your grandma talked. Almost every day I would go down to her house. I was not a pretty child and I wasn't clean, but she always acted like she was glad to see me. 'Treasure,' she'd say, 'come on in. Go wash your hands and then come to the table. How about we have us a piece of cake and a glass of sweet milk?' "

"She made the best cakes in the world," said Charlotte. "Coconut with lemon filling and a chocolate one she made with cocoa and hot coffee were the ones I liked best."

"I loved her spice cake with the brown sugar glaze," said Treasure.

"That one was good too. You know, I've got all her recipes, but mine have never turned out as good as hers."

"Your grandma cooked with love and butter." Treasure chuckled. "She always said Gold Medal flour was the secret to her baking success, but I know better."

"How long did you know her?" asked Charlotte.

"From the time I was five until I married at fifteen. I moved off and only saw her a few times after that. Ten years is all, I guess. But I never forgot her. That's why it hit me so hard when I saw you today. Brought ever' bit of that back. Seeing your face looking so much like hers, watching you tend to those little girls made me feel like I was that little lonely five-year-old all over again. Some things never leave you."

"Grandma just passed away last year."

"My condolences. May she rest in peace. Up in years, was she not?"

"Eighty-four when she died."

"A good long life."

"It's Grandmother Ruby's money that bought this house."

"You don't say."

"Granddaddy did well."

"Man was a hard worker."

"Actually, no. He suffered with a bad heart and

could never do much. What he did do was buy Frito-Lay stock when it first came out. He's been gone more than twenty years. My mother and dad were killed in a car accident my first year in college. I never had any brothers and sisters. Just Grandma. When she died, I was the only relative left. She willed everything she had to me."

"The Lord makes good out of bad. What a blessing. I know your grandmother would approve of what you're doing."

"I hope she would. I think so. Well—all except for one thing."

"What's that?"

"The color of the house. She never did like pink."

Treasure laughed. "Guess you had to put a little of yourself into this place."

"Where do you live now?" asked Charlotte.

"Edmond. Just north of Oklahoma City."

"I know the town. My husband and I lived west of there."

"He's gone too?" asked Treasure.

"Died less than a year ago."

"Why, bless your heart. You don't have any of your people left at all. No parents. Lost your husband and your grandmother. Honey, you've shed lots of tears, haven't you?"

Charlotte swallowed. "It's been hard. But getting settled in Ruby Prairie, getting my home for girls up and running has helped occupy my mind."

"I'd say so. This is a big place to take care of. When

you get all those pretty bedrooms full of little girls, you're going to have your hands full. You'll have help, won't you?"

"Not planning on it," said Charlotte. "I figure the Lord has brought me this far; He'll continue to be with me. Losing my folks at nineteen made me grow up fast. Taught me to be resourceful. I learned not to depend on other people, not even on my husband—which was a good thing, since in the end it was I who took care of him."

"Bless your heart."

"Don't feel sorry for me." Charlotte sat up straighter in her chair. "I haven't found anything yet that I couldn't handle if I was willing to work hard enough to accomplish it."

"Sugar, you're not nineteen anymore. You don't have to prove yourself to anybody," said Treasure.

"Folks in town have been friendly and nice, but I suspect some of them think I must be crazy to take this on all by myself. The way I see it is this: I'm healthy. I'm fairly young. And I have lots of energy. I believe I can take care of this place and the girls who come to me. If I thought I couldn't do it myself, I would have never tried it."

"I believe every word you say," said Treasure. "But keep in mind—there are times when even the strongest among us need help." She drained her glass. "Could I trouble you for another glass of tea?"

"Of course. In the kitchen. I'll bring the pitcher out."

Just as Charlotte got up, Vikki bounded up the

wooden porch steps. "Where's your sister?" asked Charlotte.

"Back there." She pointed. "We need you. She fell out of the tree." When Charlotte and Treasure reached Nikki, she was crying and writhing on the ground.

Was her leg broken? How far did she fall? Should she call 9-1-1? Apply some kind of a splint? Charlotte had taken first aid at the Red Cross, but her mind raced past all the jumbled-up knowledge she'd gleaned.

"Shhh. Hush now. You're going to be fine." Treasure knelt in the grass. She held the child's bony knee in her hand. "What's your name? Nikki? How do you spell that? And you're nine years old? What pretty fingernail polish you've got on. Is that color red or dark pink? Now tell me: Does it hurt here? How about here?"

Nikki stopped crying.

Treasure gently touched and pressed. "I believe you fell on a rock. Looks like a stone bruise to me. A little ice for your knee and maybe some ice cream for your stomach—I think you'll be good as new. Let's see if you can stand up."

Nikki could.

"Who are you?" asked Vikki.

"I'm Treasure. Your moth—I mean, Charlotte is my friend."

"Are you a doctor?" asked Nikki.

Treasure smiled. "No. But I know a little bit about taking care of hurts. Speaking of which, seeing as how

I'm down here on the ground and you're standing up, how about you girls give me a hand. My old knees don't work as good as they used to. I gained some pounds when I went through the change. Reckon that made things worse."

Charlotte and the girls, even Nikki, who appeared to be fine by now, extended their hands.

"Are you a nurse?" asked Charlotte.

"No, but I've studied in that direction. Anatomy. Physiology. How everything fits together and works."

"Really," said Charlotte. "But you're not a nurse."

"No. I'm a masseuse. These days we call ourselves massage therapists. I've been at it going on twenty years. Work out of a little shop right next to my house. I give massages and sell vitamins and supplements on the side. It's been good to me. Past few years, Edmond has grown up so much I've got more customers than I know what to do with. Used to be, if you hung out your shingle saying you would give massages, folks thought you were some kind of a pervert. Not anymore. I've even got some doctors what send folks to me."

"You do it full time?"

"Can't anymore. Got a touch of carpal tunnel that gives me fits if I work too much. Long as I hold it to no more than twenty hours in a week, I do pretty fine."

Nikki and Vikki sprinted toward the house, eager for promised bowls of Blue Bell Cookies 'n Cream. Charlotte and Treasure watched them go. About every third step, Nikki remembered to limp.

"Your knowledge came in handy today, Treasure. Thank you. I'm so glad you were here. You were so calm. I get rattled when unexpected things happen," said Charlotte.

Treasure threw back her head and roared with laughter. "Dear, you'd better get used to all kinds of shenanigans taking place in this house. If you're gonna have a mess of children around, nothing is ever going to happen according to plan."

Charlotte looked down.

"Honey." Treasure gave her a big hug. "Don't get your feelings hurt. You're going to be just fine. You've only got to remember one thing. No matter what you think, you're not going to be able to do this thing alone. You're not supposed to. God puts people in the places where He needs them to be. He put you here for these little girls. But there's something else. Why would He put me here on your porch today? Be honest. You were about to take that child to the hospital in your car—were you not?"

Charlotte nodded.

"Would have cost you a bunch of money. And you'd have been there for the rest of the day, probably half the night."

"You're right."

"Look at her now. Fine as frog hair. Prancing up those steps. God knew I needed your grandmother when I was a little girl. In a small way, you needed me today. That's why I'm here." She took Charlotte's hands in her own. "Honey, pretty soon you're going to figure out that's why we're all here. Now—" Treasure looked at her watch "—it's getting to be late. I best be getting on my way."

"You're not driving to Edmond tonight, are you?"

"No. Just as far as my sister's house in Telephone. You know where that is? Wide place in the road, just south of the Oklahoma border." She dug and dug in her multi-pocketed purse. Once she'd excavated what she wanted, she called to Nikki and Vikki.

"Girls, I've got to go. Y'all come hug my neck. Here's some gum for when you finish your cream." Treasure hugged them and kissed them on their foreheads, leaving behind Jungle Rose lipstick prints. "Be sweet now. Study in school. Mind Charlotte."

"We will. Bye."

That night, after baths and supper, Charlotte stood in the doorway of the girls' darkened bedroom. "Good night, you two. Sweet dreams."

"Good night."

"Will you leave the hall light on?"

"Yes."

"Is Treasure coming back tomorrow?"

"No. She went home to her house."

"I wish she was still here."

Later, staring up at the ceiling in her own bed, Charlotte wished the same.

Chapter Nine

"Do you pick the girls up from school, or do they ride the bus?" asked social worker Kim Beeson. She sat with Charlotte at the kitchen table and made notes on a yellow legal pad.

"Neither. They walk."

Kim didn't hide her surprise. She pushed her hair behind her ear and chewed the end of her pen.

Was letting the girls walk home from school a breach of some rule? Charlotte racked her brain, then spoke quickly to explain. "The first two days I took them in the van. After that they begged me to let them walk. Seems that here, that's what all the kids do. For Nikki and Vikki, it's only three blocks. I asked around. Everyone I talked to insists that it's safe. Folks up and down know what time school lets out. They watch out for everyone's children—not just their own."

Kim made a note, then turned to a new page.

"So you've had Nikki and Vikki for just over a week now. I'm sure you've had lots of adjustments. You feel as though everything's going well?"

"I do."

"How are they doing in school?"

"Pretty good. According to the records from their last school, they read slightly below grade level. They've had no problems in math—which is a great thing, because I'm not sure I would be much good if they needed help with that. Their teacher tells me they're behaving. She thinks they're a little socially immature compared to other fourth graders, but I don't agree. They're just a bit shy around children they don't know. Who can blame them? They'll make friends in time. The last couple of days they've come home talking about other students in their class."

"Do they seem to be comfortable here at home with you?"

"I think so. Not having ever had children of my own, there are a few gaps in my education. Currently I'm working on learning how to do hair and how to make oatmeal with the right amount of sugar and butter."

"Are they sleeping?"

Charlotte smiled. "Together. In the same bed."

"Eating?"

"No problems. Three meals a day, and they come home starving after school."

"Did their mother call?"

"Their grandmother did. Saturday. They talked for about half an hour."

"Did her call upset the girls?"

"Not that I could tell."

How could anyone know what went on inside a child's mind? Soon as they'd hung up the phone, Nikki and Vikki had grabbed juice boxes and crackers and made a beeline for their secret backyard retreat. Watching from the window over the kitchen sink, Charlotte had longed to follow them. Instinct told her to leave the two of them alone.

They'd stayed hidden in the green arbor for the better part of an hour before coming back inside and heading up the stairs to their room. Charlotte was just about to go up and check on them when they came back down, showing no outward signs of distress. It seemed that between the two of them they'd worked things out in their minds.

Dinner that evening had been upbeat and silly, though the twins' chirpy around-the-table talk had been punctuated with repeated references to "when we get to go home."

"They miss their mother and their grandmother. I know they do. It's good that she called. They need to hear from their family. Having each other, I believe, is what makes them able to handle the separation."

"I'm sure it does," said Kim. "You have any questions for me? Any problems we need to discuss?"

"None that I can think of."

Kim closed the twins' folder and paused for a moment.

Was something wrong? Maybe the walking home from school thing?

"I want you to have plenty of time to adjust to Nikki and Vikki," said Kim, "and not to feel in any kind of a rush. But just so you know—when you're ready—I have another girl in need of a placement."

Charlotte's heart sped up. "Really? That's great!"

"Her name is Beth."

"How old is she?"

"Fifteen."

"Where is she now?"

"She's currently in a Dallas homeless shelter," said Kim.

"A shelter? Why?"

"It was my only option. All my emergency foster homes were full. Sometimes this happens. Beth's need for placement came up quickly."

"What's her situation?"

"Sweet girl. Been in foster care on and off for more than ten years. I thought this last family would work out. Everything appeared to be going so well that I thought they might keep her until she turned eighteen. I was wrong. They've terminated the placement."

"Did she cause problems?" Charlotte had Nikki and Vikki to think of.

"Nothing like that. Three weeks ago, Beth's foster mom found out she was pregnant. She's in her late thirties and didn't think she could ever have kids. When she got the news of the pregnancy, her feelings for Beth changed. Maybe hormones are to blame. I don't know. Practically overnight, she decided she wanted Beth gone. Her husband is in such shock at all of this that he went along with her."

"So they just told her they didn't want her any-more?" Charlotte's heart hurt. How could someone do that to a child?

"Worse than that. Knowing full well they weren't going to take her back, they sent Beth to church camp. Once she was there, they called and told me they were not going to pick her up. There was nothing I could do. I tried to talk them into reconsidering. To at least pick her up, take her home, and explain things to her. They refused. Nothing I said made a difference. They sent her belongings UPS. to my office and told me they didn't plan to see her again."

"That's awful! They didn't even tell her good-bye?" *Which room should be Beth's? Which quilt would a fifteen-year-old like best on her bed?* "So—she's been at the shelter how many days?"

"Almost a week."

"You should have called me."

"You'll take her?"

"Of course. Bring her today."

"I'm glad you want her, but it'd be best for you to think about this overnight," said Kim. "You're still adjusting to Nikki and Vikki. There've been lots of changes for you and for them. You need to know, Beth is going to be a difficult placement. She's older, and she's been terribly hurt. I expect she will do some acting out. There's no need for you to rush into a decision. As of right now, she's in a safe place."

"You call a shelter safe?" Charlotte hadn't meant to snap. "I'm sorry, but I've been to those places. I used to volunteer. They're awful."

"Not ideal. But they have regulations. And this one's better than most. I know the director. Teens and adults are kept in separate areas."

"I don't need time to think. I appreciate you not wanting to overwhelm me, but I'm fine. The twins are fine. The reason I opened up this home is to care for girls just like Beth. I'm ready. When can you have her here?"

"If you're sure, I can bring her tomorrow, around noon."

Once he'd heard from the insurance adjuster, Pastor Jock called for an emergency business meeting of Lighted Way's deacons. Since the church was still in a mess, he told them all that the meeting would be held at his house. In preparation he ran the vacuum, put on a pot of coffee, and set a Sara Lee layer cake out on the counter to thaw.

"Gentlemen, we've got two options," he explained after prayer. "Stretch and reinstall the carpet that got wet, or spend the extra to put down new."

"Hold on," said Catfish, whose gout was slightly improved. "There's a lot to consider here. How old's that carpet we already got?"

"Two years, I best recall," said Gabe.

"Should have a good bit more wear left in it," said Catfish.

"About two more years is what the carpet restoration people told me," said Pastor Jock. "Its getting wet shortens the wear we can expect to get out of it."

"Can't go by that. They're wanting to make a buck selling us new. That carpet's got at least five more good years from where I sit."

"How much'll it be to replace it?" asked Dr. Ross.

"Above what insurance will pay, around twelve hundred dollars," said Pastor Jock.

"How much will we spend when we put down what we've got now?" asked Ben.

"Four thousand," said Pastor Jock. "And that was because Hardy's agreed to order it and sell it to the church at cost."

"Plus freight," reminded Catfish.

"Looking at those amounts, I believe we should bite the bullet and put down new. Save us a bundle in the long run," said Chilly. "I agree," said Ben.

"Me too," said Gabe.

"I'll go along, but tight as the church budget has been, taking on this carpet deal means we'll have to be cutting some other financial corners. Making some sacrifices. Lord's money don't grow on trees." Catfish looked square at Pastor Jock. "Can't be always asking folks to dig deeper. Lots of members on fixed incomes. Most others have got wives, little ones to raise."

Pastor Jock knew exactly where this was leading.

"May as well bring this up," Catfish continued. "I know he's been looking for it but don't see as how we can give the pastor here any kind of a raise next year."

"Should I step out?" asked Pastor Jock.

"Won't be any need of that." Dr. Ross jumped in with both feet. "Catfish, we all here appreciate your budgetary concerns, but you've gotten off track. This is neither the time nor the place to be discussing the pastor's wages. Carpet's our concern tonight, and looking at these figures, I say we've got enough to cover putting down new without too much of a strain." He locked eyes with Catfish. "Men, shall we put it to a vote?"

"All in favor."

It was a unanimous aye, except for Catfish, who, arms folded across his chest, declared at the last minute that he would abstain.

"Fine," said Dr. Ross when the voting was done. "That was the easy part. Now we've got to get the ladies to agree on what color to get this time around."

Groans were heard around the room.

"Can't we just go on and order beige?" said Gabe.

Dr. Ross acknowledged Gabe's suggestion with a grin but, being a married man with forty years' experience, wisely ignored him. "Chilly, can you talk to Hank Hardy and see what kind of deal he can give us?"

"No problem. I'll get down there tomorrow."

"Good," said Dr. Ross. "Now, tell me I wasn't dreaming, Pastor. Didn't I see a cake sitting on your counter when I came in?"

Alone in his kitchen, Pastor Jock rinsed out coffee mugs and threw paper plates in the trash. Catfish's comments played over again in his mind. Seventeen years of ministry, and nearing his fortieth birthday, Pastor Jock was accustomed to pointed comments about his status as a single man. Still, they rubbed.

Five years gone since Lighted Way called him to serve. First, of course, they'd heard him preach. They'd also wanted answers to a host of questions about what had brought him to this place in his life. He'd answered their queries as best he could.

There were specifics a church needed to know about a person being considered for a position—items one of the older men, now passed on, referred to as general housekeeping details. As was to be expected, Lighted Way Church required facts that could be written down in black ink, backed up with framed documents, diplomas, certificates, and such.

Easy enough.

He'd told them the truth. How he became a Christian at twenty-four. Having already obtained a bachelor's degree in history, he'd entered seminary at twenty-six, graduated on time with honors, number three in his class. The résumé he offered revealed the names and locations of three satisfied churches where he had served.

And yes. Of course. He was happy to provide references upon request.

That part was short and to the point.

It was the other stuff, the personal side of his life, that Jock Masters could never figure out how to share and explain in a neat, tidy way.

Single. Divorced, actually, he had learned to add quickly. Married at nineteen, before coming to the Lord. She, pretty and pregnant at the time; he, foolish and fond of having everything his own way. Their marriage wheezed along for eighteen months. By the time it ended, his bride had miscarried their baby and discovered that he was having an affair.

Single again.

And single still.

Back when he was nineteen, Jock had never intended to be married. Nor had it crossed his mind that what he was doing might lead to his becoming a daddy. Fun was all that had mattered. It had come as a shock to wake up one day next to a wife with morning sickness and the sound of a toilet that wouldn't quit running—a fixture that he, a husband now, was somehow expected to know how to repair. At the time of his divorce, only twenty-one years old, Jock had felt no guilt, only relief to be shed of the whole confusing and confining mess.

The way he saw it, he could now get back to his regular life. Except he never did.

When Jock looked back, he saw, beginning soon after the loss of his unwanted, unplanned-for wife and child, God repeatedly casting for his heart. That year, and the next one too, time and time again, his path crossed with folks who'd once been like him, but who'd become something new. Honest co-workers. A passionate college professor. A pair of helpful neighbors in the apartment next door. To their credit, not one of them thumped a Bible at him. None of them preached to him about his sins. Instead, they told him stories about how God had mended their broken lives and healed their scarred hearts. When the times that felt right came along, they told him how Jesus had died to take away everything wrong a person had ever done.

Not feeling a bit broken or scarred or burdened at the time, Jock listened and enjoyed their company and their stories. But he didn't see how any of that had to do with him. He was like a fish in a pond that's come upon a baited cane pole—one who nibbles, fiddles with the worm, but manages to avoid getting hooked.

The year he turned twenty-four, Jock was visiting his mother at her house on a Sunday afternoon. They'd had KFC for lunch and were watching the Cowboys on her living room TV. It was during the fourth quarter that she chose to tell him about her cancer. "*Pass the popcorn, please.*" She'd shifted in her recliner, crossed her other leg, and scratched at a chigger bite on the back of her hand. "*Right lung. Not to worry.*" Things would be okay.

Jock had stopped chewing and wondered if maybe he should turn off the game.

"*Don't be silly. Score's tied. Eleven minutes left to play. But bring me another Pepsi, would you—and a handful of that peanut candy in the covered yellow bowl.*"

Chemo, radiation—nothing worked. It was after the third long night spent in the fold-down chair beside his mother's hospital bed that Jock stood up, stretched, and told her he was going downstairs to get some fresh air. Instead of taking the elevator as he usually did, Jock took the stairs. Close to the ground but not quite there, he exited the stairwell, stumbled into the bright lights of the wrong floor, and found himself standing directly in front of the hospital's poorly marked, tucked-out-of-the-way, closet-sized chapel.

For reasons known only by God, Jock entered the little room.

Went down on his knees.

And told God he was ready to give it all up.

The hospital's part-time chaplain, Grady Moore, had come in on his day off to pick up his paycheck. He found Jock in the chapel. He'd been on his knees for half an hour but was to the point of wondering what exactly it was he was supposed to do next.

Grady bought Jock breakfast at Denny's, baptized him, and gave him a Bible.

Two weeks later he preached his mother's funeral.

Grady stayed Jock's friend and mentor. Spotting a gentleness of spirit and a deep desire to serve, Grady encouraged Jock to go to seminary. They never lost touch. Over the years, he helped guide Jock's career, prayed for him, listened to him, and advised him how to deal with the inevitable sticky situations pastors find themselves in.

It was Grady, who knew everything about his past, to whom Jock turned when he was flooded, yet again, with remorse over all that he had done back then. Jock knew he was forgiven. He understood the grace that flowed over him every day that he lived. Yet he was haunted by what he had done to his wife, more so by the loss of a child he hadn't even mourned at the time. After all these years, he looked back aghast. What kind of a person was he, that he could do something like that? Could he ever be sure he wasn't still that same selfish guy?

He'd never been convinced.

For Jock Masters, eighteen months of his youth held a lifetime of heartbreak. Those months were the source of an infected sore, a wound that he wouldn't allow to heal. Though his ex-wife remarried and from all accounts was doing well, he regretted to his core that he could never go back and fix the thing that he had done.

Single then.

And single since.

Grady told him he needed to let the past go, but Jock disagreed. He couldn't undo the past, but he could surely protect the future. Consumed by fears that perhaps he was the possessor of a character flaw or weakness, Jock had not, since that day in the chapel, trusted himself to get close to a woman. Not in seminary, not at the other churches where he served, not in Ruby Prairie or at Lighted Way.

Jock had dated. A man would have to be more skilled and less attractive than he to avoid the romantic snares set by matchmaking church ladies eager to marry off granddaughters, nieces, and nice, single neighbors. He'd taken the young and not-so-young ladies out, but he was always careful not to allow things to go too far emotionally. As soon as a paramour indicated more than a casual interest in him, Jock found some good reason not to see her again.

Most days Jock thought he did fine without a wife.

Didn't the apostle Paul say that being single is a desirable state? He could certainly see how that could be true. Being alone made things easier in lots of ways. He had more time to study, and a quiet, peaceful house in which to pray. He could stay at the hospital or nursing home till late without needing to call and explain to anyone.

Not having children wasn't so bad either. He could play ball with church members' kids, then send them home to their parents when they began to fight.

At least that's what he told himself.

Tomorrow being garbage pickup day, Pastor Jock tied up his trash and took it to the curb. He made his way carefully in the dark.

Could two really live as cheaply as one? Catfish wasn't the only member at Lighted Way who believed a single pastor should be paid less than a man with a family; he was only the most vocal of the bunch. Perhaps there was some truth to the view. Hard to see how. Lately, every month something either went up or something else went out. Gas prices, property taxes, insurance premiums, the heater in his car, the fillings in his teeth. Ends didn't always meet.

"Pastor? That you?"

"Wha—at?" Jock jumped at the unexpected sound. It was Alice Buck, dressed in a lavender jogging suit with reflective trim down both sleeves. "Hi there. You startled me."

"Out taking my walk."

"A little late, isn't it?"

"Got caught up watching a movie on TV. Then the phone rang. Didn't realize the time. Don't worry. I'm just going round the block once; then I'm turning in."

"Be careful," said Pastor Jock.

"Don't worry about me." She stepped in place. "By the way, Pastor, Nomie and I just talked on the phone. We're thinking mauve with a light blue fleck would look nice."

"Excuse me?"

"Why, for the new carpet, of course!"

Despite a heavy caseload, made worse by her inexperience, Kim Beeson had found time to call the hundred-mile-away shelter every single day to check on Beth Hollis. Each conversation with the woman who answered the shelter phone yielded a breezy assurance that Beth was just fine. So quick were the woman's answers, Kim wasn't convinced that she even knew which kid she was asking about. The third day she called, Kim went over the phone-answering person's head.

"May I speak to Holly Payne, please?" The shelter's director was a personal friend from recent university days.

"Holly who? Uh, don't think she's here anymore.

No. No director right now. They haven't hired anybody yet. I'm filling in."

Great.

Kim tried to console herself on the drive to pick the teen up. It wasn't as though she'd had any choice. And at least Beth hadn't been at the shelter all that long—just over a week. What a relief it would be to have her placed in Charlotte's home, to know for sure she was safe.

Had she taken care of all the details involved in moving the girl to Tanglewood? File and school records in her satchel, personal belongings sent by her former foster parents, Tim and B.J., in the trunk. She'd made sure Charlotte knew they were coming, and she'd informed the shelter that Beth would be leaving today.

Kim could think of nothing she'd overlooked.

At the shelter, without even checking her ID, a young woman with pale eyes and droopy blond dreadlocks showed Kim to the hack.

"Let's see. I think she's in this section." She stood, hand on hip, in the doorway of a poorly lit living room and looked all around. "Hey! Anybody seen that girl—what'd you say her name was—Beth?"

Half a dozen teens slumped zombie-like on stained couches in front of a snowy-screened TV. Some of them slept. Not one looked up. Bob Barker was on. Some woman in shorts won a red Impala.

"Guess not." She shrugged. "Who'd you say you were with again?"

"Kim Beeson. With Social Services."

"Gotcha. Guys! Anybody know where Beth is?"

No one in the next room had seen her either.

The woman appeared unconcerned. With every minute that passed, the raw feeling in Kim's stomach grew.

"Kids aren't allowed in the sleeping area during the day, but maybe she sneaked back. We could look."

"Let's do." Kim struggled to control her fury at the woman's slump-shouldered nonchalance as she followed her to another room.

The woman flipped a switch. Overhead fluorescent lights flickered, then came on. "There she is. Wonder how she got back here. That door's supposed to be locked."

Kim spotted Beth across the room.

She was curled into a ball, asleep on one of a dozen cots. Her head was cradled by a makeshift pillow she'd fashioned from a T-shirt stuffed with her dirty clothes.

"Beth, wake up, sweetie. It's me. Kim. You okay? I've come to take you to your new placement."

Beth sat up and rubbed at her eyes. "Wha-at? Are Tim and B.J. here?"

"Who's that?" asked the woman.

Kim ignored her. "No, they're not here. Just me. Let's get your things together. You hungry? It's going to be a long drive. How about we go get something to eat? Mexican sound good?"

"I guess so. I gotta pee."

Dreadlocks woman suddenly became Miss Rules. "Before you leave you've got to fill out some papers." She looked up at the wall clock. "Sorry, but you'll have to wait. Time for my break."

Nikki and Vikki sat at the kitchen table, snacking, doing homework, and kicking the legs of each other's chairs. "When's she gonna get here?"

"Late today. Could be after you two are in bed." Charlotte was standing at the cupboard trying to think up something to fix for supper. The solitary days when yogurt or cereal, munched while leaning against the kitchen counter, passed as dinner were no more. Vikki and Nikki required balanced meals. Did pork and beans count as a vegetable? Probably not.

"Can't we stay up?" asked Vikki.

"Please?" said Nikki.

"I don't know. Maybe. If it's not too late."

Nikki popped a grape into her mouth. "Are we going to get lots of girls in this house?"

"Not a whole lot. Maybe six," said Charlotte.

"That would be us and the new girl and three more," said Vikki. "Plus you. You're a girl."

"Uh-uh, Charlotte's not a girl," said Nikki. "She's a woman."

"Yes, she is. That makes seven."

"You're right," said Charlotte.

"Just girls. No boys."

"We should make a sign that says *No Boys Allowed,*" said Vikki.

“We could paint it on the gate,” said Nikki. “Then everybody could see it. I’ve got a red marker.”
“How about you write a sign and tape it on the door to your room? That might be better,” said Charlotte.
“Okay.”
“What’re we having for dinner?”

Kim took her eyes off the road to glance over at Beth. Full of fajita nachos, she was buckled in, sound asleep again. Dark circles rimmed her eyes. Her lips looked swollen and chapped. Amazing how much the girl’s appearance had changed in the past eight days. While at the shelter she’d cut her blonde hair. A short, spiky do had replaced formerly long, face-framing layers. Her ears had been pierced two more times, reportedly courtesy of some guy named Kirby, a teen also staying at the shelter. When Kim asked her how he did it, Beth told her he’d used a safety pin—sterilized by holding it in the flame of a lighter. She’d numbed her ears by applying ice to them until just before he poked. She traded a girl a pair of jeans for the earrings.
Kim cringed, looking at those red ears. She hoped they weren’t infected. Shouldn’t she have some kind of ointment to put on them? Antibiotics? Maybe Charlotte would know what to do.

Charlotte looked at her watch for about the fiftieth time. Past nine o’clock. The twins were already in bed, though she guessed not asleep. Where was Kim? What about the new girl? Was she coming or was she not? Charlotte knew Kim had said today. No way had she misunderstood. Still, she'd not received a single phone call.

Maybe her phone line was out. She could have even knocked it off the hook. Nope. Dial tone was there. She started a bag of popcorn in the microwave, turned on the TV, turned it off, burned the popcorn, tried to read. Nothing eased her nerves.

Charlotte thought about Beth and all she had been through—realized that she didn't and likely never would know the half of it. What would Beth look like?

What kind of temperament would she have?

She'd be angry, most likely. Who could blame her—shuffled from home to home for most of her life? At age fifteen, the child deserved to go someplace knowing it would be a home where she could stay. Charlotte decided one thing. Tanglewood was going to be that place. It didn't matter that she'd expected most girls would come to stay for a year or less.

Sight unseen, she would keep Beth until she was eighteen. Charlotte looked at the clock.

If, that is, she ever arrived.

At 9:25 Charlotte heard her next-door neighbor's dogs begin to bark. She peered out the lace-curtained window beside her front door. Kim's car was parked at the end of her walk.

Not nearly as apprehensive as when Nikki and Vikki arrived, Charlotte flung open the front door and stepped out to meet them.

"Charlotte, I'm so sorry!" said Kim. "I didn't mean

to be so late. We got a slow start. It took forever to check Beth out. Then we got lost coming out of Dallas. Went the wrong way on the loop. I'd have called you, but today of all days, I left without my phone."

"That's okay." Charlotte reached out to hug Beth but caught herself as she saw the girl's rigid stance. Their gazes met for an instant before Beth averted her eyes.

"Hi. I'm Charlotte. I've been waiting all afternoon to meet you. I'm glad you're finally here."

"Sorry," said Kim. "I'm so worn out I can hardly remember my name, much less how to do proper introductions. Beth, this is Charlotte. Charlotte, this is Beth."

"Hi," said Beth. She and Kim followed Charlotte inside.

The front door had been closed for less than five minutes when Kim looked at her watch. "I hate to do this, but I really need to go. I've got a meeting at eight in the morning, and my dog should have been let out three hours ago. Charlotte, all of Beth's records are here. We talked on the way over about Tanglewood. I've told her all about you and the other girls and as much as I know about the town." She handed over a thick folder, then turned to Beth, who was still holding her bag.

"You have everything you need, right? Did you think of anything you wanted to ask me before I go?"

Beth shook her head.

"She's got plenty of clothes, but probably everything's dirty by now. Did they do any laundry for you at the shelter?"

"No."

"I didn't think so."

"Not a problem," said Charlotte. "We can run a load of clothes tonight if we need to."

"I hate to rush off, but it's an hour to my house. You two okay with me going?" asked Kim. She hesitated with her hand on the doorknob. "Charlotte, I'll call you first thing tomorrow just to make sure everything's going all right. You and I'll talk too, Beth."

Charlotte and Beth stood on the porch and watched her go. "Be careful," called Charlotte. And then Kim was gone.

"Are you hungry?"

Beth shook her head. "We ate on the way."

"How does a hot bath sound?"

That brought a smile. "Okay."

Charlotte guessed Beth hadn't had a shower in a couple of days. "Come on upstairs and I'll show you your room. Then I'll show you the bathroom, where the towels and shampoo and all that stuff is. I bet you need something to sleep in till we get your things washed. Pair of my pajamas be okay for tonight?"

"Sure."

"Hold on a second." Charlotte left Beth at the bottom of the stairs while she retrieved pajamas from her downstairs bedroom. When she returned, Beth was studying a framed photo of her and J.D.

"This your husband?"

"Yes."

"Does he live here too?"

"No. He died."

"I'm sorry." Beth bit her lip.

"It's okay. There are pictures of him all over the house. His name was J.D. We were married for twenty years."

"That's a long time. He looks nice."

"He was. Really nice." Charlotte swallowed.

Since J.D. had died, at the oddest, most unpredictable and inconvenient of times Charlotte had found herself feeling physically squeezed, out of air, rendered unable to speak. They stood looking at the picture of J.D. Not a sound passed between them. Finally, as quickly as it had overtaken her, the sensation was gone. If Beth thought the long moment odd, she didn't let on.

"Will these pajamas fit?" Charlotte held up a pair of flannels, size medium, light yellow background with baby blue stars.

"I think so."

"Good. I've never worn them. I knew better than to order flannel; it always makes me hot. But they looked so cute in the catalogue." Charlotte smiled. "You can keep them if you like them. There're several sizes of new underwear in one of the closets upstairs. Socks too, in case your feet get cold. We'll wash your things tomorrow. Let's go on up. We'll get you settled in."

• • •

An hour and a half later, under a purple and blue quilt, Beth looked around the room and took pretend snapshots of the walls and windows, the furniture, the closet door. She willed herself to remember everything about where she was sleeping so maybe this time she'd know where she was when she first woke up.

Not that it would work. Nothing she tried ever did. That dizzy, disoriented feeling of panic always overtook her on the first morning in a new place.

It must be awful for babies. Happened to them all the time. They fell asleep in the car or the store or on a warm lap, only to wake up somewhere totally different, like Grandma's house or the baby-sitter's bed, covered up with different blankets, sometimes not even wearing the same clothes.

No wonder they cried.

Would it be so hard to wait—to let them wake up in the same place where they were laid down? One thing was for sure. If she had a child, once it went to sleep, she wouldn't move it until it woke up on its own.

Sure enough, when Beth opened her eyes ten hours later in her bed at Tanglewood, she couldn't remember where she was. The room spun. She feared throwing up but squeezed her eyes shut until the sensation passed.

Finally it came to her. Caseworker Kim. Charlotte Carter. Two-story house. Tanglewood. What kind of a name was that? Beth opened her eyes but lay still.

Curled on her side she saw in the chair next to the bed the nearly empty juice glass, the cracker crumbs, and the remnants of the sliced apples she'd found waiting there last night after she'd gotten out of her bath. On the floor next to the chair was her backpack. Wasn't much in it. Dirty clothes, comb and toothbrush, shoes, a jacket, and the letter Kirby had given her on the morning she left the shelter.

Beth stretched and turned over onto her other side. "Ahh!" she yelped.

She was not alone.

Quiet as cats, Nikki and Vikki—up, fed, and dressed—had crept into the room. They stood looking down at the new Tanglewood guest.

"You've got blood on your ear."

Beth felt her lobes.

"Just a little bit. Charlotte's got Band-Aids."

"Are you going to get up?"

"I guess so," said Beth.

"We can help you." Nikki tugged at the covers Beth clutched. "You need some socks to wear? We've got lots of socks. All colors," said Vikki.

"We've got two cats too. You want to see them?"

"Our room is right next to yours. Want to see it?"

Beth sat up in bed and hugged her knees to her chest. "What are your names?"

"I'm Nikki and she's Vikki."

"Is Charlotte your mother?"

How hilarious. "No," they giggled.

"She's not a mom. She's Charlotte," said Nikki. "Our mom's sick. Charlotte's taking care of us until she gets well."

"Have you been here a long time?"

"Not too long." said Nikki.

"Pretty long," said Vikki. "Are you going to get up now?"

"I guess so." Beth eased out of bed.

The twins took her by the hands. "Come with us. We'll show you all the rooms we have up here. Charlotte says if you don't like this one, you get to choose any one you want."

"I'm sure this one's fine."

Charlotte stood at the top of the stairs. "Did they wake you up?"

"No. She was already awake."

Charlotte smiled. "I bet. Did you sleep okay, Beth?"

"I slept fine."

"If you think you'd like another room better, you can change," said Charlotte.

"This one's okay."

"You can move the furniture if you want, put some of your own things up on the wall, arrange things the way you want them," said Charlotte.

"Thank you. It's nice the way it is right now."

Why should she change anything? None of it mattered, not the room, the bed, the cute little girls, or even Charlotte, who was trying so hard to make everything okay. None of it mattered because she, Beth Hollis, would not be around for long. At the first opportunity, she would be gone from this place.

She and Kirby had it all planned out.

Chapter Eleven

Nomie Jenkins called to order a special gathering of the Ruby Prairie Women's Culture Club. The group was meeting this evening at Alice Buck's house.

Alice's husband, Boots, had promised Alice he'd make himself scarce during the meeting by doing some work out in the yard. "Scouts' honor, honey, I'll leave you gals alone," he'd told her.

Alice knew better.

A man who loves company better than cake and who, given a choice, would pick ironing his wife's Lycra underpants over spending an afternoon with no one to talk to, Boots kept finding excuses to come back inside. First he was thirsty. Needed a glass of water. With ice, of course, dropped into the glass one noisy cube at a time. Then WD-40 for a sticky tool. Finally, a can of wasp and hornet spray from way back under the kitchen sink. On every trek he made through the house, Boots grinned and waved at the room full of ladies. "Just me. Back again."

Alice returned Boots's smile the first trip he made. Smiled a little less his second time through. Finally her husband's disruptive comings and goings got on her nerves. "Boots! We're trying to have a meeting here. Do you mind?"

Boots ducked his head and headed out the back door. Alice rolled her eyes. Ginger, married to Lester, who was turned the same company-loving way as Boots, shot her a look of sympathetic understanding. Alice knew she'd hurt his feelings, but what exactly was a wife supposed to do?

Ignoring Alice and Boots's marital rub, Nomie cleared her throat and tried again. "Culture Fest is the last weekend in November. Ladies, we've lots yet to do. Let's start off with a report from our committee chairwomen. Ginger, you're in charge of food. How's it all shaping up?"

"Locally, so far we've got Rarity Real Estate with their kettle corn, the Debate Club from the high school grilling turkey legs, and the Methodist men churning homemade ice cream. Lester, of course, is doing his fried peach pies."

"Don't forget," said Nomie, "this is our major club fund-raiser for the year. Every organization hosting a booth has got to pay its fee. Best to collect when we sign them up."

"We charging out-of -towners double?" asked Alice.

"Yes. Same as last year. How many do we have so far?"

"The Martinez family's coming for sure," said Ginger. "Bringing their tamale cart. They were very popular last festival. This year, they tell me, they'll be offering chips and salsa too. Still waiting to hear from the funnel cake people. Since that grease fire incident at the Okra Festival over in Ella Louise, they've slowed down a bit."

"Don't know about the rest of you, but all this talk of food is making me hungry. You've done a nice job, Ginger. We appreciate your efforts. Alice, could you give us a rundown on the entertainment?"

"Glad to. High school band and choir are coming. Drama department says they'll do two performances of their play, one at ten, the other at three. Did y'all know those kids won the bi-district competition last week? Performed *A Midsummer Night's Dream*. They're really good," said Alice.

"What is that drama teacher thinking—having those children do foreign programs year after year?" interrupted Sassy Clyde. "I, for one, would enjoy seeing something done in regular English. This is America, after all."

Nomie knew that Alice's granddaughter had the lead. Hoping to head off hurt feelings, she quickly cut in. "I'm sure we'll all enjoy the play. Anything else?"

"Hardy Boys Quartet says they'll sing."

"Something patriotic?" asked Sassy.

"I'll ask," said Alice.

"See if they'll do 'Home on the Range.'"

Alice wrote it down.

"Kerilynn's in charge of arts and crafts. Anybody know where she is?" asked Nomie.

"I'm here," hollered Kerilynn. "Boots told me to come in through the kitchen. He's spraying for wasps out front. What's the matter with him, anyway? Man looks like his dog just died." The screen door slammed shut behind her.

"He must have got stung." Nomie winked at Alice.

"Don't pay him any mind, Kerilynn," Alice declared. "Boots is fine."

Sassy moved her purse so that Kerilynn would have a place to sit down.

"Sorry I'm running late. The afternoon I've had! Today was cupcakes for the kindergartners. I took chocolate—frosted with that good seven-minute icing I do—takes forever, but they all just love it. Got the cupcakes there just fine, but the teacher forgot to tell me she's got two new children allergic to chocolate. When she told them they couldn't have treats, they started crying. Near broke my heart. So I ran over to the Quick-Stop and bought two packages of Twinkies. That satisfied them just fine, but it put me behind. Didn't have time to go home and change. Not only that, I ran out of sweet tea at the 'Round the Clock. You never heard such a fuss. Thought there was gonna be a riot. I tried, just this once, putting some sugar into the unsweetened, but that went over like sand in a swimsuit."

"Never tastes right if you don't put the sugar in while the tea's still hot," said Sassy. "May as well throw it out and start over fresh. I always do."

"So tell me, what have I missed?" Kerilynn fanned herself with a church bulletin she pulled from her purse. "Y'all hot in here or is it just me?"

Ginger Collins got up, went to Alice's kitchen, and

got Kerilynn a cold Coke. Alice turned on the ceiling fan.

"Kerilynn, aren't you already fifty?" said Sassy. "I would have figured you'd made it through 'the change.' "

"Fifty-two," said Kerilynn. "You all know I've been late for most everything all of my life."

"Take your time, honey. Nobody's in any rush," said Nomie. "When you're ready, we'll hear your report."

Kerilynn took a swig of Coke, leaned back in her chair, hiked her pant legs up over her skinny calves, and fanned a bit more. Finally she was ready to go on. "Let me see. I've got it all written down right here." She dug in her purse for a flowered notepad, which she held out at arm's length. "Lands. I can't read my own writing. Sassy, let me have your glasses." She snatched the pair right off Sassy's nose.

"Much better, thank you. Little smudged, though." She gave Sassy's glasses a good wiping with the tail of her blouse. "First off, we've got the ladies at the New Energy Rest Home with their crocheting. Believe they're offering house shoes and those tight little caps all the teenagers are wearing. Activity director said they're trying something new—using variegated yarn. Wal-Mart donated three dozen skeins. Of course the Nimble Thimble Quilting Club is displaying their latest project. They're also planning on demonstrating some new techniques. I don't know exactly what all."

"They doing a raffle?"

"Yes. For a Log Cabin Twin. Two dollars a ticket. But the biggest news is I've got hold of a fellow from Louisiana, a wood-carver. Does animals. Bears, bobcats, deer—anything you want. Uses nothing but a chain saw. Catfish saw him at some flea market last year. Says the man does beautiful work. I've about got him talked into coming."

"A chain saw? Won't that be loud?" said Nomie.

"I reckon so," said Kerilynn. "Long as we put him a ways away from where the band and choir'll perform, I don't think there'll be any problems."

"Got anything special for the children?" asked Alice.

"Sure do. Lila's House of Beauty is doing face painting and Pastor Jock from Lighted Way is making balloon sculptures. Oh, and I nearly forgot. My cousin Nell has agreed to come with her sand art stand. She's wonderful with children. I've never seen one that didn't take to her. Course all kids love to mess with sand. She helps them pick out their colors and layer them in a jar."

"How much does she charge?" asked Sassy.

"A dollar for a small jar, two for the next size up."

"Two dollars! For dirt?" said Lucky.

"Not dirt—colored sand," said Kerilynn. "Sterilized. Plus they get a choice of ribbon or that raffia stuff to tie around the top when they're done. Not that it matters." She gave Sassy a withering look. "Seeing as how part of every penny made goes to a good cause."

"I was just asking." Sassy took her glasses back.

Kerilynn stuffed her notepad back down into her purse. "Sassy, no offense, but what's the matter with you? You're as testy as a snake. Honey, have you gone off your hormones again?"

"Since you ask, as a matter of fact, I have." Sassy teared up. "I'm tired of taking those pills every day. Article in the *Reader's Digest* says they're bad. Give you old-timer's disease or cancer or something like that. Nothing I want. I've been off them going on a week."

"Bless your heart. No wonder you're so nervous," said Ginger. "I'd rather give up iced tea than my hormones. That woman on *Good Morning, America*—think her name is Katie—she says if you can't take them, soy powder's supposed to be good."

"My sister swears alfalfa tablets helped her," said Alice. She handed Sassy a tissue.

"I don't mean to be short with y'all. I just don't feel like myself." Sassy blew her nose. "Go on, Nomie. I'm all right."

"You sure?" Nomie patted Sassy on the knee. "All right. From our reports so far, I'd say we're off to a great start. All that's left is the commercial booths. Who was it we assigned that to?" She studied her notes.

"Wasn't it Charlotte?" asked Ginger.

"Believe it was," said Nomie.

"Why isn't she here?" asked Sassy. "Seems to me she would take her responsibilities a bit more serious."

"Now, Sassy—" said Ginger.

"I'm sure Charlotte's got everything under control," said Nomie. "But she's got a lot on her plate. Y'all may not know this, but she's got three girls now. One of them may be sick. We all remember how it is with children at home."

"I've been meaning to stop by her house," said Kerilynn. "Think I'll do that tomorrow. See how she's coming along with her assignment. Nomie, I'll give you a call."

Charlotte's plans for the day kept getting interrupted. First, the phone.

"Mrs. Carter? Ben Jackson here."

Ben Jackson? Who is Ben Jackson?

"I'm calling about Beth."

Right. Santa Claus man. Principal of the school. Ben Jackson.

"I'm sorry to bring this up, but I hope you'll understand. Ruby Prairie is progressive in a lot of ways, but basically we're a small town with small-town values. As such, I suppose you could say we're a bit conservative about some things—things that in a bigger place would likely be overlooked."

What in the world was he talking about?

"Beth's not the first student—well, actually she is the first girl as far as we know. But I'm positive she won't be the last." He cleared his throat. "Here's what we're looking at. Far as the student body goes, policy doesn't say we can't have them, only that they can't be out in the open. Guess you could say we've got your basic 'don't ask, don't tell' rule."

Charlotte's mouth fell open. *Don't ask, don't tell? Wasn't that the military's policy in regards to dealing with . . . ?* Oh my.

Kim hadn't said a word. How was she supposed to handle a situation like this? Charlotte twirled the phone cord around her wrist. "Mr. Jackson, I had no idea. I've had Beth for less than a week.

Honestly. Her caseworker didn't say a word."

"You weren't aware? I would have thought you'd get some kind of a report or something."

"Yes. I would have thought so too."

"Sorry, then, to be the bearer of bad news. I know you're probably a little shocked, but honestly, I wouldn't worry too much. There's lots of worse things kids can do. Least it's not drugs. Some of that goes on, even around here."

Charlotte took little comfort in his words. Hating to ask, she steeled herself. "Mr. Jackson, I need to know. How did you find out? Did Beth tell someone? Did she, I mean did she act out in some way?"

"Beth? Act out? Oh no. She's been a model student. Quiet girl. Not giving anyone any trouble at all. If it hadn't been for the coach being in the locker room when the girls were getting dressed for PE, no one would have known."

Charlotte's mind raced. She had vowed to keep Beth as long as she needed a home, but that was before she knew about this. What about the other girls? What a thing to have to think about. Goodness. Maybe Kim didn't know about Beth either.

"Mrs. Carter, I don't want to embarrass Beth. I haven't approached her because I didn't think it would be appropriate, considering the delicate nature of this thing. Everything's been handled by the girl's coach, who is a woman, and by the school nurse. Here's what they've come up with, and I agree. If Beth wears long enough shirts and keeps them tucked in or pulled down, there shouldn't be a problem. All we ask is that she keep it out of sight."

"Out of sight," Charlotte repeated. What was he talking about? Her head hurt. She supposed she had led a sheltered life. Never in her life had she felt so dumb.

"One more thing," said Mr. Jackson. "The school nurse said to tell you that it looked to be pretty new. She said tattoos are easily infected. Might be a good idea to put alcohol or some kind of antibiotic ointment on it at night."

Tattoos.

Beth had a tattoo.

That's what this was about.

Charlotte struggled to keep relieved laughter out of her voice. "I appreciate your call, Mr. Jackson. You have no idea how much. I'll talk to Beth when she gets home. I assure you we'll keep this, shall we say, under wraps."

"Appreciate it, Mrs. Carter. If I can ever be of service, you let me know."

She hung up the phone. She and Beth would talk tonight. When would she have found an opportunity to get a tattoo?

Charlotte looked up at the clock. The morning was half gone. She'd planned to run errands today, to go to the grocery store and the bank. She needed to pick up furnace filters at Hardy's, and her hair was driving her crazy. Kept falling into her eyes and had gone flat on top. Maybe Lila could work her in for a trim. Charlotte dug in her purse for her keys. If she left right now, there was still time.

She was turning off the overhead light when someone knocked on her kitchen door. She stretched on her tiptoes to see out the window over the sink. Standing on her back stoop was the peach tree man. What was his name? Her mind was a blank.

"Morning, ma'am. How're you?"

Lester. That was it. Lester Collins. Married to Ginger. Lived just down the street. Unbidden, the man planted and tended peach trees all over town—in the churchyard, at the library, next to the school, and at randomly chosen private citizens' houses—whether they truly wanted peach trees in their yards or not.

"Didn't want you to be startled when you looked out and saw me tending to your trees. Just making my fall rounds. I'll be using a little diluted orange oil mixed with a bit of compost tea today." He spoke like a gourmet. "Scattering some cornmeal too. Your cats won't like it much, but it won't hurt them none. All organic. Nontoxic to pets and kids. Good thing, since you've got some of both. Just so you know, I'll be back next week to put down a nice thick layer of mulch. We want to discourage disease and get everybody tucked in for the winter. From the look of the coats on the squirrels this year, we're in for a long one. Wouldn't be surprised if we have a hard freeze before Thanksgiving."

"Thank you. Thank you very much. It's so nice of you to do all this." Charlotte was never sure exactly how best to express her appreciation to Lester for his unbidden horticultural good deeds.

Pastor Jock had advised her not to try to pay him. "You'll hurt his feelings," he'd explained.

Kerilynn had said the same thing. "Just say thanks and send him on his way. Honey, one thing you need to know ahead of time: Lester is a fine man, but he loves to talk. Don't ever get him started unless you've got the better part of a day."

"Don't want to hold you up." Charlotte flashed Lester a cheery smile. Though she didn't invite him in, she gave him coffee in a throwaway cup to sip while he worked. She stood at the window watching him tend the trees as if they were pampered, well-to-do children. Charlotte finally put down her keys and began to unload the dishwasher. It didn't seem right to get in her car and drive off with Lester out there working for free. How long would all of this take?

Not long. Within thirty minutes Lester had finished with the half-dozen peach trees and left in his truck.

This time Charlotte made it to her front porch before she got sidetracked.

Kerilynn was parking her baby blue station wagon out front. She gave Charlotte a big wave, then got out.

Charlotte saw that she was carrying a cake.

"Hey there! How're you? Just thought I'd drop in and see how you were getting along. Saw you on Sunday but didn't get a chance to say hello."

"Good to see you," said Charlotte.

Kerilynn spotted Charlotte's car keys in her hand and her purse on her shoulder. "You were just about to leave, weren't you? I'm sorry. I won't stay. Bet you've got a million things to do. I'll leave you this cake and come back another day."

"No, don't go. Come on in. I was planning on running some errands but nothing that urgent. I'd rather visit over a pot of coffee. What a beautiful cake."

Could the bank wait? If she'd subtracted correctly, nothing would bounce for at least two more days. The furnace would be fine for another day or two. Pork and beans could pass as a vegetable tonight. And she could trim her bangs herself.

In the kitchen Charlotte filled the carafe with water. Kerilynn made herself at home. "Where's your coffee?"

"In the cupboard to the left." Charlotte would have preferred that Kerilynn sit down instead of helping herself.

Kerilynn measured out six scoops. "Honey, you have any cream?"

"Sorry, no. Milk okay?"
"Skim?"
"Two percent."
"Perfect."
The two of them sat at Charlotte's kitchen table. Kerilynn declined Charlotte's offer of a sandwich. It was, after all, nearly noon. "Let's just have cake. It's coconut with lemon filling. Made with four whole eggs. Practically health food."
Charlotte's sweet tooth thought cake for lunch was a fine idea. "You're a great cook," she said, cutting herself a second piece. "I enjoy it. Started when I was a little girl. My specialty back then was no-bake chocolate oatmeal cookies."
"The ones made with peanut butter? I haven't had those in forever. You have the recipe?"
"Got it memorized. If you've got a card, I'll write it down for you."
"I imagine for someone who loves to cook, owning a cafe is a dream come true. How long have you had the 'Round the Clock?"
"Ten years. Opening it was like a dream all right—a nightmare, is what I would call it."
"I suppose opening a restaurant's a bigger undertaking than people realize," said Charlotte, not understanding.
"It is harder than it looks, but it wasn't just that. It was all the stuff that led up to it. Up until then, I was your basic housewife, a stay-at-home mom. Never worked except volunteer. PTA, band boosters, library

board. I also helped out at the rest home some. My husband, Paul, and I had our children young—two rowdy boys. We were only forty-three when the second one graduated high school and took off for college. Looking forward to having some time to ourselves. Paul especially. Loved those boys, but he couldn't hardly wait to have me to himself." Kerilynn took a sip of coffee and grinned.

"He was like most men. If you'll notice next time you go to a graduation, it's the mamas doing the crying, especially if it's their last kid to fly the coop. The daddies—while they're busy squeezing their wives' shoulders, most of them can't hardly wipe the grins off their faces."

Charlotte poured them each a third cup of coffee.

Kerilynn's face changed. "It was in the fall that we found out Paul was sick. Like your husband, he had cancer. Doctor gave him three months at the most."

Charlotte's eyes clouded. "I didn't know. I'm so sorry."

"On top of being sick, Paul was scared to death about me having to support myself and get our boys through school. I tried to hide it from him, but I was scared too. He was a plumber. Had his own business. We did okay, but never managed to put anything away. Right after he got sick, I applied for jobs in Ruby Prairie and in little towns all around. Didn't take me long to figure out I was one of those women who had what they call 'no marketable skills.' Wasn't much call for a cookie baker or a nose wiper. Paul and I got married right out of high school and I never went to college. We had those boys right off. Truth is, I can't even type."

"That must have been awful, to have to be concerned about making a living along with your husband being sick. We didn't have children, so I worked all the years J.D. and I were married. Our finances were in pretty good shape, and we had life insurance on J.D.—but it was still hard."

"We were lucky that we had some insurance, enough for Paul's funeral and to get me through about two years. It was what would happen to me and the boys after that ran out that had us both worried. Paul and I spent many hours talking about what I should do. We thought about me starting to beauty college. I could finish in a year, but I've never been very good with my own hair. We looked into Avon and Amway, but they both seemed like something to do on the side rather than full time. Paul's the one who came up with the idea for the cafe. He knew I was a good cook and that it was something I would enjoy.

" 'Don't have to have any college degree to flip pancakes or fry steak,' is what he said. At the time, Ruby Prairie didn't have any place to eat except the grill at the Chevron Station, and they were only open for lunch. Before I hardly had time to think, Paul had cashed in his life insurance, bought the building and all the equipment I needed to get a cafe up and going. I wasn't sure I could run a business, but Paul was. He never doubted."

"How long did it take you after he died to get the 'Round the Clock open?"

"It opened before. Paul held on so as to be at the grand opening. I think looking forward to it was what kept him alive four months longer than the doctors predicted. He was skinny as a rail, on oxygen, and in a wheelchair by then, but he wheeled around and greeted everybody that came in. We hung balloons and streamers all over the place. Chamber of Commerce came and did a ribbon cutting. It was quite a big deal. Paul had a blast, but it was a sad day for me. Felt more like some kind of closing. I knew exactly what Paul seeing me open the restaurant meant. He died a week later."

Charlotte blew her nose.

Kerilynn got up and rinsed out her cup. "So that's how I ended up with the 'Round the Clock. Paul was 100 percent right. It's not made me rich, but it got my boys through school. Course I wouldn't have made it if it weren't for the help of folks around town. First year, broken water pipes flooded everything. Right after that, I got laid out flat with a bad case of the flu. I still don't know everything that was done to help me out.

"Not just then either. I can't tell you how many times my boys and I would be needing something we didn't have and that I had no idea how we would get. I'd get on the phone. Never failed. In the most unexpected ways, the very things we needed would turn up right when we had to have them. Days when I thought

I would die of loneliness—when I missed Paul and my old life so bad my teeth hurt—a friend would call or stop by."

Charlotte arranged cake crumbs on her plate. "Were you embarrassed when you had to ask for help?" she asked.

"Embarrassed? Why would I be embarrassed? I didn't have it all together then; some days I can't hold it all together now. Way I look at it, at the time I was the one needed help. Time would come, and it has, that somebody else'd be needing something from me."

"J.D. teased me about being a perfectionist. For feeling like a failure if I couldn't do whatever I set my mind to perfectly, all by myself, the first time I tried."

Kerilynn nodded. "My cousin Sharon used to be that same way. Nearly drove herself crazy 'fore she got over it."

"What happened?"

"She had kids."

"Oh."

"Anyway, in another two years I'll have my duplex paid off. These days I've got good enough help that I can afford to take time off now and then. Makes it nice." Kerilynn pushed her plate back. "Sugar, I didn't mean to run on. How are you? That's what I came to find out. How're things with the girls? You feeling at home? Anything you need?"

"We're doing fine. You know I've got three girls."

"Nikki and Vikki?"

"And Beth."

"How're they all doing?"

"The twins are tons of fun. They come home from school talking ninety to nothing and don't stop until they're asleep. Sometimes not even then. My newest girl, Beth—she's the opposite. She's doing okay too, I think, but she's quiet. Has had some rough things go on in her life. Hard to know what she's thinking."

"She's how old?"

"Fifteen."

"It's partly her age. Teenagers keep you guessing what's going on inside of their heads. She'll come around."

"I hope so."

"My boys talked my ears off until they turned fourteen; then they clammed up. Didn't hear much out of them for the next half a dozen years. But you know—they talk to me now, though. Call most every Sunday afternoon."

"That's good to hear."

It was three o'clock before Kerilynn left Charlotte's home. Looking up at the clock, both of them were startled at how much time had passed.

"Lands! Your girls will be home from school any minute. I didn't mean to stay all afternoon."

"So glad you came," said Charlotte, returning Kerilynn's front porch hug.

It was not until she was back home that Kerilynn realized it had slipped her mind to ask Charlotte how things were coming along with her Culture Fest commercial booth assignment.

Keeping her promise, she called Nomie up and told her only the smallest of fibs. "I'd say there's no need to worry. Charlotte's doing great. She's got everything all under control."

Chapter Twelve

Charlotte's pen hovered over yet another required-by-social-services form. This was actually one of the shorter pages she'd been asked to complete. Nothing on it was hard; nor did any of the questions require research or thought. *Please print. Use black ink only. Sign at the bottom. Return to the address below.* The form in her hand, like others, asked for the basics—name, address, sex, race, date of birth, marital status.

That last one was where she always got stuck.

Single.

Married.

Divorced.

Widowed.

How could the act of checking some silly box on some unimportant form cause a person to feel as if she'd been hit by a train in the middle of her chest?

Today would have been twenty-one years with J.D. Their custom was to scrimp on birthdays but do anniversaries up big. Dinner out sometimes a whole weekend away. Always gifts. Every year some surprise.

Near their fifteenth, J.D. told Charlotte he had to work late on their actual anniversary date. He was sorry, really sorry. They would simply hold off on celebrating till the weekend. She'd been okay with that—no other choice. But she was tickled to death when she arrived home from work that day to find dinner J.D. had made and her husband hiding under the candlelit, draped-to-the-floor table, holding a bouquet of red roses.

Lots of good memories.

Some regrets.

If she'd known J.D. was going to go so soon, she would have never been sharp or short with him as she sometimes was. She would have fussed less about the house, fussed more over him. Toward the end, she had the opportunity to tell him as much. To apologize, to make it a little bit more all right.

"What are you talking about?" he'd said. "I don't remember any of that. We've had lots of fun, don't you think?"

Truly they had.

But she was having none today.

There was more to Charlotte's melancholy than remembrances of anniversaries past. Since her nineteenth year, October had been anything but a celebratory month. Six weeks into her first semester at an out-of-state university, she'd been enjoying the freedom of being away from home for the first time.

Her bliss was short-lived.

English Comp. Dr. Rich. Second floor, Baxley Hall. Room 204. That's the class she was in when the dean of women came to the door, called her out, walked with Charlotte to an office across the campus.

Charlotte feared she was in trouble for missing curfew, or for a parking ticket she'd paid too late.

No.

Life-altering news.

Her parents. Car crash. Dead. Both the same day.

A tornado couldn't have rocked her world more. Her mom and dad's only child, she'd been cuddled and cared for all of her life. That very morning she'd received a package of homemade cookies from her mom, a silly card from her dad, a statement from the bank showing an unexpected hundred dollars deposited in her account.

Other people planned their funeral. Charlotte only came. Three days after burying them, she was back at school. Life insurance covered tuition. She got a job. Grandma Ruby sent checks.

Everyone marveled at her maturity, her strength. Grandma Ruby told her it would be okay to cry.

She graduated in three years.

Did really well.

But something happened to her along the way.

After a couple of early testy years, J.D. learned to take Charlotte's quirks in stride.

"I don't need any help. I can do it myself," she told him about bank statements that didn't balance,

Christmas decorations in the attic, hard-to-open pickle jar lids.

"I can't believe I did that. What was I thinking?" She'd beat herself up for days, even fight tears over a misplaced, unpaid, and now-late bill, a forgotten haircut appointment, a rusted garden tool accidentally left out in the rain.

Independence and perfection. Charlotte craved the one, demanded of herself the other.

Where was God in all this?

Still there.

A Christian since age twelve, Charlotte didn't lose her faith. She always believed in God. After her parents died she just started believing in herself more.

It was how she coped with her parents' deaths.

How she coped with losing J.D.

How she held herself together today.

Charlotte finished the form, signed it, sealed it up, and put it out in the mailbox on the front porch. No time for self-pity. Kim Beeson was coming in a couple of hours, bringing Tanglewood's fourth girl. Her name was Donna, and she was fourteen.

Four girls. Her house was filling up. Two more due next week. Upstairs, Charlotte blew her nose, then readied Donna's room.

"Come in." Charlotte was an old hand at this by now. "I'm so glad you're finally here."

Kim and Donna made their way up the walk.

"You must be Donna. What beautiful hair you

have." It was shiny, straight, dark brown, and hung halfway down the girl's back. Charlotte reached up and pushed a stray strand from Donna's face.

As if the touch were too much to bear, Donna instantly began to sob.

"Honey, I'm sorry." Charlotte met no resistance when she gathered her into her arms. "It's been a bad day, hasn't it?"

"I want to go home. Please. Let me go home."

Charlotte's eyes met Kim's over the girl's head.

"Let's go inside. We'll talk," said Kim.

The three of them sat on Charlotte's living room sofa, Charlotte and Kim on the ends, Donna in the middle.

"I miss my dad. When will I get to see him again?"

"You can call him tomorrow," said Kim. "Remember? Just like we said."

"It's not right I have to come here. I don't see why I have to."

"We talked about this," said Kim. "With your dad's new job, he can't take care of you right now."

"I can take care of myself. I've been doing it anyway. I did our laundry. I cooked supper. I cleaned up. I know how to do everything."

"That's wonderful," said Charlotte. "I know your dad must be really proud of you. And I'm sure he misses you." She turned to the social worker. "Kim, is there any reason Donna has to wait until tomorrow to call her dad? Why don't we let him know she made it here all right?"

Donna quit crying, called her dad, cried some more, stopped for a while, then started up again when Kim left. Charlotte held her, talked to her, glanced at her watch.

The other girls would be home any minute.

There were snacks to be fixed, three loads of clothes yet to be washed, homework to be done, supper to be planned.

And a sobbing girl in her arms.

Kim called the next day. "Going okay?"

"Better," said Charlotte. "She's settling in. A bit clingy but better. Really eager to help."

"And the other girls?"

"Doing well. Nikki and Vikki already love her. She's like a little mother to them. Beth's polite, still holding herself off a bit."

"You ready for two more?"

Charlotte gulped. This would make a full house. "Sure," she said.

Kim hesitated. "There is one thing you need to know."

Charlotte's mind raced through a thousand possibilities.

"One of the girls is black. I mean she's African-American. I hope that's all right."

"Is that all? I thought you were going to tell me something terrible."

"We've never exactly talked about how you felt about taking girls of a different race."

"Nor do we need to."

"Her name is Sharita. She's thirteen and she loves to sing."

"Wonderful. Lighted Way has a teen choir. They'll love to have her."

"The other one is Maggie. She's a year older."

"So when are you bringing them?"

"Monday afternoon."

Charlotte tried to remember who had what appointments next week. Somebody had a doctor's appointment on Monday—or was that a counseling session at the school? She swallowed. "Sure. Monday will be great."

"See you then."

Monday was a school holiday. Charlotte had forgotten.

When Kim and the new girls arrived, Beth was up in her room, Donna in the kitchen making brownies from a mix, Nikki and Vikki outside on the porch.

"Hi, girls," said Kim. "What're you doing?"

"We've got walkie-talkies," said Nikki. "See?"

"We're calling the cats," said Vikki. "Watch." She grabbed a walkie-talkie out of her sister's hand. "Here, kitty, kitty, kitty." She kept her voice low.

At the sound of Vikki's transmitted voice, Snowball and Visa bounded across the yard toward what they expected to be dinner. When they got to the middle, they stopped and looked around, both of them confused.

"Here, kitty, kitty, kitty."

The cats looked even more bewildered. Snowball sat down and wailed.

"Where's the other walkie-talkie?" asked Kim.

"We hid it in that tree."

Nikki and Vikki couldn't stop laughing.

"You girls," said Kim. "Those poor cats. Where's Charlotte?"

"She's inside," said Nikki. "I think she's taking a bath."

"Did she tell you two more girls were coming today?" asked Kim. "She told us," said Vikki. She looked up at one of the newcomers.

"What's your name?"

"Maggie."

"You have a cat?"

"No. One time I had a pet snake. I took it to school with me. The principal made me let him go."

"You don't get your own cat," said Nikki. "There're only two."

"You have to share," said Vikki.

"I don't really like cats," said Maggie.

"What's your name?" Nikki asked the other girl.

"Sharita."

"We've got two rooms left," said Vikki.

"Want to see?" said Nikki.

"Welcome to Tanglewood," said Charlotte, when the group came inside. "You two look like you're already friends. Did you know each other before today?"

"Nope," said African-American Sharita. "Never saw the girl before in my life."

"They bonded over chocolate shakes and onion

rings on the way," said Kim.

"Yeah," said red-haired Maggie. She burped a loud burp. "We bonded."

"You should smell my car," said Kim.

"How old are you girls?" asked Charlotte.

"I'm thirteen," said Sharita. "She's fourteen. But we're in the same grade."

"I got to go," said Maggie. "Bad. Where's the restroom?" Charlotte showed her the downstairs bath.

When she came out, Nikki and Vikki dragged the new girls upstairs. Charlotte stayed downstairs with Kim.

"Pretty lively pair," said Charlotte.

"You have no idea," said Kim, shaking her head. "They've been giggling and singing for the past two hours." She glanced up the stairs. "Like the others, their records are in these packets. I'll give you a quick rundown. Maggie's lived in the country—I mean, way back in the woods—for most of her life. No dad, just she and her mom. Really rural. I'm not sure they had indoor plumbing. The two of them moved to Dallas six months ago. Mom thought she could make it. Couldn't. Lost her job and her apartment. She's worn out her welcome at any of her relatives' houses several times over. They had no place to go. Two weeks ago, somebody reported them at a state park, living in their car."

"Poor things," said Charlotte. "Where's her mom now?"

"Jail. Outstanding warrants. Nothing violent. But

without anyone to pay bond, she'll stay locked up for the next several months."

"I'm glad Maggie's here," said Charlotte.

"A bit rough around the edges," said Kim. "From what I've seen, she has no concept of manners, and her standards of hygiene leave something to be desired."

"Probably hard to keep clean living out of a car," said Charlotte. "What about Sharita?"

"She's a city girl through and through. Raised by two good, loving, hardworking parents who happen to be poor. They live in an area of Houston where gangs are a big problem. Sharita's brother was killed in a drive-by shooting two years ago. According to her parents, gang members have had their eyes on her for more than a year. Her mom and dad are scared to death of her getting involved. They can't afford to move, but they're willing to do anything to keep her safe."

"Even send her away," said Charlotte.

"That's right," said Kim. "There's more info in the packets. If you have any questions, give me a call." She gathered her things. "Tanglewood's full now. Six girls—that's a lot of estrogen floating around. You see any problems ahead?"

"No," said Charlotte. "We're fine. Got it all under control."

Kim left, and Charlotte went up to help Maggie and Sharita get settled in. As soon as she was back downstairs she remembered. Today was the fourteenth. Tonight in the church fellowship room an appreciation reception was being held for Pastor Jock. She'd read about it in last week's church bulletin. Something about his being at Lighted Way for five years. Six o'clock. Coffee and cake.

Should she and the girls go? Probably not. A quiet night at home would be better for the two new ones. They needed time to settle in before facing the attention of Ruby Prairie folks.

But Pastor Jock had been so kind—to all of them.

Charlotte waffled. They really should go.

"Girls," she called them all together. "We're going to church tonight. At six o'clock. There's a party for Pastor Jock."

"Is it his birthday?" asked Beth.

"They gonna have food?" asked Maggie.

"No, not his birthday. More like an appreciation party. There'll be cake. Probably punch too. We'll eat supper and then leave right after. Everybody be ready."

They were a good twenty minutes late. "Come on, girls." Charlotte urged them out of the van. "Remember. Be polite. Say hello to Pastor Jock. Only one piece of cake each. We won't stay long."

The room was really crowded. Hardly a place for Charlotte and the girls to stand. She looked around the room. Unfamiliar faces looked back. Where was Pastor Jock? Kerilynn? They must be sitting down somewhere.

"Can we have cake now?" asked Nikki.

"I guess so. Remember to say thank you."

Charlotte didn't know the woman doing the cutting. Nor the one pouring punch.

Seven pieces of cake. Seven cups of punch.

Charlotte overheard the two servers discussing the dwindling refreshment supplies. Had they prepared enough? Perhaps they should have brought more than one cake.

She found a place where all of them could sit down. Maggie spilled her punch. Then Nikki turned her chair over and upended a potted plant. Sharita got the hiccups. Donna saw a man who reminded her of her dad and started crying.

Folks stared.

This was a bad idea. She would find Pastor Jock, apologize for leaving early, and take them all home. "Don't move," she told the girls. "I'll be right back."

"Excuse me," Charlotte said to the woman cutting cake. "Can you tell me where Pastor Jock is?"

"Who?"

Maybe the woman was hard of hearing. "Pastor Jock." Charlotte spoke up louder. "The man this reception is for."

The woman looked confused. "Honey, I don't know anybody named Jock. This is the quarterly regional meeting of the Retired Teachers Association. Don't take this the wrong way, but you look awfully young to be retired. Where did you last teach?"

Charlotte looked up then at a calendar pinned on the

wall behind the woman's head. Today was the seventh.

Not the fourteenth.

Oh my.

It really was time to go home.

Chapter Thirteen

Charlotte was bent down comparing prices on peanut butter, wishing she hadn't forgotten her glasses and wondering why it was the economy sizes of everything were stocked on the lowest possible grocery store shelves, when she heard a distinctive voice chatting it up in the next aisle over.

Lila Peterson.

Charlotte straightened up and pushed her overgrown bangs from her eyes.

Shortly after arriving in Ruby Prairie, Charlotte had heard about Lila from several well-groomed residents. "Town treasure," is how Kerilynn had described her. "Only twenty-eight, but she's got a gift with hair."

According to Kerilynn, even though she was only three years out of Mr. Freddy's College of Beauty, Lila was already an expert when it came to color and cuts and perms. Not only that, she knew just what chemical processes worked best on what kind of hair and which style flattered which shape of face.

Lila's grateful customers were generous. Not only did they tip her with dollar bills stuck in the empty jam jar next to her styling station, but they surprised her with frequent gifts of appreciation. On her last visit to Lila's shop, Charlotte had noticed two loaves of banana bread, a jar of bread-and-butter pickles, and a set of crocheted pot holders custom-done in Lila's kitchen colors, aqua and peach.

"Not that I'm trying to drum up business or anything, but a person can only cut on her own hair for so long and get away with it." Lila had rounded the corner and was heading up the peanut butter aisle toward Charlotte.

"Lila! I thought that was you I heard," returned Charlotte. "Guilty as charged. I've been meaning to call."

Lila grinned. "Just kidding, honey. You look fine. That pink sweater's cute on you. How're those girls? I hear you've got a full house."

"I do. Six now. And all of us need haircuts. Desperately."

"Seven heads of hair—that's the kind of household I like. May as well set you and your bunch up on a regular schedule, the way they do your cleanings at the dentist. Every six weeks whether you need it or not. Why, with that many girls, you should put me on retainer like they do those lawyers on TV. I could be your personal on-call stylist. Anybody at Tanglewood needing highlights? A perm or straightening?" She gave Charlotte's brows a quick scan. "You know I do waxings too."

Upon moving to Ruby Prairie, Charlotte had been

shocked by two things. The high price of groceries at Rick's, the family-owned and only grocery store in town, and the unbelievably low prices at Lila's beauty shop—almost half of what she had been accustomed to paying.

"You want me to call you at the shop?" asked Charlotte. "I really do need to make some appointments."

"No. I don't need my book. Just give me a second to think." Lila scratched her ear with an artfully French-manicured nail. "Tell you what. Kids are out of school again on Friday—teachers have another workday or something. I know for a fact I'm booked real light. Let's do five of you then. As for the other two, how about they come in after school today? I'm booked, but it won't be a problem to work them in."

Charlotte wrote it down on the back of her grocery list. "That'll be great. I'll send the twins this afternoon. All they need is a trim. The other girls and I will come on Friday. I've got a couple that could really use your help."

"I love a challenge."

"What time?"

"Let's say nine. I imagine we can be done by two. I've got a snack machine in the back room, but you'd better bring y'all some lunch. Just think," said Lila. "Come Sunday, you'll be a good-looking bunch. Seven lovely ladies in one pew. Pastor Jock may have a hard time keeping his mind on his sermon notes."

"What I'll have a hard time with is getting six girls and myself up and to church anywhere near on time," said Charlotte. "Somebody's been late to school every day this week."

"I don't wonder," said Lila. "How many bathrooms you got?"

"One downstairs, two up."

"There's your trouble. Three girls trying to get ready all at once. I grew up with two sisters in a house with just one bathroom. We never made it anywhere on time. Two out of three of us were late to our own weddings, and we lived next door to the church. See you Friday."

Charlotte hurried home and rushed to put away her groceries. In between stashing the canned goods in the pantry and the frozen stuff in the freezer, she switched a load of clothes from the washer to the dryer. After that, she changed the sheets on her bed, vacuumed the living room, and ran a dust mop over the entry hall. Her goal every school day was to get her housework—cleaning, laundry, errands, and such—completed by the time the girls arrived home. She tried to have it all done and have a snack ready for them—sliced apples and warm-in-the-microwave caramel dip today—so she could spend the last remaining private minutes of the day rocking on her front porch and gathering her thoughts. She didn't always accomplish her goal, but when she did manage to carve out the time, it was among her favorite half hours of the day.

Today, zipped into a fleece-lined jacket, Charlotte stole twenty minutes to sit, rest, wait, and watch for the girls to come into view. It being fall, most of the yard's massive maple trees, ones whose leafy branches had obstructed her view only a month ago, stood bare, making it easy for her to see almost a block in three directions.

Tanglewood sat at the top of a T formed by two streets, Main Street, which ended at the sidewalk leading to her front door, and Betty Lane, which ran east and west in front of the house. So quiet was this part of town that when the wind was right, the sound of the bell signaling the end of the school day three blocks away and the revving of the engines of the school's six rural route yellow buses could sometimes be heard from Charlotte's front porch.

Most days, Visa and Snowball joined Charlotte on her afternoon vigil. While she watched for the girls from a rocker or the wicker swing, they kept their eyes peeled from their perch on the porch railing.

Charlotte knew the two cats differed in their reasons for keeping watch. Visa, her company-loving cat, craved the attention of the house full of girls. She liked Charlotte, but she adored the girls and could scarcely bear the long hours they were gone, choosing to sleep and mope the day away. Lest she hurt anyone's feelings, Visa diplomatically slept with a different girl each night. Her rotation was amazingly precise. Charlotte, who sometimes forgot which girls were asleep in which rooms, had no idea how the cat kept track.

Snowball, on the other hand, had little use for anyone other than Charlotte. Queen cat for a half-dozen years, she'd grudgingly tolerated the arrival of the twins, but had appeared thoroughly miffed when Beth moved in. The recent additions of Donna, Sharita, and Maggie had just about pushed her over the edge. The cranky cat spent her evenings either curled up on Charlotte's bed or snootily perched on top of the refrigerator. Not only was it warm up there, but she was well out of reach of the dozen hands that longed to stroke, pet, and scratch behind her ears.

"Won't be long now, girls," said Charlotte to the cats when she caught the sound of the bell. She yawned. Caring for six girls meant a never-ending succession of estrogen-fueled, late-night dramas. Many midnights she was up rubbing someone's back, drying someone's tears, listening to someone talk.

Last night it had been Donna. Charlotte had found her crying twenty minutes after she'd told her good night and turned off all of the upstairs lights.

"Donna? What's wrong?" Charlotte asked.

Shrouded by darkness, the girl spilled out her worries about her dad. "I know he's missing me. He hates to be alone."

According to her file, it had been just Donna and her dad baching it since her mother had left them two summers before. From what Donna told her, and from observing her competent, eager-to-please helpfulness around the house, Charlotte gleaned that the girl had taken on the role of chief home tender for her still stunned and brokenhearted dad. When he'd taken a job on an offshore drilling rig, one which required him to be gone for six months at a time, Donna suddenly had no place to live.

What was the man thinking, taking a job like that with a teenage daughter and no mother in the picture?

"Daddy says he'll make more money in six months that he could make in two years at home. When he gets back, we're going to move to Oregon because it's really pretty up there. He says we can get us a nice house and that when I'm sixteen he'll buy me a car."

Charlotte prayed that Donna's dad would be true to his word. She couldn't help but wonder why he had placed her at Tanglewood a full week before he had to go.

"He leaves on Friday. Can I call him tomorrow?"

"Of course you can. How about a foot rub? You think that would feel good?"

It had been well after one o'clock before Charlotte had gone to sleep, the scent of peppermint foot cream on her hands.

Out on the porch, Charlotte yawned and stretched and ran over in her mind the agenda for the rest of the day. Phone call to Donna's dad. Homework. Teen choir practice tonight. Haircuts. She'd almost forgotten. She'd feed Nikki and Vikki a quick snack, then send them on down to Lila's. They could walk. Maybe she'd make one of the older girls go with them. Maybe not. Lila's shop was only a couple of blocks away.

Visa and Snowball, snoozing on the porch railing,

were suddenly awake. Snowball put her ears back, not even trying to hide her displeasure. Visa jumped into Charlotte's lap, where she began to purr and pad back and forth. It was the approaching girls, still half a block away, that had stirred the cats.

First came Nikki and Vikki, swinging their backpacks, kicking at rocks and chattering away. Had they had kept their bras on today—or like yesterday and the day before that, taken them off while at school? They were still too far away for Charlotte to tell.

An early bloomer herself, Charlotte could relate to their reluctance to accept the contrary contraptions. "I know they feel funny, but really, you'll get used to them," she told them when they'd come home with their bras stuffed into their backpacks. "You're young women now. Becoming a woman is nothing to be embarrassed about. It's really a special thing."

"Okay," they'd both said. "Can we watch cartoons now?"

The next day Charlotte had driven to school to pick up the girls for dentist appointments. Nikki had come out first. Even with the windows of the car rolled up, Charlotte could tell she was singing. Lost in her own gleeful world, Nikki kept time with the bra she had in her hand, holding it by one strap and swinging it around like a prop.

That day Vikki had left her bra in her locker at school.

As the girls got closer, Charlotte saw that today she was one for two. Looked like Vikki was wearing her bra. Nikki was not.

Donna walked a pace behind the twins. This morning she'd helped them with their hair. Last night she'd played eight rounds of Uno with them. Charlotte prayed that Donna's dad would be home when she called.

Beth came next. Tanglewood's most difficult-to-read girl, she did everything asked of her. But she still kept all her thoughts to herself.

"Beth, do you have a tattoo?" Charlotte had asked on the day she'd received the call from the school.

"How did you know?"

"The school called."

Beth's transparent face showed instant fear.

"Honey, it's okay. You're not in trouble. I just want to see it." Beth lifted her shirt to reveal the image on her side—a nickel-sized, oddly shaped star, permanently inked in blue.

Charlotte touched the design with her thumb. "It's pretty. I've never seen a design exactly like that. But don't you have to be eighteen?"

"You're supposed to. They make you sign a form or something."

"Who signed for you?"

"Nobody. It's homemade. I got it at the shelter."

"Someone there did it? How?"

"This guy did it with a safety pin and some ink we got out of a pen. Other kids did it too."

Did it hurt?" Charlotte struggled to keep her face

and voice neutral. *Keep it light. Don't look shocked.* A lot. I almost changed my mind."

Was this the same guy who pierced your ears? What was his name . . . Kirby?

"Yeah." Beth's face went pink.

"Sounds like you two got to be good friends. Was he at the shelter the whole week you were there?"

"Not the whole week. He came the day after I did."

"It must have been good to have someone to talk to."

"It is. I mean, it was." Beth looked down at her lap. "I think I've got some homework to do. I'm going upstairs to do it in my room."

"Beth, just one more thing," said Charlotte.

Beth chewed a fingernail.

"Try to keep your tattoo out of sight—just while you're at school. Okay?"

"Sure."

"Uh—and maybe at church too. Wouldn't want any of the old ladies to need prayer or anything."

Beth grinned and disappeared upstairs.

Charlotte could hear the girls' voices as they grew closer. Nikki and Vikki, still ahead of the rest, were at the far end of Tanglewood's front walk.

Sharita and Maggie lagged behind the rest of the girls. Best friends since their arrival, they made quite a pair—Sharita with her cropped black hair and medium brown skin, and Maggie, freckled, fair, and as redheaded as Charlotte had ever seen.

Charlotte's quiet time was over. The porch was full of girls—girls talking, girls laughing, girls needing her attention. Feeling like a shepherd in the midst of a meandering herd, she dispensed hugs to the huggers—Nikki, Vikki, Donna, and Sharita—and pats and smiles to nonhuggers Beth and Maggie.

She held open the screen door as the girls trooped inside and headed toward the kitchen. "Backpacks and coats on the stairs, please," Charlotte reminded them. "Take them up with you when you go."

The stairs were quickly covered up.

"School go well? How were your days?" Charlotte asked.

"Mine was okay." Donna scooped Visa into her arms.

Charlotte gleaned from the look on her face, half hidden in Visa's white fur, that Donna's day had actually been less than okay. She'd probe a bit when the two of them had a few moments alone.

"What's for snack?" Vikki made a quick grab at Snowball, but the cat slipped out of her grasp and made a successful run for the underneath of Charlotte's bed.

"Cookies?" asked Nikki.

"Nope. Apples," said Charlotte.

"Plain apples?" Vikki made a face.

"With caramel dip," said Charlotte. She popped the bowl in the microwave and hit reheat.

"Any mail for me?" asked Beth, fiddling with one of her earrings.

"Two letters. On the breakfast bar. Next to the napkins."

"Is tonight choir practice?" asked Sharita.

"Six thirty. Pastor Jock said he would come by and pick you up." Charlotte stirred the caramel and set it on the table next to the plate of sliced apples.

"What kind of a name is *Jock* for a pastor?" asked Sharita.

"I guess it's the name his mother gave him," Charlotte replied. "Sounds dumb to me." Sharita always had to have the last word.

"What should I wear?"

"What you've got on will be fine."

Sharita dropped a big glob of caramel on the front of her shirt. "Then again you might want to change your shirt," Charlotte said with a smile.

"Don't have to." Sharita scooped at the dip with her apple slice and popped it into her mouth. "See?" Her eyes dared Charlotte to disagree.

Successful parenting supposedly involved not making mountains out of molehills. But how was one supposed to tell which were which?

"Suit yourself," Charlotte said.

Maggie held her tummy "Oh, man. I've got killer cramps. You got any Tylenol?"

"Extra strength." Charlotte handed her the medicine, retrieved from a top kitchen shelf.

Maggie opened the bottle. "Do I take one or two?"

"One. Who wants something to drink?"

"I do."

"Me too."

"Milk, water, or juice?"

"Maggie!" said Sharita, her mouth full of apple. "Don't double-dip. That's gross."

"Goodness," said Charlotte. "I nearly forgot. Nikki and Vikki—you're getting haircuts today. Finish up. I told Lila you'd be there soon as you got out of school. Any volunteers to go with them?"

"I've got homework," said Donna.

"Me too," said Sharita.

"Cramps," said Maggie.

"Where's Beth?"

"She went outside. To the secret arbor," said Donna.

"To read her lo-o-ove letter," said Nikki.

"From her boyfriend." Vikki made a gagging sound.

"She writes his name all the time," said Nikki. "I saw it on lots of little pieces of paper she's got in her desk."

"She even writes it on her hand sometimes," added Vikki.

Charlotte looked out the window. Sure enough. She could just barely see Beth's red sweater, partially hidden by the evergreen branches of the arbor.

"We don't need anybody to go with us," said Vikki.

"We used to walk to school by ourselves," reminded Nikki. "Okay. But go straight to Lila's and come straight back home."

"We will," said Vikki.

"Promise," said Nikki.

They would be fine.

After all, Lila's was only three blocks away.

Chapter Fourteen

Dear Beth,

I miss you so much. All I can think about is you. The day that I told you good-bye at the shelter was the worst day of my life. This may sound dumb, but I cried all the way to my uncle's house. He kept joking and punching me in the arm, asking me what was wrong. (Like I would know where to start.) Even though we were together for only six days, I swear I have never felt about any other girl the way I feel about you. I can't wait until we can be together again. Don't worry. I'm working on our plan. It won't be long now, I promise.

Love,
Kirby

P.S. I'm sorry your ear got infected.
P.S.S. Write back soon.

Beth read the letter, then folded it up, put it back in the envelope, and stuffed it into the pocket of her jeans. She sat Indian-style on the ground, her shoulders hunched. With sweaty hands, she rearranged fallen pine needles into three neat little piles. She ringed each pile with pine cones, then lined up a row of small rocks around the whole configuration.

Back at the shelter, no particular staff member had been in charge of locking inside doors, which meant that they were rarely secured. So while other teens lounged in the recreation area watching TV, playing Ping-Pong, eating donated day-old doughnuts, and making calls on the pay phone, it had been easy for her and Kirby to sneak into the supposedly off-limits female living quarters.

They spent the first day sitting cross-legged on Beth's cot, eating strawberry Pop-Tarts and talking nonstop. Kirby wanted to know everything about her. Where was she from? Did she have a family? Why wasn't she going back to her old foster home? When she cried telling him about Tim and B.J., Kirby cried a little too. He'd been through some of the same stuff himself. The more they talked, the more it felt to Beth as if she'd known Kirby all her life.

Once they discovered how easy it was for them to slip away, they went back to Beth's cot every single day. On the two occasions they found that the door had been locked, Kirby, steely determined, had jimmied it open with hardly any trouble at all. *"So we can talk,"* he'd assured her, when Beth hesitated the first time. *"That's all."*

No one ever knew.

Beth took the letter out of her pocket and read it again three more times. *Our plan.* She wished Kirby had been more specific. It was the not knowing that made it so hard.

She shivered. This was different. In ten years of living in foster homes, she had never had a plan. Not a real one—not unless you count it a plan to be as good as you can be so that maybe, just maybe, the folks you are staying with will like you and let you stay.

A lot of good that had done. If such a plan were ever going to work, it should have been with Tim and B.J. What an act they had put on. She was so stupid—actually believing them when they told her she was like a daughter to them, the daughter they had always wanted and never been able to have.

She would never fall for that line again.

Charlotte looked out her kitchen window. Beth was still in the arbor. Had her letter contained bad news?

"Anybody talk to Beth?" Charlotte asked. "Did she seem all right when she went out?"

"She wasn't crying or anything," Maggie called from the couch. "She looked okay to me," Sharita added with a shrug.

Add Beth to the mental list of girls she needed to connect with one-on-one. Some days there was not enough of her to go around.

Charlotte looked at the clock on the stove. Three forty-five. "Nikki and Vikki, you finished with your snacks? Good. Go wash. You two need to get to Lila's pronto." Charlotte tossed crumpled napkins into the trash while Donna put empty glasses into the dishwasher.

"I don't want to get my hair cut," said Nikki. "I want it to grow out. Like Donna's."

"That's fine. You don't have to get it cut, just

trimmed. Your bangs are in your eyes, and you've got raggedy ends."

"If you get it trimmed, it'll make it grow faster," said Donna. "Is that true?" asked Vikki.

"Absolutely. I get mine trimmed all the time." Donna turned around so they could see the back. "See? And I drink at least two glasses of milk every day. Milk makes it grow faster."

Nikki and Vikki finished their glasses of milk.

Charlotte gave them twenty-two dollars. "Your haircuts are ten dollars each. That's what the twenty is for. The singles are to leave for a tip. I want you to go straight to Lila's and come straight back home. Understand?"

"We understand." Nikki had her hand on the doorknob.

"Wait. Either of you have homework?" asked Charlotte.

"Math," said Vikki.

"English," said Nikki.

"Take your backpacks. Get your homework done while you wait for your turn; then you won't have to worry about it later."

Charlotte stood on the porch and watched the twins until they disappeared from her sight. Inside, she dialed Lila's number to let her know they were on their way. The line was busy.

"Hi, girls," called Mr. Collins. He was out raking leaves in his yard as they passed. Ginger had gone in to put something on for their dinner, leaving him all alone with no one to talk to.

This made three times he'd seen Nikki and Vikki today. Like other eagle-eyed Ruby Prairie residents who lived along the school route, mornings and afternoons, either he or Mrs. Collins—oftentimes both of them—made it a point to be outside during the half hours students walked to or from school. Sometimes they sat on their porch. Other times they did outside work, like sweeping the walk or hanging out a load of sheets or pulling up weeds.

"Aren't you two heading the wrong direction? Tanglewood's that way," he teased, pointing back toward Charlotte's. "Then again, maybe I looked at my watch wrong. Is it tomorrow already?"

"We're going to Lila's," said Vikki.

"To get our hair cut," said Nikki.

"So it will grow faster," said Vikki.

"Why, you two have pretty heads of hair," said Mr. Collins. "Not like me." He stroked his shiny bald head. "When it's windy like today, I can't do a thing with my hair. Year or so ago, I decided to just part it down the middle and be done with it."

The girls giggled.

"Be careful now. Watch out when you cross Abney Street." He decided to stand in his yard and keep an eye on them until he was sure they'd made it safely across.

"We will," said Vikki.

"Bye, Mr. Collins," said Nikki.

• • •

South of Abney, Main Street was lined on both sides with houses. Tanglewood sat at its farthest end. Near the edge of town, way out the opposite direction, were located the Four Paws Pet Clinic; Hometown Tire and Implement; Catfish Martin's Video, Snack, and Bait Shop; and the New Energy Rest Home. It was in between, north of Abney but still on Main, that most of the rest of Ruby Prairie's businesses were located. On the east side of the street stood the 'Round the Clock Cafe, the Chamber of Commerce office, Field of Dreams Florist, and Rick's Grocery.

On the opposite side was Hardy's Hardware, run by the four fifty-something Hardy brothers. The hardware store sold everything from toilet seats and copper wiring to fifty-pound sacks of dog food, deep freezers, and matching six-piece living room suites. One of the brothers' wives sold Mary Kay, so they kept some of her best sellers, especially that bath oil that was also said to repel bugs, on a display cabinet next to the register. Most days, the store did a good trade. However, when things got slow, and there wasn't too much backed-up stock to put away, the Hardy Boys Quartet put in a little practice time.

Next to the hardware store was Angelina's Attic. It was a gift shop run by a small-boned Asian woman named Rita, who had recently begun teaching herself to play bluegrass on the banjo. The shop boasted a wonderful selection of china and crystal, as well as a wide variety of candles, decorative pillows, potpourri, and such. Every bride who married in Ruby Prairie registered her selections at Angelina's.

Just past Angelina's was Joe's Italian Restaurant. Open for a year, Joe's had proved to be the 'Round the Clock's only real competition for the eating-out crowd. Tuesday through Sunday, Joe Fazoli cooked up the best lasagna, manicotti, and spinach chicken pasta a person could ever dream of putting in his mouth. Not only that, his basic spaghetti—$4.50 for meat sauce, $5.25 for sauce with meatballs—was pretty good too. Joe baked his own garlic bread and was saving up for a soft-serve ice cream machine. He figured offering a light dessert to his patrons would be a real draw.

Down from Joe's was an antique store called Grandma Had One. Sassy Clyde ran it, renting out space to anyone who had some old stuff they wanted to get rid of. Sassy's store was frequented by out-of-towners, who didn't seem to mind poking through harvest gold seventies kitchenware, dusty Beanie Babies, and twenty-year collections of *National Geographic* to get to the good stuff.

Right inside the door of Grandma Had One sat a decoratively carved oak church pew. It was such an interesting piece that, despite its *Not for Sale* sign, two or three times a week someone tried unsuccessfully to talk Sassy into parting with it.

Several folks in Ruby Prairie had been afflicted with what the folks at the rest home referred to as old-timer's disease. For example, Jerietta Rollins, who came in twice a week with her husband, Ralph, from their home in the country to take care of his business in town. Jerietta tired easily. If she was on her feet for long, she grew more confused and fretful. So Ralph, when he had to buy groceries or load up at the feed store or take care of some matter down at city hall, brought Jerietta by Grandma Had One. He greeted Sassy, settled his wife on the church pew, then went about with his errands, knowing that Sassy would keep a close eye on her.

Occasionally Sassy could be found handing out cold Dr. Peppers to three or more elderly folks, all of whose behinds were resting on the pew while their grateful family members raced around town, taking care of their errands.

"Sorry, not for sale," explained Sassy to hopeful customers. "That there is a reserved seat."

When Nikki and Vikki passed in front of Hardy's, they heard the strains of "Let Me Call You Sweetheart." They stopped for a moment to listen, but when the men spotted the girls and waved, the twins walked on.

The twins knew all about Joe's. Charlotte, who loved Italian food and who was not a creative cook, treated herself and her girls to dinner at Joe's most Thursday nights. Nikki and Vikki considered the Open sign in the front door a personal invitation. The scent of baking garlic bread welcomed them in.

"Hi there! What you two doing?" asked Joe. Behind the counter, he was busy wrapping knives and forks in paper napkins. "Is too early for dinner. You come in to give me some help?"

"We're getting haircuts," said Nikki.

"At Lila's," said Vikki.

The two of them smiled brazenly at the gum ball machine Joe kept next to the front door.

"You girls don't need any gum today, do you?" asked Joe.

"Yes, we do," said Nikki.

"I thought so." Joe opened up the register and handed them each a quarter. "Here you go."

The girls knew better. They also knew that Joe would not tell. He gave away quarters for his gum machine to every child who came in, though generally to children whose parents had just paid for meals.

Last Thursday night, the twins had watched a little girl cry when she didn't get a pink gum ball. Joe had kept handing her quarters—six in all—till she got her desired hue.

"Thank you," said Nikki.

"Thank you," said Vikki.

They got their gum, said good-bye to Joe, and went on.

Nothing about Grandma Had One appealed to the girls. They walked right on by. However, an elderly man in overalls sitting on the back of a pickup truck in front of the store did catch their eyes. On his bony knees he was balancing a good-sized cardboard box.

"Good afternoon, young ladies. How are y'all?" said the man, smiling and tipping his cap.

"Fine," said Nikki.

"What you got in that box?" asked Vikki.

"Something I bet you'll like." The man winked. "Want to see?" The girls nodded, and he lowered the box so that they could peek inside.

"Puppies! Four of them!"

"They're so cute!"

"Can I hold one?"

"Sure, you can. You girls be needing a good dog?"

"Oh, yes. We need a dog really bad."

"We've just got two cats at our house."

"No dogs."

"Well, then, let's fix you up with one of these pups. Which one you like best?"

The girls picked up each fat, cuddly pup in turn. The puppies made soft little grunting and whining sounds. They wiggled their noses and licked the girls' hands.

"Are they girl dogs or boy dogs?" asked Vikki.

"All of 'em's girls 'cepting the little black one. He's a male."

"Where's their mother?" asked Nikki.

"Had to leave her back at the house."

"Oh." Nikki and Vikki fell silent. They understood. She would not be happy about her children going to some other house. "Are they free?" asked Vikki.

"Well, no, sugar, I'm sorry, they ain't."

"How much do they cost?" she asked.

"Twenty-five dollars apiece."

"Oh. We don't have that much." Nikki moved to put her dog back into the box.

"Now, just hold on," said the man. "Why don't you

two tell me how much you got, and we'll see if we can't work something out?"

Vikki buried her face in the fur of the puppy she was holding. "We've got twenty dollars."

"And two more dollars for a tip," added Nikki, nuzzling one of the girl dogs.

"Well, now. Seeing as how it's getting on in the day, I sure do hate to take these dogs back home with me. Tell you what. You two pick you out which puppies you want. I'll give you two of them for your twenty-two dollars. That'd be, what now—eleven dollars each."

"Really?"

"Go on now. Pick you out one apiece 'fore I change my mind. Now you'll give these dogs a good home, won't you? They've had they first shots but be needing they second set coming up next week."

"Yes, sir. We will."

"We'll feed them and give them water and play with them every day," promised Nikki.

"We'll even take them swimming," said Vikki.

The old man chuckled. "Might wait till they get a mite bigger 'fore you go and do that." He opened his wallet and put their bills inside. "You girls go to school, don't you? You study your lessons real hard? Course you do. Now, tomorrow, I'll be back here in this same place. Tell all your friends that if they want them a good dog, come see me. I'll fix them right up. Shoot. If they kids, I'll give them a discount, same as for you."

"Thank you," said Nikki.

"Thank you," said Vikki.

The two of them, carrying the puppies close to their chests, started toward Lila's, still half a block up ahead. It was Nikki who figured out first that the two of them had a problem. She stopped walking. "We can't go to Lila's. We don't have any money."

Vikki's puppy wet on her hand. She set the pup on the sidewalk, then squatted down and wiped her palm off on some grass. "You think Charlotte'll be mad?"

"I'm pretty sure," said Nikki. "She gave us money to get our hair cut, and we don't have it anymore."

"We told her we wanted to let our hair grow out."

"She's still going to be mad."

"You think she'll like the puppies?"

"I don't know. Maybe she just likes cats."

"We could tell her we got them for her. Like for a present or something. Then we could offer to take care of them for her."

"I'm not sure," said Nikki. "We had money to get haircuts, not to buy dogs."

The two of them sat down on a curbside bench.

"What are we going to tell her?"

They petted the puppies and chewed on their gum.

"You got your scissors in your backpack?" asked Nikki.

"I think so. Can we sell them?" Vikki dug in her backpack, though she didn't think Sassy would pay them enough.

"No, silly! Not that. I'll cut your hair, and you cut mine. Charlotte'll think we spent our money at Lila's.

We'll tell her somebody gave us the puppies."

"But that'll be a lie."

"Not really. Remember, the man gave us a discount. He *ga-ave* it to us. It's almost the same thing. Besides, we'll still have haircuts. We won't have the money, but we'll have puppies. Two things for the price of one. I bet Charlotte will be glad we got such a good deal. She'll be proud of us. Give me your puppy. I'll hold her while you cut my hair; then we'll trade."

Vikki held the scissors as though they were a snake that might bite her. "I don't know how to cut hair."

"It's not hard. Remember? We used to cut Barbie's hair all the time. Just go across." Nikki sat up tall and straight. "Start right here." She pointed to her bangs.

"This is kind of hard," said Vikki, after the first couple of whacks. The scissors weren't very sharp, and neither of them had a comb. "Aren't you're supposed to wet your hair first?"

"Sometimes they do it dry," Nikki assured her. The puppies were getting heavy and squirmy in her lap.

Vikki kept cutting. She stepped back to get a better look. "I think I should do some more in front of your ear." She sawed a while on the other side. "It's kind of short."

Nikki reached up and touched her bangs. "Feels okay."

"Should I do the back?"

"I guess. Just a little."

Vikki sucked at a blister on her thumb.

"Your turn," said Nikki, handing her the two pups

when she was done. After a few minutes of work she stepped back. "These scissors don't work very good," she announced.

"Told you." Vikki fidgeted. "Hurry up. My neck itches."

"We need one of those capes to keep all the hair off." Nikki brushed bits of hair off her sister's shoulders.

"Are you done?"

"Almost. Just got to do the back."

It was Beth, coming in from the arbor, who first saw the twins. They had cut across the yard and were sneaking toward the back door. "Where have you guys been? What happened to your hair?"

"We got it cut," fudged Nikki, clutching her middle.

"At Lila's?" asked Beth. She didn't want to hurt their feelings, but she'd never seen anything quite like the asymmetrical styles the girls wore.

Vikki reached up and touched her hair. "Does it look bad?"

"No-o. But it's pretty short," said Beth. She looked more closely at Vikki's middle. "What's under your shirt?"

Nikki looked at Vikki. They pulled out the dogs.

"Puppies? How cute! Where'd you get them?"

"A man gave them to us. Said we could have them if we gave them a good home," said Vikki.

"Is that right?" said Charlotte, who had heard their voices and stepped out the back door to greet them.

"Anything else you think I ought to know?"

Nikki looked at Vikki.

Vikki looked at Nikki.

Both of them squirmed.

"There might be one or two more things."

"Lila? This is Charlotte. I know, I know. The twins didn't show up. . . . I'm so sorry, and I know it's late—but could they come now? It's sort of an emergency. . . No. Really. It is. If I can just bring them in, you'll see exactly what I mean."

Chapter Fifteen

"What do people do at the Culture Fest?" asked Sharita, between ruthless Monopoly moves.

"I'm not exactly sure, since I've never been before." Charlotte rolled the dice, moved four spaces, and handed over Park Place rent.

After she'd received her fifth and sixth girls, Charlotte's request to be relieved of her position as chairman of the commercial booths had been graciously granted by the ladies of the Culture Club. She'd been grateful at the time, but tonight, knowing how hard the other club members had worked—and were likely working even at this late hour—she felt a stab of civic guilt.

"From what I hear, it's lots of fun. There'll be music and crafts, lots of food, and some of the businesses will be giving out free samples." She got up to stir the dying coals in the fireplace.

"What kind of music?" asked Maggie.

"What kind of food?" asked Nikki, her mouth full of microwaved popcorn.

"What kind of free stuff?" asked Donna.

"I don't know any of that. What I do know is that all the money the club takes in goes to good causes, like to buy school supplies for kids that don't have them and presents at Christmas for families who don't have money to buy gifts."

"Kids like us?" asked Maggie. "I mean, like we were before we came here?"

"Yes," said Charlotte. "I suppose it would be kids like that." She pictured Maggie and her mother, homeless, celebrating Christmas last year in a van.

"My mom and I used to get Christmas boxes every year," said Maggie. "Thanksgiving too."

"What was in the boxes? Presents?" asked Sharita.

"Mostly food. Same thing every year. Big turkey. Those things come frozen hard as a rock. Stovetop Stuffing Mix, instant mashed potatoes, a few apples and oranges, a can of cranberry sauce, and a can of green beans. Sometimes we'd get a package of rolls. You know—the kind you cook to make them get brown."

"You ever get ramen noodles, Maggie?" asked Sharita.

"Don't remind me. We got lots. Not at Christmas, but from the food bank in between."

"One time we had a food drive at my school," said

Sharita. "All the homerooms tried to collect the most food. Whichever kid donated the most food got a free movie pass. My mom gave me ten dollars, and I spent it all on ramen noodles. I got eight packages for a dollar! My mom said I should have gotten some other stuff instead, but I thought I got a good deal. I won the contest."

"You ever eat ramen noodles?" asked Maggie.

"No."

"Believe me. You did not get a good deal."

"What time does the Culture Fest start?" asked Vikki. She wasn't playing Monopoly but was working at teaching Jasmine, one of Tanglewood's two dogs, to sit and shake hands. The dog's sister, Mavis, slept on the rug by the back door.

"Nine o'clock," said Charlotte.

"Can we get there when it opens?" asked Sharita.

"Got to. I'm an official greeter from nine until noon."

"What are we gonna do?" whined Vikki. "Do we have to be greeters too?"

"That won't be any fun," said Nikki.

Beth, curled up on the window seat, looked up from her book.

"No, you don't have to be greeters," said Charlotte with a smile. "I'm giving you twenty dollars each. As long as you stay together, or at least in pairs, you can explore the festival on your own."

"Twenty dollars?" said Maggie.

"Man!" said Vikki.

“Out of your twenty you’ll have to buy lunch. Other than that, you can spend it on whatever you want. There’ll be vendors selling all kinds of stuff—like T-shirts, hats, probably CDs. Everybody needs to check in with me at eleven and again at two. We’ll stay until the end and help clean up.”

“I’m out,” said Sharita, tossing down a wad of Monopoly money. “Me too,” said Charlotte.

“I’m going to bed,” said Beth.

“I’m not even tired,” said Vikki.

Across town, Pastor Jock yawned. He should have volunteered to sell hot dogs for the 4-H club or take tickets at the gate. Making balloon animals was harder than it looked.

So far, he had mastered inflating the balloons with the cool little pump that had come with the kit. What was supposed to come after that? He was unsure. He studied the spiral-bound how-to book’s illustrations and read the step-by-step instructions one more time. Knot. Bend. Twist.

Simple enough.

Pop.

He tried again.

Down the street, under a handmade quilt, Ginger and Lester Collins snored in tandem. In preparation for an early start, they had turned in before ten. Last year, the demand for Lester’s made-on-the-spot, fried peach pies was so great a line had snaked all the way around to the back side of the concert area—which had proven terribly distracting for the middle school choir, who were off-key under the best of circumstances.

This year, Lester had it all laid out. He would have three kettles of grease going at once. Ginger, hearing of Lester's plan—and worried about the high blood pressure the doctor had warned him about—chided Lester about it being altogether too much for one man. To make her feel better he'd cajoled Boots Buck and Chilly Reed into giving him a hand. The three of them would get a head start by having the filling fixed and the grease hot by 5:00 A.M.

In the activity director's office at New Energy, boxes of tissue-wrapped crocheted items were stacked by the door, waiting to be loaded first thing in the morning into the rest home's 1977 baby blue Care Van. Creative residents had outdone themselves this year, completing five dozen pairs of house shoes and nearly as many little caps. When they'd realized there was yarn left over, and being of a generation not given over to waste, the ladies combined the multi-colored snippets with the contents of a box of used greeting cards to create lovely, wide-tasseled bookmarks. At only fifty cents apiece, they ought to be a good seller.

On Main Street Catfish Martin and Gabe Eden, in charge of security and parking, drank coffee and cut clandestine pieces of pie at the 'Round the Clock. The cafe had been closed for two hours, but Catfish had a key.

Two of the out-of-town vendors, the sand-art lady—Nell Something-or-other, Catfish recalled—and Grizzly Gates, the chain saw artist, had made arrangements to arrive after the designated 6:00 P.M. check-in time. She, because her truck was in the shop and would not be out before 5:00, he because of a carnival gig somewhere off across the state. Both had asked if there was someone available who could meet them late and direct them to where they were supposed to set up.

"No problem," Catfish had told them. "Just come on when you can. We'll be watching for you."

Catfish and Gabe hunkered over their coffee at a booth near the front where they could see the well-lit but deserted street that ran in front of the cafe. So little traffic came through town at night, spotting a pickup truck pulling a motor home and a van toting a small red trailer would be easy. Soon as they saw either of the vehicles, they would hop into Catfish's pickup, drive the two blocks to the grounds, open the gate, and let the folks in.

Nomie Jenkins, Sassy Clyde, and Alice Buck, hopeful that everything that needed to be done had in fact been done, punched their pillows, rechecked their alarms, and got up to get themselves something to drink.

Mayor Kerilynn took a Benadryl and went right to sleep.

At ten minutes after seven, Dr. Lee Ross had just finished his breakfast of bacon and eggs when his phone rang.

"Doctor Ross?"

It was Miss Lavada Minter. He could tell by the quavery, eighty-eight-year-old voice. "Yes, Miss Lavada?"

"I know this is Saturday, but are you real busy right now?"

"Actually, Miss Lavada, I was on my way to the festival."

"Oh, dear." Miss Lavada was prone to fret. "Something is wrong with Elizabeth. I was hoping you could see her today."

"I'll be in my office on Monday. Reckon it could wait until then?" Dr. Ross was president of the Ruby Prairie Jaycee Club, and he really should have been at the festival already, setting up the club's soft drink stand.

"I really don't know."

"What seems to be the problem with Elizabeth?"

"She won't eat. And she's prowling around the house looking very strange. This morning I found her way back up under my bed. Elizabeth never acts like that. I had to shoo her out with my broom."

Didn't sound too unusual, but Dr. Ross knew better than to put Miss Lavada off. Sometime today he'd have to see that cat, either now or at an even more inconvenient time.

"Tell you what, Miss Lavada. You know I don't normally make house calls, but how about I stop by in, say, ten minutes, on my way to the festival. Would that be okay?"

Miss Lavada coughed politely. "Dr. Ross, I'm still in my housecoat."

"Twenty then?"

"That would be better."

Miss Lavada, fully dressed, including stockings and shoes, graciously offered Dr. Ross a cup of tea soon as he was inside of her house.

"Thank you, but I believe I'll take a rain check this time. Let's take a look at our patient."

Miss Lavada showed Dr. Ross to the utility room, where she kept Elizabeth's bed.

"How long have you had this cat?" asked Dr. Ross.

"Five months. She was my sister's pet. When her children put Rose in the home, she asked me if I could take Elizabeth. I'd never had a cat before, but how could I turn my sister down in her time of need?"

"You couldn't, of course. It was kind of you to take her in." Dr. Ross peered into the dimly lit room. Elizabeth lay on her side in her cat bed, panting a bit. He knelt down and put his right hand on the cat's abdomen. "Miss Lavada, have you noticed Elizabeth putting on weight?"

"Now that you mention it, I suppose she has. She's hungry all the time. Have I been feeding her the wrong kind of food?"

"No, ma'am. You've been feeding her just fine. That's not the problem. You see, Miss Lavada, Elizabeth is—well, Elizabeth is in the family way. Matter of fact, I believe she's going to deliver kittens sometime today."

Miss Lavada put her hand to her mouth. "But that's not possible."

"Why is that?" Dr. Ross tried hard not to smile.

"Elizabeth doesn't have a husband. She's an inside cat. I never let her outside."

"Never? What about when she has to—?"

"She has one of those boxes."

"Maybe she got out accidentally—just once or twice."

"Dr. Ross, I can assure you, Elizabeth has not been outside this house. You should examine her more closely to see what's wrong." She began to wring her hands. "It will break my sister's heart if anything happens to Elizabeth. Are you sure I didn't feed her something that wasn't good for her?"

Dr. Ross tried to soothe the elderly woman. "Okay, so Elizabeth hasn't been out. Then you must have another cat in the house."

"I told you, until my sister went to that home, I'd never had a cat."

"She's not been out of the house in four months, and there aren't any other cats in the house."

Dr. Ross scratched his head and wished his home number weren't in the book. He looked at his watch. Already way late to the festival. That was not good. Young people these days drank sodas all day. There were probably folks at this very minute lined up, needing cold Dr. Peppers to wash down their breakfast biscuits.

"Miss Lavada, I don't know what to tell you except that Elizabeth is going to have kittens. I'm sure of it. Here's what you need to do for her. Keep her closed up in the utility room all day today. If you let her out, she's likely to run back up under your bed, and you don't want that. Make sure she's got water. Check on her every once in a while. She probably won't eat, but leave her a little food where she can get to it. My best guess is that by this afternoon nature will most likely have taken its course."

"I see," said Miss Lavada in an unconvinced voice.

It was at that moment that Elizabeth let out a menacing hiss.

"Elizabeth, darling, what's wrong?" said Miss Lavada.

A big tabby tomcat, unseen by either Dr. Ross or Miss Lavada, had crept into the utility room and ventured to give the mother-to-be a sniff.

"You *do* have another cat in the house," Dr. Ross said. "I misunderstood. That explains everything."

"Oh, Dr. Ross." Miss Lavada blushed. She bent down and picked up the big boy cat. "This is Edward."

"You'll need to keep Edward away from Elizabeth and her babies," Dr. Ross warned. "Cats aren't like people. Papa cats can be mean."

"Dr. Ross." Miss Lavada spoke as if she were addressing a rather slow-witted child. "Edward can't possibly be the father of Elizabeth's children."

"Has he been neutered?" Dr. Ross took a closer look at the longhaired cat.

"I certainly don't know about anything like that, but Edward couldn't be—well, you know. Why, Edward here is Elizabeth's *brother.*"

Dr. Ross scratched his head. Sometimes this job did beat all.

Even though the festival grounds were within walking distance of Tanglewood, to save time Charlotte decided to drive the van. "Everybody in?" she asked. "Buckle up."

Outside the gates of the festival grounds, directing cars to the inside of the fence, stood Gabe. Catfish collected the two-dollar parking fee and saw to it that everyone parked in neat rows.

When Charlotte pulled her red twelve-seat van through the gates, she returned the scowl on Catfish's face with a smile. "Morning! How are you?"

"Two dollars," he said. "Need to keep moving. Don't want traffic to get all backed up."

There was no one in line behind Charlotte.

Charlotte parked where she was told. "Okay, girls," she told her sleepy, Saturday-morning bunch. "It's a quarter to nine right now. Remember when I said you're to check in with me?"

"Eleven and two," said Nikki and Vikki in unison.

"Right. I'll still be greeting at the gate at eleven, so I'll be easy to find. Now at two—how about let's meet at the performance area. There're some picnic tables there. We can hear the high school choir perform and watch the drama club's play. Everybody got a buddy?"

Except for Nikki and Vikki, nobody did.

"Y'all just want to stay together?" asked Donna. "All four of us?"

Beth shrugged. "Sure."

"Okay," said Maggie and Sharita.

"Fine," said Charlotte.

Mayor Kerilynn had assured her that the festival grounds were a safe place for kids to roam and enjoy a bit of semi-independent fun. Members of the Ruby Prairie Police Force manned both the exit and the entrance; and eagle-eyed, walkie-talkie-toting Culture Club members roamed the area, prepared to assist with any needs festival goers might incur.

"If you decide to split up later, make sure you stay in pairs." She watched as Nikki and Vikki set out at a dead run for the children's area. The older girls strolled behind.

By ten thirty Charlotte had greeted more than two hundred festival goers. The crowds came in waves. Soon as she'd think perhaps no one else was coming, another bunch would arrive. Out-of-town church and club groups came in vans. Families from out in the country arrived packed into cars. Her admiration for the ladies of the Culture Club grew. What a task it must be to pull off an event like this year after year.

"Been coming every year for the past twenty," said one man. "Don't remember seeing you here before."

"Charlotte Carter. New to town." She'd figured out after only a week that unless a citizen's grandparents had made their home in Ruby Prairie, that person would forever be considered a newcomer.

"Nice to meet you, sugar. They ain't run out of peach pies yet, have they?"

"Not that I've heard."

As each person entered, Charlotte gave out a canvas tote bag, courtesy of the Ruby Prairie Chamber of Commerce. "Welcome to the Culture Fest. Thank you for coming," she said. "Don't miss the commercial booths. Over this way." She pointed. "There's lots of free stuff. This bag will come in handy."

From what Charlotte could see, Sassy Clyde, who had taken over the commercial booths, had done the Culture Club proud. Word was, Sassy had demonstrated unprecedented success in her quest to extort goods and services from nearly every business in town.

The gratis goodies that attendees received included a lavender-scented votive candle from Angelina's Attic; three plastic-bagged, complimentary minnows from Catfish's bait and video store; and a trial-size bottle of shampoo from Lila's beauty shop. Not only that, but Annie Woods from the Home's Best Home Health Agency was offering no-charge blood pressure checks and giving away free pens and key chains to everyone who sat down and offered her a pulse. Nomie's niece, Daphne, a new Avon consultant, sprayed everyone who walked by with the company's latest scent. Joe Fazoli handed out bite-sized bread sticks and tiny paper cups of his famous marinara sauce, along with a coupon good for fifty cents off his spaghetti-and-meatball lunch special.

Charlotte hoped they didn't run out of goodies before she had a chance to glean some freebies for herself.

Kerilynn, making her rounds, stopped to check in with Charlotte at her post. "You doing okay?" she asked.

"Fine. How about everybody else?"

"Great. Good crowd so far. Everyone who was supposed to be here has shown up. Had a little glitch when the Jaycees were late getting their soft drink stand opened up, but other than that things are running smoothly."

"That's wonderful," said Charlotte. "I can't wait till my shift's over so I can see everything."

From her spot at the gate, Charlotte could smell an array of delicious aromas—hot dogs, tamales, turkey legs, and roasted corn. Her stomach growled, and she looked at her watch. Like the man who'd been coming for twenty years, Charlotte hoped Lester Collins didn't sell out of peach pies before she got her share.

Finally, at straight up noon, Nomie arrived to take her post, and Charlotte was free to explore. She strolled first to the children's section. Pastor Jock was a hit with his balloon animals. From the looks of it, he had perfected the crafting of a snake but was still working on making recognizable wienie dogs.

"You've got talents I never knew you had," said Charlotte.

"Thanks," he said. Just then the balloon he was

working on popped, causing him to jump and the waiting children to laugh. "This is harder than it looks. I'm getting blisters in my thumbs from tying. How about you? Had a peach pie yet?"

"Not yet."

"Don't miss out. They're as good as people say."

Charlotte walked on. Most every child sported a flower, a lightning bolt, a butterfly, or a bug on his or her cheek, courtesy of Lila and her pallet of face paint.

Most popular of all was the sand art stand. Along with her helper, a deeply tanned, pony-tailed young man wearing—in spite of the chill—Hawaiian print shorts and red flip-flops, proprietor Nell Bell kept the children busy layering colored sand into widemouthed canning jars.

Charlotte stood and watched.

"How many colors would you like? . . . Three? Okay, which ones? . . . Good choice. That'll be really pretty. . . . For your mother? Oh, she'll like that. Pour it in very slowly. . . . That's right. . . . No, sugar, don't. Don't shake it up. . . . Sweetheart, don't cry. You can do another one."

Over at the arts and crafts section, New Energy's crocheted items were practically flying off the table. Charlotte was disappointed to find they'd already sold out of bookmarks.

"Honey, folks were snatching them up half a dozen at a time," explained the lady in charge. "We had them underpriced. Next year we'll start them at a dollar apiece."

Vendors selling T-shirts appeared to be doing well. Those offering shirts with patriotic themes had the longest lines. Also popular was the booth where a man sold clocks handcrafted from two-inch cross sections of highly polished oak.

One of those would look nice over the mantel at Tanglewood.

Triple-scented candles were a hot item, with three booths in competition. Charlotte sniffed several. What unusual scents. Birthday cake. Harvest afternoon. Charlotte finally bought a vanilla and a mulberry.

While the chain saw artist did indeed do some beautiful work, only those citizens who'd already suffered hearing loss could stand to get close enough to watch without putting their fingers in their ears. Charlotte didn't linger long. She watched Catfish Martin buy an American bald eagle. "For my living room," she heard him say.

Lester Collins, taking a break from frying up his pies, strolled over in time to see the man finish carving a bear poised on his hind feet with a fish in his mouth. "I'm going to buy that," he told Ginger.

"No, you are not. We don't have anyplace to put it. Got too much stuff as it is," said Ginger.

Lester went back to his grease, slump-shouldered and disappointed.

"Poor thing," said Ginger to Charlotte. "Looks like he lost his last friend. I'm getting him that bear; he just don't know it. Got the perfect place for it. Going to store it at Gabe's until his birthday, twelfth of next month."

At two o'clock the girls met up with Charlotte. She bought them all fried peach pies, and the seven of them sat down at a picnic table near the concert stage. She was so hungry she couldn't wait for her pie to cool, and she scorched the roof of her mouth.

"What all have y'all done? Are you having fun?" asked Charlotte. "Have you spent all of your money?"

"I learned how to crochet a chain," said Vikki. "See? An old lady showed me how. She even let me keep this hook."

"How pretty," said Charlotte, fingering the twisted yarn. "Maybe you can teach me. What about you, Nikki? Did you buy anything yet?"

"I did the cakewalk twelve times, but I didn't win a cake. I bought something for you, but you can't see it. It's a surprise."

"How nice! I love surprises. Did you have any lunch?"

"I gave her some money," said Vikki, " 'cause she didn't have enough."

"The cakewalk costs a dollar every time you go," explained Nikki.

"What about the rest of you? Have you had fun?"

"Maggie and I did karaoke," said Sharita. "You should have seen us. We got up on the stage, and everyone clapped when we were through."

"What did you sing?" asked Charlotte.

"Crazy'—you know, by Patsy Dime," said Maggie.

"Patsy Cline," corrected Charlotte. "That's an old song. I'm surprised you two know it."

"My grandma liked that song," explained Maggie. "When my mom and I lived with her, she played it over and over."

"I never heard it before in my life," said Sharita. "I just followed along."

"Beth, did you buy anything?" asked Charlotte.

"Just a hot dog for lunch. I haven't decided what I want yet," said Beth.

"I bought a poster for my room," said Donna. "Cost eight dollars, but I got a free frame." She unrolled the poster for them all to see. It was a picture of two little girls, dressed in old-fashioned clothing, picking flowers in a field.

"That's pretty," said Sharita. "They got any more?"

"Not like this."

"Where're you going to put it?"

"Over my desk," said Donna.

"It'll look great there. I'll help you hang it up when we get home."

"When are we leaving?" asked Nikki.

"You're not ready to go, are you?" Charlotte surmised the Culture Fest was not as much fun once a person was broke.

"No!" said Vikki.

"We want to stay till the end," said Sharita and Maggie. "I'm still having fun," said Donna.

"Me too," said Beth.

"Sorry, sweetheart, you're outnumbered," Charlotte said, looking at Nikki. "How about this? The concerts and the play start in an hour. After that, there's the parade.

Once that's over, we'll go home. That gives everybody an hour to see anything they've missed and to buy whatever they've got their eyes on. Sound good?"

Everyone except a pouting Nikki agreed that it did.

As time for the parade approached, festival goers poured back out through the gates, leaving their cars parked on the festival grounds so as to snag prime viewing spots up and down Main Street. Charlotte and the girls decided on a spot in front of Grandma Had One. A late afternoon wind had come up, and a cloudy, darkening sky had replaced the day's bright sunshine. The twins shivered and huddled one under the shelter of each of Charlotte's arms. "How long is this going to last?" asked Donna.

"I wish I'd worn my bigger coat," said Sharita.

"Cold front's come through," said Gabe, who was standing nearby. He looked up at the sky. "Temperature's dropped a good twenty degrees in the past hour. Bet we get a hard freeze tonight."

"At least we had pretty weather for the day." Lester worked his way through the thickening crowd to claim a spot next to Charlotte. "Did your girls have a good time?"

"A great time," said Charlotte. "The festival was wonderful."

"Looks like the ladies did real good," agreed Lester. "Won't know till they pay all the bills, but I'm betting they netted a nice sum this year."

Folks were lined up two and three deep along both

sides of the street up and down four blocks of Main by the time the faint sounds of the high school bass drum's thump, thump began to be heard, followed by the high-pitched whine of the town's new fire truck.

"Won't be long now," said Gabe.

"Charlotte," said Beth, "I've got to go to the bathroom. Can I go across the street and use Joe's?"

"Sure, but you'd better hurry; the parade's almost here. You won't be able to get back across once it's started."

By the time Beth came out of Joe's, the band and baton twirlers were in the middle of the street. They were followed by Mayor Kerilynn riding in a black convertible. Behind her crept the town's brand-new fire truck, siren blaring, lights flashing. Charlotte motioned to Beth to stay put till the parade was over.

After the fire truck came the floats, flatbed trailers decorated with tissue paper and all sorts of creative props, some illuminated with twinkling colored lights. Leading was the 4-H club, followed by Dina's Day Care, then the high school football team. Last in the lineup was the float sponsored by the Culture Club. Perched in lawn chairs, surrounded by pots of fake mums, the officers of the club smiled and waved and tossed candy to the kids. They looked tired to the bone but very, very pleased.

The crowd up and down the parade route gave the ladies huge applause.

Behind the floats inched a line of almost a dozen tractors of various makes and models. Up close the machines were much bigger than they looked out in the fields. Some had enclosed cabs, and all had been scrubbed and shined in preparation for their trek through town.

Wisely positioned at the end of the parade were the horses and riders. Steeds of all colors and sizes, from ponies on up, were ridden by proud cowboys and cowgirls. There were even a few old-fashioned buggies and wagons. While most of the horses behaved themselves, a few appeared skittish and frightened by the crowds and commotion.

"Yuck. They stink," said Maggie.

"They're beautiful," disagreed Donna.

"Can we get a horse?" asked Nikki.

"Horses need lots of room," said Charlotte. "More room than we have at Tanglewood."

As soon as the parade was over, everyone headed back to the festival grounds and toward their cars. With only one bottlenecked exit, it would take forever to get out of the parking lot.

"Can't we just walk home?" asked Maggie. "We'll get there faster."

"I don't want to walk," said Nikki. "I'm tired."

Charlotte dug out her key. "Whoever wants to walk can go on home. Whoever wants to stay with me, can." She handed Maggie a house key. "Who's walking and who's riding?"

"I'm walking," said Sharita.

"Me too," said Donna.

"I'm staying with you," said Vikki.

"What about Beth?" asked Sharita.

Charlotte looked across the street to where Beth had been standing the last time she had looked. The chilled crowds, three deep on the sidewalk only minutes ago, had dispersed quickly to the warmth of their cars. The only person remaining in front of Joe's was Joe himself, sweeping up.

Charlotte glanced up and down the street.

And saw no sign of Beth.

Chapter Sixteen

Dr. Ross willed himself to let the answering machine take the call. His wife was out of town visiting her sick sister, so he had the house to himself. After cutting out on the Jaycees a bit early, leaving the task of taking down the booth to some of the younger members, he was settled into his recliner with his feet up and the TV remote in his hand. Surely whoever was calling would be able to wait.

"Dr. Ross. Are you there?" It was Miss Lavada, speaking up loud. "You were right. Elizabeth became a mother today. She has three poor fatherless babies. Two of them look just fine, but I'm afraid the other one is sick. I was hoping you could come doctor the little thing because I don't want Elizabeth to lose one of her children. But since you're not at home . . ." Her grieved voice trailed away. After a long while she hung up, and the machine clicked off.

A guilty moment of silence passed before Dr. Ross's footrest came down with a resigned thud. Miss Lavada had been about to cry. He could tell. Woman had a heart condition. Arthritis too. He had no choice but to call her back.

"Yes, ma'am. I understand. Is the kitten taking nourishment from her mother? . . . Sometimes that happens. Usually nothing to worry about. It can take a while for nature to take its course."

Dr. Ross looked out the window. A light, misty rain was starting to fall.

"Now, Miss Lavada, don't you go to worrying. Elizabeth and her kittens are going to be just fine."

She was getting worked up. He could tell.

"I suppose that I could. In the meantime, you had best set yourself down. Make yourself some tea. Have you eaten today? . . . That's what I thought. Now you go on into the kitchen and fix yourself a bite. Do you recall taking your heart medicine today, Miss Lavada?"

Dr. Ross hung up, put on his coat, grabbed an umbrella, and reached for his keys.

Charlotte's cell phone was dead. She crept in her van toward the exit gate of the Culture Fest. At least twenty cars inched along in line ahead of her. Rain, moments ago a light mist, was changing to big plopping drops. She turned on the wipers and turned off the radio. Because of the coming thunderstorm, it was broadcasting little more than an agitating static. In the backseat, the twins whined and bickered over which sand art jar belonged to which girl. The driver in line ahead of her kept letting other cars cut in.

Why in the world was there only one exit out of this place? Wasn't there some kind of a law against that? Charlotte drummed her fingers on the steering wheel and willed herself to calm down.

There was no reason to be worried. Beth had to be at home. It made sense. She got cold and tired, and when she saw the parade was nearly over she walked home. It was not what Charlotte feared. *But please, God, oh, please. Let that be what happened.*

This was all her fault. Problem was, she had been altogether too lenient with the girls. Given them way too much freedom. What had she been thinking, letting them roam as she had today? She would no longer let it matter to her what other community kids were allowed to do. Was there anyplace truly safe in the world? Of course not. From now on there would be rules at Tanglewood. Strict ones. She would not be swayed. She was going to run a much tighter ship. Yes, definitely. That is what she would do.

Finally, the street. She turned the van in the direction of Tanglewood.

Please, God. Let Beth be at home.

Catfish Martin waved cars out of the parking lot, directing them toward the exit. He looked up at the sky and was thankful he'd remembered to bring his plastic poncho. Good thing the rain had held off until now. Seeing as how the parking area was nothing more than a hardened patch of dirt, if the coming gully washer had arrived a couple of hours earlier, he and Gabe would have been busy all night pulling stuck vehicles out of the mud.

Judging by the wad of bills in his pocket, the ladies of the club had done real good this year. Too bad they'd spend the funds throwing good money after bad. He and Kerilynn had had this discussion many a time. It was not that he personally held anything against helping out kids. He loved kids. It was their no-good, deadbeat parents he had no use for. Folks shouldn't expect help year after year the way some of them did. He'd seen it with his own eyes. Same families showing up for Culture Club handouts two times a year—in the fall for school supplies, at Christmas again to get free stuff for their kids.

Folks ought to work for what they had, pull themselves up by their bootstraps. Wasn't that the American way?

Take that Carter woman, for instance. He didn't wish her no ill will. None at all. Not that he knew her personally—didn't care to—but by all accounts she appeared to be a nice enough person. Problem was, Ruby Prairie had no business welcoming in someone from outside who was bringing in kids that their own parents ought be raising themselves. Why did folks have kids if they couldn't take care of them?

Treasure Evans couldn't get Charlotte Carter off her

mind. The Lord did that to her on occasion—laid a person on her heart, then left that person there to languish for days upon days. Her response to such a weighty thing was always to pray. Sometimes she'd find out later that the person had been going through some terrible patch. Other times, from the accounts that came to her, she would learn that things had been altogether good. The person she'd spent so much time praying for would have gotten a raise the month before or their kids had been given some kind of an award for their work in school. Used to, when Treasure would hear such news as that, she would wonder if perhaps she'd wasted all those prayers on someone who hadn't needed them after all.

Not so anymore. She'd come to believe that few of the battles folks face are those that can be seen of the eye.

On the day Charlotte came to mind, Treasure was booked to give four massages, three in the morning and one in the afternoon—a full day, sure to leave her own muscles tired and worn out. Her first client was a girl, five months in the family way. Treasure had done extra work to learn how to give a pregnancy massage. It had turned out to be one of the things she liked best to do. Later in the morning she worked on a nurse with a sore shoulder, then a young man training for some kind of a race. Her afternoon client was an attorney's wife who always came for a massage the same day she got her nails done.

Most folks didn't care to talk during their massage.

They preferred instead to lie quietly, listening to the soft piano music Treasure kept on continuous play. Sometimes they even went to sleep. The silence suited Treasure fine today. While her hands were working over her clients' muscles, her spirit was in prayer, working over whatever it was Charlotte and her girls were needing just now.

Treasure wasn't a woman prone to meddling in other folks' business, but ever since she'd visited that big, pretty, pink Ruby Prairie house, she'd felt a nagging concern. Caring for all those girls was a big task—to her mind more than what one single woman should take on by herself. Having been a troubled girl herself, Treasure knew of what she spoke. After her own mother died she'd pitched her share of fits, lots of them during her teen years. She'd been sassy and had made bad choices, ones that caused no telling how much grief to folks who loved and tried to help her. Some of those same troubles most likely lay ahead for Charlotte and her Tanglewood girls.

What nagged at her the most was Charlotte's stubborn independence. She seemed to think that no matter what came up, she, with God's help, could handle it all alone. Years of living had taught Treasure that while God does mighty works, He generally chooses to do them through the hands of His local folks.

Pastor Jock stopped by Lighted Way on his way home. As was his Saturday evening habit, he checked to make sure all was in order for the next day's service.

In his office he reviewed his sermon notes, arranged in order the numerous announcements he'd been asked to make, and updated the prayer list.

In the closet-sized kitchen located next to the first-grade classroom he made sure there was plenty of unleavened bread and grape juice for Communion. While he was there, he gave the brass offering trays a quick polish.

Then he stood in the darkened sanctuary and prayed over each of the pews.

"Hey! What're you doing? Slow down, you idiot!"

Catfish hadn't seen the motorcycle coming. It was one of the last vehicles out of the parking lot, and just as the machine got to the gate near where he was standing, the driver had cut a sharp left and gunned it, leaving Catfish splattered with mud. Once on the street, the crazy driver had been in such a hurry that he and his rider had skidded sideways, nearly missing the surprise curve that came up in the road.

"Serve you right if you wreck!" Catfish yelled after the pair. "Gonna get yourself killed!"

Out-of-towner acting a fool. Probably some kid high on dope.

Treasure Evans dialed the phone.

"Hello?"

"I'm calling long distance. Who am I speaking to, please?"

"This is Donna."

"Donna, honey, are you one of Charlotte Carter's girls?"

"Yes, ma'am."

"Is she at home?"

"Not yet, but she should be soon. May I take a message?"

"Would you please tell her to call me soon as she gets in? And, sugar—I'm long distance. You tell her to make it collect."

It didn't take long for Dr. Ross to soothe Miss Lavada and assure her that Elizabeth and her ill-gotten brood were going to be just fine.

"She's going to make a good mother. See? Elizabeth knows just what to do, doesn't require a bit of help from either one of us. Fact, what the little family needs most is some privacy. Time to get used to each other. As for you—well, Miss Lavada, I think it best you get to bed early tonight. Get a good night's rest."

As if on cue, Elizabeth, her three hungry babies attached to her side, looked up, yawned, and began a loud purr.

When the veterinarian left Miss Lavada's, it was with thoughts of his warm house and a heated-up can of chili in mind. Surely there would be no more calls tonight.

As he steered in the direction of his home, he spotted a couple on a motorcycle, parked in the bay of the car wash a block from his house. It looked like the pair had stopped there in hopes of waiting out the storm. From the appearance of the sky, they might be waiting a good little while. Maybe he ought to stop and make sure they weren't having some kind of a mechanical problem. He slowed down, signaling to turn in. But when he did, the motorcycle took off, disappearing into the night quick as a cat running out from under a bed.

Pastor Jock turned out all the lights and locked up the front and the back doors of the church. Then, ducking his uncovered head against the rain, he crossed the churchyard to his truck parked out by the curb. Stepping carefully so as not to slip on the wet grass, he crossed a single deep rut cut into the soft, soggy turf.

Who would have done such as that? From the size of the rut, it had to have been someone on a motorcycle, someone who had been in too big of a hurry to go to the corner and stop, someone who had instead cut across the churchyard to save a few seconds of time.

Pastor Jock shook his head. Not a man generally given to pride, he nonetheless put a lot of stock into Lighted Way having the prettiest, most well-kept grounds of any of the churches in town.

Once the last car was out of the parking lot, Catfish made his way over to where Kerilynn and other Culture Club members were still, in the fading light, overseeing the taking down of the booths.

"Any of my minnows left?" he asked, not given to waste.

"Half a dozen or so." Kerilynn held up a limp and leaky plastic bag. "Looks like they may be dead, though."

"Not surprised. Throw 'em out," said Catfish. "How about Lester's peach pies?"

"Sold out two hours ago."

"Not surprised at that either." He began loading folding chairs into the back of Kerilynn's car. The Culture Fest, like a wedding, was much quicker to take down than it was to put up.

"Looks like y'all did real good," he said.

"If the count was right, biggest attendance we've seen yet," said Kerilynn. She sat down on an ice chest. "And I am worn out. Won't bother me if we don't do this again for a whole 'nother year. I'm getting too old for such nonsense."

"I second that," said Nomie, rubbing her back.

"I agree," said both Ginger and Sassy.

"4-H club kids'll be here tomorrow afternoon to pick up trash," said Nomie. "They're needing a service project."

"Wonderful," said Kerilynn.

"Port-a-Potty folks'll be here on Monday."

"Anything else we need to take care of tonight?" asked Kerilynn.

"Nothing I can think of. For sure, nothing that can't wait. Let's go home, girls."

Kerilynn stood. "See you tomorrow."

"You planning on making it to church?" Nomie asked the others.

"Probably. But I may not get there in time for Sunday school," said Ginger, knowing all the while that she would.

"Kerilynn, I'll be along in a bit," said Catfish. "Gonna stop by the shop before I head home."

"Suit yourself. I'm taking a hot bath and going to bed."

Catfish couldn't believe he'd left the back door of his shop unlocked. He never did that.

It was when he stepped into the stock room that he saw something was wrong—wet footprints, two sets of them, leading to the front of the shop.

"Who's there?"

Silence. Then the sound of someone letting out a breath. The hair on Catfish's arms stood on end.

"I said, who's there?" He set his feet and flipped on the lights.

"We—uh—we thought you were open."

"Stop right there," ordered Catfish, his voice cracking.

It was a couple of punk kids. A boy and a girl. They'd been in his cooler. His snack box too. Both had Dr. Peppers and packages of cheese crackers in their hands. The boy was wearing some kind of a black jacket. Catfish didn't believe he was from around here. The girl—well, she kept her head down—but he had the sneaking suspicion he'd seen her somewhere before.

"Who are you? What are you doing in my store?"

"Look, mister," said the boy. "No harm done. We didn't take nothing but a couple of sodas. Here. I'll pay you for what we've got." The boy pulled two dollars from his pocket.

"I'm calling the police," said Catfish. "You stay right where you are."

"No, old man. You're not calling anybody." The boy grabbed the girl by the hand and pushed Catfish against the wall.

"Kirby, don't hurt him."

It was then that Catfish got a good look at the girl's face. Yes. He had seen her somewhere. "I knew it. You're one of that Carter woman's no-account girls."

"She don't know you," said the boy. "You don't know nothin' about her."

The girl raised her head to face Catfish for the first time. Her mouth opened, but no words came out.

"Come on," said the boy. "Let's get out of here."

"You do that. Go on. And good riddance, missy. This town don't need the likes of you!" Catfish yelled after them as they fled out the back door of the shop.

Once they were gone, he sank to the floor, willing his breath to slow down. This was embarrassing. He'd never been robbed, never in his life. Most Ruby Prairie residents only locked their doors at night. His neighbor on the other side didn't lock up ever. Man bragged about losing his house keys twenty years back and never bothering to get a new set.

Not Catfish. There'd always existed the possibility of some criminal element infiltrating Ruby Prairie.

That's why he took care to lock up his house, his business, even his car every time he left it. Kerilynn had protested when he had a security system installed in the duplex they shared. Unable to remember her code, she'd had the thing disconnected from her side within six months. Foolish, foolish. A person could never be too careful. Shoot. If it weren't for the liberals and all their complicated rules he could never figure out, he would have been of a mind to carry on his person a concealed gun of his own.

How in the world was he going to explain his incompetence, his security lapse, his downright forgetfulness to folks when they found out about this? Gabe would be sure to give him a hard time. Chilly would never let him hear the end of it. He'd be the butt of jokes at the 'Round the Clock for all of next week.

Catfish rubbed at the stubble on his chin. Then again, why did anyone else have to know about it?

Slowly, he got up from the floor. Looking out the front window of his shop at the deserted street, he made up his mind that no one would.

Chapter Seventeen

The front door swung open as Charlotte stepped onto the porch. Donna's face spoke before her lips. "She's not here."

"You're sure?" Charlotte stepped inside, shed her coat, and dropped her bag.

"Some of her stuff's gone," said Maggie.
"But not all of it," said Sharita.
"We even looked in the arbor," said Maggie.
"But she's not there," said Sharita.
"Were there any messages on the answering machine?"
"Just one, but they hung up," said Maggie.
Nikki and Vikki, unaware until now that something was wrong, stood confused and blinking in the light of the hall. "What's wrong? Who's not here?"
"It's Beth," said Donna. "She's gone."
"Gone where?" asked Nikki.
"Is she coming back?" asked Vikki.
Like actors waiting for their next cue, five pairs of questioning, expectant eyes fixed on Charlotte.
She struggled to meet their gaze, stalled while she fiddled with a loose button on her shirt.
They waited.
"Of course she'll be back. And we need to pray that it'll be really soon." She was only partially successful in her attempt to feign calm.
Sharita began to chew on her thumbnail, Maggie to twirl her hair, and Nikki to cry.
"Did Beth run away?" asked Vikki.
"I don't know, honey. Maybe she did."
"Didn't she like us?" asked Nikki. "We liked her."
"She liked you just fine. You didn't do anything wrong."
"Are we going to go look for her?" asked Sharita.
Charlotte didn't answer; she was trying to think. She had to call Kim.

The phone rang before she had a chance.

"Oh, I forgot to tell you—a lady with a funny name called. I can't remember what she said it was. She wants you to call her back," said Donna.

Charlotte picked up the phone and solved the puzzle.

"Honey, I don't mean to disturb you, but you've been heavy on my mind of late."

Treasure Evans.

"I have to know, are you all right? Are all those little girls you've taken in all right?"

"Can you hold on a second?" asked Charlotte. She covered the phone with her hand. "Girls—go on into the kitchen and get out stuff for sandwiches. I'll be off the phone in a minute."

"Something's not right," said Treasure when Charlotte was back. "Tell me what it is."

"I'm sorry. I can't believe you called. You—have—no—idea." For a long moment Charlotte could not speak. It was the kindness in Treasure's voice that was more than she could take.

"Maybe I do. You talk when you're ready. I'm sitting here at my kitchen table, and I've got all the time in the world."

Finally Charlotte got herself under a semblance of control. She blew her nose, then spoke. "I've got six girls now, but one of them has run away. At least I think she has. I don't know for sure."

"Bless her, Lord Jesus," said Treasure. "I knew it. All the way from Oklahoma I could tell something was not right at your house. Have you called the social worker?"

"Not yet."

"What about the police?"

"I haven't called anyone yet. All this just happened within the last hour. I don't want to upset the girls here in the house, but I'm scared to death about the one who's gone."

"What's her name?"

"Beth."

"Okay. I'm going to take this out of your hands. You stay on this phone, and we're going to give her to the Lord right now." Treasure ratcheted her voice up a notch. "In the name of Je-sus, Father, we ask You to watch over this child. . . . What did you say her name was again?"

"Beth."

"Yes, Father, Beth. Keep her in Your care. Protect her from harm. Bring her home safe and soon. Amen."

"Amen," whispered Charlotte. "Thank you. I can't believe that you called just now, of all times."

"I can. Lord's using me. And, honey, He's fixing to use me some more. You got an extra bed in that big house of yours?"

"Well, yes—of course," stammered Charlotte. "Are you coming for a visit?" *Not to be rude, but now of all times?* "You know I'd like nothing better, but maybe it'd be better for you to wait until things settle down."

"No, ma'am. I'm not waiting. Matter of fact, on the chance that I was hearing the Lord right, I packed my bags while I was waiting for you to call me back. They're ready for me to load up in my van. Sugar, I'll be to your house by noon tomorrow."

"But—"

"No buts, missy. You need some help whether you've got sense enough to know it or not. You need an extra set of hands and an extra pair of eyes. I've got both. Not to mention the fact that I'm a decent cook."

"I don't know what to say," stammered Charlotte.

"Don't say nothing. Just fix me a place to lay my head."

"Who was that?" asked Maggie when Charlotte was back in the kitchen.

"An old friend," said Charlotte, still a bit stunned. "Well, she's sort of an old friend and sort of a new one."

"I made you a sandwich," said Donna. "You want me to cut it in half?"

"Thank you. No. It's fine like this."

"I got you some milk," said Nikki.

"Here's you a napkin," said Sharita.

Charlotte needed to make calls, not take time to eat. But looking around the table she saw five girls, all unsettled and unsure and trying to be very, very good. She pulled out a chair and sat down at her usual place.

"What's your friend's name?" asked Maggie.

"Treasure," said Charlotte. "This sandwich is good."

"I remember her," said Nikki.

"I do too. She was nice," said Vikki.

"She's coming here. For a visit."

"When?" asked Nikki.

"Tomorrow."

"How long's she staying?" asked Donna.

"She didn't say. Probably a couple of days."

As soon as she'd choked down the last crumb of her sandwich, Charlotte dialed Kim Beeson's pager number, then hung up and waited with dread for the return call. She knew Beth was special to the social worker.

Kim would be angry. She had every right. She would have questions about how Charlotte had let this happen. But nothing Kim might say would be any worse than what she'd already said to herself. Charlotte hoped she'd be able to talk without crying.

If she'd kept a closer eye, if she'd gone with her to the bathroom, if she'd insisted the girls all stay together—she'd still be here. Why had they gone to the Culture Fest anyway? They should have all been at home, reading books or playing games together or something like that, not traipsing all over town.

The state would probably come investigate Tanglewood. And they should, for there was no telling what else she was doing wrong. For sure the girls weren't eating enough fruit. She'd forgotten Donna's dentist appointment twice now, making her a month overdue for a cleaning. Not only that, even though Kim had reminded her, she had not yet engaged the girls in a fire drill.

They might even close Tanglewood down. Who would blame them? Certainly not Charlotte. If she'd been doing things right, this never would have happened.

Oh, Beth . . . where are you? Please, please be safe.

• • •

Beth could not feel her hands or her feet. Her teeth would not stop chattering and her mouth had never felt so dry. She kept her head tucked down to stave off as much wind as she could. Her cold limbs were growing stiff. But she didn't dare shift her position.

She had never ridden a motorcycle before. Once when she'd had to go to the emergency room with a cut finger, she'd overheard a doctor and a nurse discussing a badly injured motorcyclist who had just been brought in. "Only two kinds of motorcycle riders," Beth remembered the doctor saying. "Those who've been in bad wrecks and those who're going to be."

It had all happened so fast, there was no time for Beth to hesitate before climbing on the motorcycle. When her hands wrapped around Kirby's waist, they were trembling and cold. "You'll be okay," he had said over his shoulder to her. "Lean forward into me. Hold on tight." For a quick second he covered her hands with his own. "I won't let anything happen to you. I swear to God I won't. Ready?"

At first it seemed like it might be okay. But then they nearly wiped out on that bad curve. She sure wished Kirby had a car.

Through lots of letters and two clandestine phone calls, the two of them had planned their getaway for weeks. Beth was surprised when leaving Tanglewood turned out to be harder than she had thought. It seemed every day for the past two weeks Charlotte had been nicer than the day before. So much so that Beth had almost come to believe that she cared. Kirby set her straight, telling her that Charlotte got money from the state for every girl she took in.

"Is that the way it works?" Beth questioned.

"Of course. You don't think people do it for free, do you?"

She supposed not.

Only six months into the job, this was Kim Beeson's first experience dealing with a runaway child.

"Okay, Charlotte. Sit tight. You did the right thing letting me know. Since she took some of her personal belongings, that tells us she's run away and not been abducted. That's good. Let me check the procedure and notify my supervisor. I'll get back to you right away."

The procedure was grim.

First Kim needed to notify local law enforcement and supply them with a bio and a recent photo of Beth, along with the names and addresses of friends, family, and previous foster homes. While the list of homes where Beth had lived was long, the list of concerned biological family was short. Her mother had to be notified; that was required. Would she be able to find the woman? Recent attempts at contact by letter had been returned, marked *No forwarding address*.

If Beth wasn't found within a specified length of time, Kim would have to notify the courts that she was no longer under the state's supervision.

Surely, Beth would be back to Tanglewood before then.

• • •

By nine o'clock, folks began to knock on Tanglewood's front door.

"We just heard. What can we do?" They bore, along with their concerned expressions, warm cookies, cans of coffee, stacks of paper plates, and not-quite-thawed, nine-by-thirteen disposable pans full of food. Every Ruby Prairie woman given to good works kept—at the very least—a King Ranch Chicken Casserole and a layered lasagna at the ready in her freezer for such times as this.

Ruby Prairie residents filled up Charlotte's living room, took over her kitchen, and crowded into her dining room—upsetting the cats, exciting the dogs, and overwhelming the girls. Any thoughts of keeping Beth's disappearance quiet dissipated in the face of community curiosity and concern.

"Wasn't she the one with all the earrings and the short hair?" asked Nomie. "I thought so. I saw her at the festival this afternoon. At the time, she looked to be enjoying herself. Did something happen to upset her?"

"Bless her heart," said Lester. "Out there on a night like this. Was she wearing a warm coat when she took off?"

Gabe and Chilly offered their help. "Got spotlights at the house," said Gabe. "Chilly's got him a pair of good hunting dogs too. One of them's blind in one eye, but they both run good. We can go get them, set out afoot looking for the girl right now if you think it would be of benefit. Just give us the word."

Pastor Jock took one look at Charlotte and saw that all their good intentions were just too much. He led her outside and, shivering on the back stoop, got the real scoop. Then, at his direction, Kerilynn went upstairs with Charlotte to get Nikki, Vikki, Donna, Sharita, and Maggie away from the overeager crowd.

Once Charlotte and the girls were out of earshot, Pastor Jock quieted the folks down. "I know everybody's here to assist Charlotte in her time of need. We all want to do what we can. Truth is, there's really only one thing needed. That's prayer. For Beth, the girl who's run away. For Charlotte. For the other girls here at Tanglewood. We all should keep our eyes peeled in case she's still in town, but other than that, we've got to leave the rest of it up to the authorities. Charlotte's already talked to Mark down at the police station and to Leroy at the sheriff's office. They've got pictures of Beth and other information that they'll be needing to find her."

Folks nodded in agreement. Mark and Leroy were good at what they did.

Pastor Jock continued. "Charlotte's gone upstairs. We need to be clearing out here. Charlotte asked me to thank you all and to request your continued prayers."

"Of course we'll pray, Pastor," said Sassy, and others murmured agreement.

"There's just one more thing I want to say," he continued. "Let's remember, there are still five girls in this house. Girls who've not had an easy time of it.

They've been through lots of things in their short lives, and they can be easily upset. They need for things to go on as normal for them. Everyone here's been kind to Charlotte and her girls, but from now on let's not let that be enough. Let's lavish them with our love and our acceptance. Let's treat them like they were some of our own."

Of course. That was exactly what they would do. Love on those girls. Help Charlotte out.

"Before we go, let's bow our heads in prayer."

"Where've you been?" asked Catfish. "Thought you were coming home and going straight to bed." Seeing Kerilynn's headlights when she pulled into the carport, he'd gone over to her side of their house.

"I was. But one of Charlotte Carter's girls has gone missing."

"Is that right?"

"Went over to see if there was anything I could do."

"Don't know what that would be," said Catfish. He leaned against Kerilynn's breakfast bar, pulled out his pocketknife, and began to clean under his fingernails.

"There's cause for concern. The girl's only fifteen. She could be in any kind of danger. Out on a night as cold as this—why, there's no telling what she's suffering."

"You say she ran away?"

"From the looks of it. Charlotte last saw her at the parade, sometime near five o'clock. Hasn't seen her since then."

“Kid’s probably long gone by now,” said Catfish.

“I doubt it. She was on foot.”

“That right?”

“Well, unless she stole a car or something,” Kerilynn retorted. “Been no reports of that. Course I guess she could have hitchhiked, but I don’t think so. No, to my way of thinking she’s holed up somewhere right here in Ruby Prairie. She’ll turn up. Least that’s what everyone’s praying.”

Catfish made no comments about the missing girl. He slipped his pocketknife back into his pants. “I’ll be turning in. It’s late. You planning on making it to church tomorrow?”

“Yep, I am. Pastor Jock’s offering special prayer for the girl. Once morning services are over, Mark from the station’s going to divide everybody up so we can do an organized search of the town. What about you? You gonna help?”

Catfish coughed. Twice. “Don’t know. Taking cold. Have to see how I feel.”

The motorcycle didn’t sound right. Even Beth could tell. Though Kirby’s hand was steady on the throttle, they were losing momentum. Kirby steered the sputtering machine over to the side of the deserted rural road, and they coasted to a stop.

“What’s wrong?” Beth asked.

“Don’t know. Might be a hose or a belt. Could be a plug.”

Beth slid off the back of the motorcycle while he

looked. Her legs were stiff. It was freezing, dark, and too quiet.

Hugging herself, she shifted from one foot to the other while Kirby crouched next to the machine and fiddled with some stuff. He didn't have a flashlight, only the tiny flame his lighter produced. The sky was so cloudy from the rain, neither the moon nor the stars gave off any light.

Beth heard Kirby curse.

"At least it stopped raining," she said.

He didn't answer.

"Where are we?"

Kirby didn't answer that either.

Beth sat down on a fallen tree in the ditch that ran beside the road. She was hungry and she needed to pee.

Kirby cursed again, then gave the motorcycle a kick. It fell over, breaking the quiet with a startling, metallic crash.

He came and sat down beside her, not saying a word. He spit at the dirt between his feet, then looked up at the sky. Finally he reached over and took her cold hand to rub between his own.

"Bike's nothing but a hunk of junk."

It was after midnight when Charlotte crawled into her bed. Once there, thoughts of failure haunted her. She had not gotten through to Beth. Not even once, as far as she could tell.

It wasn't that Beth had been any trouble. She'd been

none at all. That was the problem. No matter what Beth was asked to do, no matter how often she was expected to compromise or share, she complied without complaint.

She never whined.

Never disagreed.

Never cried.

Never let anyone know what was going on inside.

Looking back, it was easy to spot the problem. When Beth had first arrived at Tanglewood and it was just three girls, Charlotte felt she had come close to connecting with her once or twice. But when the other girls started coming—fast—the fragile connection had slipped out of her grasp. Soon she was outnumbered six to one, and there was never enough of her to go around.

Nikki and Vikki, so young, needed constant watch. Donna, though helpful and eager to please, struggled with depression. Her crying jags summoned Charlotte to her bedside almost every night. Sharita was full of life, but sometimes so sassy Charlotte wanted to pull out her hair. Maggie had no idea how girls were expected to behave in public; Charlotte walked a thin line trying to teach her how to be socially acceptable without making her self-conscious.

With all those urgent needs, it had been easy to neglect quiet, compliant Beth. Often, despite much better intentions, all Beth had received were snippets and scraps of Charlotte's time.

One thing was for sure. She would do better when

Beth came back. A lot better. She would start getting up at five instead of at six. That would put an extra hour in her day. Then again, there was that wasted time spent relaxing on the porch every afternoon just before the girls got home from school. That could be utilized better. From now on she would use it to prepare supper so as to have more free time later in the evening. There were other things she could do to free up more time to spend one-on-one with the girls. She was sure of it.

Charlotte drew the covers up to her chin and stared at the ceiling. Where was Beth right now? What was she doing this very minute? And what had caused her to choose today to run away? Had Charlotte accidentally said something unkind to her? Maybe Beth had gotten into a fight with one of the other girls—gotten her feelings hurt. They all said no, but there was no way to know for sure.

It was obvious Beth had planned to run. Somehow, sometime during the day, she had returned to the house for her backpack and some clothes. When could she have done that?

How bad must she have felt to leave on such a night? The rain had stopped, but temperatures were expected to drop below freezing by morning.

How far had she gone? Mark, the police officer, said she couldn't have gone far if she were on foot. He believed she was holed up at a friend's house, or maybe hiding in some vacant building. He predicted that she'd be found within a day or two.

Charlotte hoped he was right. But did Beth even have any friends? What about that boy from the shelter? That was ridiculous . . . Dallas was ninety minutes away.

Charlotte looked at the clock next to her bed. Twenty minutes after one. Wearily she closed her eyes. *God, You are in control. I know that not a sparrow falls that You don't see. Please, please, show mercy upon this house and upon these girls. Give me the strength and the wisdom to take care of them. Keep Beth in Your care. Comfort her. Give her warmth if she's cold, food if she's hungry, someplace secure to sleep tonight. God, please, please bring her back. Help her somehow to know that I love her.*

Charlotte never got to the amen. The loud jangle of the telephone jolted her awake.

"Hello?"

"Miz Carter?"

"Yes?"

"This is Mark, down at the police station. Just got a call from Leroy. I believe we've located your girl."

Chapter Eighteen

"They've found her? Already? Praise the Lord!" said Kerilynn, speaking like a woman accustomed to a 3:15 wake-up call every day of the week. "Don't apologize. . . . Of course I'll come. Stay with the girls long as you need me to. Honey, I'll be there quick as I can get my clothes on. This is just wonderful news!"

"When you get here, don't ring the bell. Just let yourself in," said Charlotte. "I don't want the other girls to wake up."

What a surprise it would be for them when they *did* wake up and Beth was home safe and sound, asleep in her bed. She would make them pancakes for breakfast. Bacon too. They would sit around the table and talk about how God had answered their prayers. If Beth were up to it, they would all go to church. If . . . Beth wanted to, that is. If Beth even wanted to come back to Tanglewood . . .

Charlotte's nervous, middle-of-the-night stomach churned. She bumped into the corner of her dresser on her way to the bathroom. Where was the Pepto? When she found the pink stuff, she swallowed a slug straight from the bottle and grimaced at the chalky taste. Nasty as it was, the medicine made her feel better. She pulled a pair of jeans and a sweatshirt on over her nightgown, gathered her hair back into a ponytail, and brushed her teeth. She hunted for her glasses in near panic before she found them on top of her head.

Her keys and her purse, for once, were where she remembered leaving them in the front hall. As soon as Kerilynn arrived, she'd be ready to go.

She heard steps on the gravel outside her kitchen window and opened up the back door. Kerilynn wasn't alone.

"Pastor Jock? What's wrong?"

He and Kerilynn stepped into the kitchen. "Nothing.

I heard the great news."

Charlotte was caught off guard. Who else had Kerilynn called? Was the rest of the town, at this moment, driving in the dark back toward Tanglewood? She remembered the chaos of last night.

"Soon as you and I hung up, I called him to come go with you," said Kerilynn. "Didn't you say she was at the police station over in Ella Louise? Sugar, that's twenty miles. Road's dark. Got lots of curves. You don't need to go by yourself."

Kerilynn was right. Though Charlotte knew which road to take, she had never been to Ella Louise. And once she got there, she wouldn't know where the station was. Though she was confident it wouldn't be that hard to find, it wasn't likely that there would be anyone up to give her directions if she needed them.

"I hadn't thought of that," said Charlotte. "You're right. Thanks for coming."

"Are you ready? I'll drive," said Pastor Jock.

"Sugar, don't forget your coat," said Kerilynn. "Be careful. Give that girl a squeeze for me when you see her. Remember, call as soon as you three are headed back this way."

Catfish tossed and turned in his bed. Finally, he got back up and fried himself some eggs. He carried the plate to his living room recliner and turned on CNN. Some fellow was carrying on about recycling trash. Blame liberals. If there was one thing he couldn't abide, it was those hippie tree-hugging folks from up

North. Catfish hit the remote. Found John Wayne. Fine American if ever there was one. He settled back and forked down his eggs, sopping up the yellow with the end of his toast.

During a commercial Catfish turned to the Weather Channel. Girl said there might be sleet on the ground by morning. Temperatures below thirty expected. Catfish doubted it. Those people were wrong more often than they were right. He wondered how they kept their jobs. Especially the women ones.

He flipped the channel again.

Motorcycle racing. If that didn't beat all. Fools. Had to be to ride one of those crazy things. Free country, though. Catfish allowed them that. If people wanted to get themselves killed, according to the Constitution that was their God-given right. Wasn't anybody's place to tell anybody else what they could or could not do.

Which was something his sister Kerilynn never understood. Always poking her nose into other people's business. Time and time again he'd told her she needed to stop sticking her neck out for folks she barely knew.

Like that Carter woman and all those girls. Kerilynn chasing over there just because that one girl had gone missing. Shoot. There were still five more.

It was too bad tomorrow after church everyone would be putting themselves out looking all over town for the kid. They wouldn't know it, but they'd be wasting their time, missing out on their Sunday afternoon naps and football for nothing. That girl was long gone by now. Probably be clear to Oklahoma by morning.

Maybe he should say something. Save them all some time. But how could he fess up now? If Kerilynn found out he'd seen the girl leaving the festival and that she'd been in his store with that boy, he would never hear the end of it.

No. Causing a stir over something of so little importance wasn't worth it. The situation would blow over on its own soon enough. Catfish went back to bed.

Charlotte had told her to make herself at home, to stretch out on the couch or to even crawl up into her own bed for the rest of the night. Like that was going to happen. Kerilynn knew she'd never be able to sleep. Instead she cleaned Charlotte's kitchen and prayed all at the same time. First, the pantry. Took everything out, wiped it down, put everything back.

Lord, get them to Ella Louise safe.

Then she started in on Charlotte's spices. What a mess. Kerilynn put them in alphabetical order. What was this? Three cans of cinnamon—all of them opened. She tossed the one that smelled old, combined the other two, then did the same with the two cans of black pepper.

Be with them when they meet up with the girl. Her name's Beth.

On to the refrigerator. Not as bad as one might have thought. Main problem was some overripe fruit. The fridge needed only a good wipe down with a rag soaked in baking soda and water.

Lord, please don't let anything bad have happened to her in the time she's been gone.

It wasn't until she had Windexed the appliances and swept and mopped the floor that Kerilynn began to wish Charlotte or Pastor Jock would call. She looked at her watch. They'd only been gone forty minutes.

She pulled out a kitchen chair, sat down, and helped herself to some cookies she'd found already opened up. Time sure flew when one was having fun.

"So who was it that called? Mark at the police station or Leroy at the sheriff's office?" asked Pastor Jock. He shifted from first into second.

"Mark. But he said something about Leroy. I didn't really understand."

"If something happens within the city limits of a town, it's police business. If it happens outside, the sheriff of the county takes care of it," explained Jock. "They overlap a lot in what they do."

"So they must have found her out in the country somewhere," said Charlotte.

"Likely near Ella Louise."

They rode along in silence for a few miles.

"I really appreciate this," said Charlotte.

"Appreciate what?" teased Jock. "I like getting up in the middle of the night. Gives me an early start on my day."

"You've been so kind. Everyone has."

"Folks in Ruby Prairie are like that. Sometimes they

come on a bit strong—like last night—but they mean well. More than anything, they want to help out."

"I never intended for Tanglewood to be a burden to anyone else. The girls are my responsibility. I should be able to handle things on my own."

"You don't feel that you have?"

"I never expected to receive so much help."

"You are an independent one."

"I thought I was." Charlotte leaned her head back. "When my husband got sick, I handled everything. The house, the yard, the bills, his care."

"What about your church?"

"It was a tiny little place, around sixty members. They did what they could. I know they prayed. Some of them called. But most of the members were elderly, in poor health themselves. Before J.D. got sick, he used to do little household repairs for the widows."

"Sounds like a kind man."

"He was. Those old ladies loved him. Every time he'd go over to change a lightbulb or tighten a leaky faucet, they would feed him. There were a few of the ladies I took to the doctor or ran errands for. They always told me thank you, but they didn't feed me the way they did him. Didn't matter what time it was, or whether he'd just eaten. He'd have to sit down at their tables and eat to keep from hurting their feelings."

"How long were you married, Charlotte?"

"Nearly twenty years."

"Sounds like you were blessed."

"We were. With everything but children. We wanted a houseful."

"You have one now," said Pastor Jock. "A full quiver, as the psalmist says."

"Minus one."

"But not for long. We'll be there in ten minutes. Are you nervous?"

"More than nervous—I'm wondering what Beth'll do when she sees me, what's the best thing for me to do when I see her. I need to know why she ran away, what happened, what I can do to help her."

"Has she had any counseling?"

"Off and on, being in foster care as much as she has."

"Might be a good idea for her to talk to someone now."

"I agree. I'm checking with her social worker about a referral next week."

"This may sound crazy, but Beth's running away may turn out to be a good thing. Maybe it'll prompt her to get the help she needs."

"You're right. She's had such a wall around her. She was quiet and polite but totally closed off. At least now it's out in the open that something is wrong."

"That's Ella Louise up ahead," said Pastor Jock. "Let's pull off right here and pray." He steered the truck off the road and into the parking lot of a car wash, then took Charlotte's hands in his.

"Father, we ask Your blessing upon this meeting. Be with Charlotte. Give her strength and wisdom and grace. Be with Beth. Let her feel the love You have for her and the love Charlotte has for her. Bridge the gap that's between Beth and the people who love and care about her. In Jesus' name. Amen."

"Amen," said Charlotte.

"Sugar? What are you doing up?" asked Kerilynn.

"Where's Charlotte?" It was Nikki, rubbing sleep from her eyes. "Is it time to go to church?"

"No, baby. It's still the middle of the night. See—it's dark outside. Charlotte's gone to get Beth. She'll be back in a little while. You need to go back to bed. Want a drink?"

"No." Nikki curled up on the window seat and began to suck her thumb.

"Come on. You're not even awake good. Let's get you back upstairs and into your bed."

Treasure Evans was awake good, thanks to her neighbor's dogs. Carrying on something awful, they were. Most likely worked up by a teasing cat.

Treasure got up and hollered at them twice. Once she gave them treats out of the stash she kept under the sink for her own pooch, Peaches. Finally, after trying unsuccessfully to tune the dogs out, she gave up, got dressed, and loaded Peaches and herself into her van.

The digital clock on the dash said 4:30 when she pulled out of her drive. "We'll be there in time to make those girls breakfast," she said to Peaches.

• • •

The Ella Louise police station was located at the far end of town. At this time of night, the small town was eerily deserted. Not a single business was open, not even a convenience store or a gas station. As they drove through the center of downtown, the only signs of life Charlotte saw were at least a half-dozen roaming, feral cats. They skulked between buildings and disappeared beneath bushes.

"Looks like Ella Louise rolls up the streets at night, doesn't it?" said Pastor Jock.

"It's really deserted," said Charlotte. "At least Ruby Prairie has the 'Round the Clock."

Pastor Jock smiled. "I hate to break it to you, but the 'Round the Clock closes at eight."

"No. Really? Then why do they call it the—?"

"Beats me. I think Kerilynn just liked the name. Why'd they name our town Ruby Prairie when the closest prairie land is five hundred miles away? There's the police station. That brown building on the corner."

Charlotte's heart, which had been gradually increasing its rhythm as they drove through Ella Louise, began to pound when she saw the brick government building. She took some deep breaths and wiped her damp hands on the thighs of her jeans.

"It's going to be fine," assured Pastor Jock. "Before you know it, we'll be headed right back the way we came. You, me, and Beth."

When they entered the building, Charlotte saw that

there were two officers on duty, a man and a woman. He was watching wrestling on TV; she was lightly dozing in her chair.

"May I help you?" The male officer turned off the TV. The woman came awake, smiled at Charlotte, and stifled a yawn.

"I'm Pastor Jock Masters, and this is Charlotte Carter. Officer Andrews called us about a girl. We've come to pick her up."

"Yes. Been expecting you. Young lady's in the restroom; she'll be out in a second. So, y'all from Ruby Prairie? How's things in your neck of the woods?"

Charlotte fidgeted.

"Everything's good our way," said Pastor Jock.

"Is—is she all right?" interrupted Charlotte. "Has she been hurt?"

"No sign of it," said the woman. "Hasn't said much, but she's worn out. Needs a hot bath and a bed more than anything else, looks like to me."

"Where did you find her?" asked Pastor Jock.

"Just down the road, asleep in a fruit stand. Officer on duty drove by and spotted her. Said, 'Are you Beth?' and she nodded and came right with him. Actually seemed grateful to be found."

Charlotte's shoulders relaxed. Pastor Jock was right. Beth's running away might turn out to be a good thing. *Amazing,* thought Charlotte, *how God can take something bad and work it into something good.*

"So there aren't any charges," said Pastor Jock.

"Naw. We'll file a report, but other than running away—and that for less that twenty-four hours—she hasn't done anything wrong."

"You have her things? Backpack, jacket?" asked Charlotte.

"Girl's got her coat with her," said the officer. "Didn't see a backpack. She didn't have a thing with her when we picked her up. Not even any ID."

The sheriff's office was tiny and not soundproof. Out of respect, the four of them continued to make conversation until they heard a flush, then the running of water, and the sound of a paper towel being pulled from the dispenser.

Finally the door opened and a girl came out.

It wasn't Beth.

Chapter Nineteen

Kerilynn, on three hours' sleep, graciously took the girls to church at Lighted Way, where a groggy Pastor Jock stumbled his way through a sermon taken from the fifteenth chapter of the gospel of Luke.

He cleared his throat. "Suppose a woman has ten silver coins and loses one. Does she not light a lamp, sweep the house and search carefully until she finds it?" Pastor Jock stifled a yawn. "And when she finds it, she calls her friends and neighbors together and says, 'Rejoice with me.' " He yawned again.

This time he lost his place.

"Sorry, folks. Let's try again."

Worshippers flashed him encouraging smiles. Punchy with fatigue, Pastor Jock was grateful for their patient indulgence.

" 'Rejoice with me; I have found my lost coin.' In the same way, I tell you, there is rejoicing in the presence of the angels of God over one sinner who repents."

Pastor Jock closed his Bible. "Most of you have heard that one of Charlotte Carter's girls, Beth, has run away from Tanglewood."

The few church members who hadn't heard began whispering to their neighbors.

"Happened sometime yesterday. Since no one saw her, we're not sure exactly when it was she left."

Catfish squirmed in his seat. He picked up his announcement sheet and began to study it carefully.

Pastor Jock continued. "Charlotte's not here this morning. She was up most of the night and must stay close to the phone today. She's worried, and as you can imagine, she's worn out. She needs our prayers. Beth, wherever she is, also needs our prayers. The rest of the girls—Kerilynn brought them, and they're sitting in this pew right here—they need them too." He left the pulpit and stepped down into the aisle. "Folks, Beth is not the only person lost today. Every one of us is prone to get off track. We all are in need of being found. Let's close this service by going to the God who knows all about finding lost things."

• • •

Treasure Evans made a pot of strong coffee. She poured a cup, doctored it with sugar and cream, and carried it into Charlotte's bedroom, where she set it on the nightstand. Quietly, she eased herself into a rocking chair next to the bed and waited. For the past hour she'd noted Charlotte stirring. Treasure figured she was soon to wake up on her own.

Within a minute, the aroma of the steaming coffee penetrated Charlotte's sleep, and she opened her eyes. "Treasure?"

"Good morning."

Charlotte reached for her glasses and fumbled with the bedside clock. "I thought you weren't coming till this afternoon. What time is it? Goodness, I've overslept. I have to see about the girls."

"Girls are fine. Somebody came and got them for church. Jerry Lee, I think she said her name was."

"I have to get up." Charlotte threw back the covers. "They'll need lunch."

"Drink your coffee. You've got a kitchen full of food for those children to have for their lunch. You and me need to have us a little talk."

Charlotte reached for the coffee mug, took a hurried sip, burned her mouth, and set it back down. "I'm so sorry I wasn't home when you got here. You must have wondered what in the world was going on. It was an awful night. Have you eaten? I can make you something."

"I know all about last night, and I don't need you to

go about fixing me anything."

"It was nice of you to come for a visit," said Charlotte. "I only wish this wasn't such a—"

"I'm sure we'll be doing a fair amount of visiting," Treasure interrupted, "but I'm not here on a social call."

"How long can you stay?"

"My bills at home are paid up for two months."

Charlotte's mouth dropped open.

Treasure laughed. "Careful now. You'll catch flies that way." She reached over and patted Charlotte's knee. "So you're surprised. Don't be. Lord put it on my heart to come up here and stay with you awhile. Give you a hand."

"But your business—"

"It's not going anywhere. Besides, my carpal tunnel's been acting up something terrible the past six months. Gets better, then it gets worse. What with numbness, tingling, some awful pain, I've suffered something fierce." She held her hands out and wiggled her fingers. "I've tried everything—salves, soaks, and creams—every remedy except for the one that would do me some good. Last week my doctor laid down the law. Told me if I didn't give my hands a rest, I could ruin myself. Might have to quit my work for good. A masseuse isn't much good without a pair of healthy hands. So you see? Timing's perfect. I didn't have a thing to do other than come up here and help you."

"Treasure, it is so sweet of you to be concerned

about me. I appreciate it more than you know. But as for you helping out—normally, there's not that much to be done," said Charlotte. "It's just this particular weekend that's been crazy. There was the festival and all that, then Beth running away, and then hearing that she'd been found, and then it turning out not to be true."

Treasure handed Charlottte a tissue and moved from the rocker to sit next to her on the side of the bed.

"What a bawl baby I'm being. It's not usually like this," said Charlotte. "Most days I really manage okay."

After letting Charlotte cry for a bit, Treasure took her hand and spoke in a gentle voice, patting all the while. "So to your mind, you aren't needing any help. Doing fine all by yourself. Am I understanding you right?"

Charlotte nodded.

"Let's see now. You've got this big old house, which—not to hurt your feelings, honey—is in need of a good dusting. You've got a yard of more'n an acre to keep up, and a shedding mess of dogs and cats to take care of."

"Where did that one come from?" Charlotte interrupted. A shaggy pooch of undetermined parentage had sniffed its way into the room.

"That's my Peaches," said Treasure. "Go on now," she addressed the dog. "You don't have no business in here. Go on back to the kitchen."

"What kind is she?" said Charlotte.

"Pound pup. Two years old. Hope you don't mind my bringing her. She's getting along good with the others so far."

"Course I don't mind."

"Now, what was I saying? . . . Sister, you've got six—well, I guess five, for the time being—girls under your care. Course that other one'll be back. Not having you a husband, you're called to be mama and daddy both to this house full of children. Ever' one of them girls be needing help with they lessons, having to be carried to the dentist and the doctor and the counselor, to play practice and music lessons and lands knows what else. I bet some of 'em are in Girl Scouts, aren't they?"

"Nikki and Vikki," murmured Charlotte. "Tuesdays at four. I forgot last week. They missed. Cookie sale starts this Thursday."

Treasure's face was both kind and smug. "You've got meals to fix, laundry to be done up, groceries to buy. Honey, I'm wore out just from talking about all you've got on your plate. I'll be needing to find me a place to lay myself down."

"Maybe I could use a little help getting organized," said Charlotte.

Treasure snorted. "It's not just me, sugar. There's lots of folks wanting to help you. That woman Jerry Lee—"

"Kerilynn?"

"Yes. That's her name. She sure is a nice person. And that sweet pastor from your church. Goodness. I may be old, but I'm not blind—that man is easy on the eyes. Is he married or just the kind what doesn't wear a ring?"

Charlotte started to answer, but it was then that they heard the front door open, footsteps on the hardwood floor, and a chorus of feminine voices in the hall.

"Where's Charlotte?" they heard Maggie ask.

"Shhh. She might still be asleep," said Donna.

"Hello?" It was Kerilynn. "Charlotte? Are you up? Where are you?"

"Be right there," Charlotte called. The door to her room was pushed to but not closed. She grabbed for her robe.

"You girls go on up and change your clothes," they heard Kerilynn say. "Then we'll get you some lunch. There's lots of food here."

"Take your time. Go on and get dressed," said Treasure. She got up out of the chair. "I'll see to them."

But Kerilynn didn't wait for Charlotte to come out of her room. She stuck her head in. "Hi there," she said to Treasure.

"Kerilynn—thank you so much for taking the girls," said Charlotte. She hugged her friend. "You've got to be tired."

"I'm fine. I'll get me a nap soon as I get home." She yawned. "Did you get some rest? Good. You may need it, because you've got a small problem. Two of them, actually."

"What? Did you hear from Beth?"

"No. I wish it was that. No, honey, it's Nikki and

Vikki. They're covered in spots. Came up during church. Looks to me like they've got the chicken pox."

"They've had their immunizations," said Charlotte. "Isn't one of those for chicken pox?"

"Shots don't always take," said Treasure.

"Charlotte?" This time it was Donna who burst into the room. "Something threw up in the hall. You want me to use a towel to clean it up?"

"Shoot. Bet it's Peaches," said Treasure, hurrying to see. "She gets carsick sometimes after the fact. Honey, you got paper towels in the kitchen?"

Lucky Jamison felt convicted in her heart. Home from church at Lighted Way, changed out of her Sunday dress, stockings, and slip and into a housedress, she was able to reflect on Pastor Jock's good message and how he'd encouraged the congregation to show compassion and love to Charlotte Carter and her Tanglewood girls.

Lucky had not done her part. Not even close. She'd intended to bake one of her famous fruit pies and take it over, but she'd never gotten around to it. And what good would one pie do in a house with so many hungry mouths? She should have baked two.

Bless that woman's heart. She and those girls would have enjoyed a pie. Bet she didn't even bake. Not many people did anymore. At least not from scratch. Dying art. Not just baking, but sewing and mending, and keeping house in general. Too many modern young women meant well but didn't know where to begin.

Lucky was sure of one thing. It was not their fault. The problem could be traced back to when the Ruby Prairie school board voted to stop requiring high school girls to take home economics.

What a sadly misdirected decision that had been. Not only had the board made home economics optional, they had done away with girls-only classes altogether. In their place, boys and girls both were prompted to sign up for odd-sounding classes like Home and Family Life and Consumer Training. Classes that attracted not eager young girls planning on having husbands and children, but slow-learning athletes who needed extra credits to pass.

Thankfully, none of that had commenced until the year after Lucky had retired from her teaching position in the Ruby Prairie schools. The girls in her homemaking classes were among the last young Ruby Prairie women to learn how to put in a straight hem and make never-fail pastry from scratch. She had gotten out at the perfect time. From what she heard at monthly meetings of the Retired Teachers Association, the current teacher was having a terrible time of it.

Lucky made herself some lunch, tomato soup and cheddar cheese on buttered wheat toast. She bowed her head. Raised it up, then bowed again with an addendum to her usual before-meal prayer. *Lord, show me what You would have me to do to help Mrs. Carter and those girls. Please look after that lost one and bring her back soon.*

After finishing her lunch, washing her dishes, and sweeping the kitchen floor, Lucky elevated her feet and took up her crocheting. She was working on a baby blanket, one of many destined to go in the mail to the county hospital in Dallas. When she'd read in the newspaper of the pitiful plight of mothers too poor to provide pretty things for their own newborns, such that some of those babies were being sent home in disposable blankets, why, her heart had nearly broken. Every child deserved a better start than that. Lucky took it upon herself to remedy at least a small part of the solution. It didn't take long for fingers as practiced as hers to do a thirty-six-inch blanket. Three or four times a year, she packed up and sent a half dozen of the pretty, delicate things, each of them stitched with love and sent off with prayers.

Lucky dozed off. Right in the middle of a row. She hated that she did that. Used to she never, ever slept during the day. Only lately did it seem that every time she got still, her lids came down. Her daytime drowsiness was a source of embarrassment, and Lucky did not appreciate it when her doctor, a woman of seventy, dismissed Lucky's narcoleptic complaints as nothing more than the expected signs of advancing age.

"It's normal for a woman your age to be needing more sleep. Not a thing to worry about. If you're drowsy, take a nap."

A woman her age. Eighty-six. Was she really that old? Lucky couldn't believe it herself. It shocked her when she looked into the mirror and saw all those wrinkles—even worse, that sagging turkey-neck chin. What an awful trick. Despite various mild aches and pains, Lucky never had begun feeling like an old person—a fact that on one occasion proved to be a dangerous thing. When she was seventy-nine, she'd been up on a kitchen chair cleaning the top of her refrigerator. Forgetting her age, Lucky had jumped flat-footed to the floor as if she were a girl. That escapade brought on an ankle twisted and broken severely enough to need surgery to fix it back up.

Sometimes, even Lucky had to admit, a nap did have a way of refreshing the mind. On this afternoon, when she woke up from her unwanted, unplanned-for snooze, it was with a wonderful idea, a plan, really—one that had come to her fully formed while she slept. There would be no procrastinating this time. She picked up the phone.

"Miz Carter?"

"Yes."

"This is Lucky Jamison. I'm calling to tell you that I'd like to do something special for the girls of Tanglewood."

"How nice of you, Mrs. Jamison."

"I'd like to invite them to come to my house. Would Thursday afternoon be all right?"

"Yes—I think so," said Charlotte.

"I'll have a nutritional snack fixed for them, and then we'll get busy."

Charlotte was quiet on the other end.

"Goodness. I've gotten ahead of myself. What I'd

like to do for your girls is give them some instructions in the art of keeping a home."

"I—I'm not sure I understand," stammered Charlotte.

"Why, of course," said Lucky. "Pardon me. Having only moved here, you have no way of knowing. Dear, I'm a retired home economics teacher. I taught in the schools for thirty-eight years. I loved teaching girls how to cook and sew and keep house. I can't imagine, with everything you have to do, that you've much time to teach them such skills." Surely her suggestion wasn't hurting Charlotte's feelings.

"What I'd like to do is, once a week, have your girls come to my house so that I can give them a lesson. Do you think they would like that?"

"Yes. I'm sure they would—at least some of them. Two of my girls, Nikki and Vikki, have come down with the chicken pox."

"Bless their hearts. Are they itching? Oatmeal baths are good for that."

"Not too bad yet, but I appreciate the suggestion. I've some oatmeal in my pantry. Instant. Will that do?"

"No, I don't believe so. You need three-minute brand. Put a quarter cup in a tub of warm water. Have the children soak for at least twenty minutes. Will do them a world of good. Now—back to our Thursday plans. That would leave three girls who could come?" said Lucky.

"Yes. Maggie, Donna, and Sharita."

"Wonderful, I'll see them on Thursday. We'll be making pies."

Charlotte hung up the phone. Homemaking skills. Now that had never crossed her mind. Of course, such things were important. But nice as Miss Jamison was for volunteering, she couldn't rely upon the efforts of an elderly woman to teach the girls all they needed to learn. She'd have to come up with a plan of her own.

Soon as she found a spare minute.

Lighted Way Church youth were going off to camp the week of their winter break from school. The cost? Seventy-five dollars apiece. Pastor Jock wondered if the Tanglewood girls would be able to pay. But instead of possibly embarrassing Charlotte, he popped in at the 'Round the Clock and asked Kerilynn.

"When is it? First week of December?"

"Kids leave on the tenth," said Pastor Jock. "Be gone five days."

"Right around the corner. Not much time to plan or put money back. I don't know exactly how Charlotte's finances are, but I suspect they're tight as everybody else's. She let it slip once that she doesn't get any money from the state."

"None?"

"Something about the way she's got it set up. Some of the children I think she could get it for, but she decided at the beginning to run Tanglewood without any help from the government. Didn't want any money that came with strings attached."

"Have to admire her for that," said Pastor Jock.

"Absolutely. She's an admirable women." Kerilynn poured him a glass of sweet tea. "Tell me, Pastor, far as Charlotte Carter goes, is there anything else you've found to admire? Other than the way she's funding her home?"

Even though Kerilynn was sitting across the table from him, he managed to avoid looking her in the eye. Instead he concentrated on positioning the tabletop salt and pepper shakers, sugar dispenser, Sweet 'N Low packets, and bottle of hot sauce all in a straight row.

Kerilynn closed in for the kill. "I've been meaning to say something. Since you brought the subject up, this is as good a time as any. Aren't you and Charlotte the same age?"

"Right at it," said Pastor Jock. He squeezed lemon into his tea. "Did I miss something? What exactly is it that I brought up?"

"Don't be going and changing the subject on me now, Pastor. Just answer the question. Either of you married?"

"No."

"You seem to get along good."

"We get along fine. She's an asset to Lighted Way. We're blessed to have her be a part of our church."

"Do you think she's cute?"

"Very cute. I also think that with everything she's going through she's in need of a pastor, not someone to take her out on a date."

"So you *have* thought of asking her out!" Kerilynn could not hide her glee. "I knew it. You two would be perfect for each other. What would it hurt to ask her to dinner, say—just as friends?"

"Not one thing. But it's not going to happen."

"Not now, you mean? Maybe at some later date?"

"Kerilynn." Pastor Jock laughed. "I came over to ask you about those girls going to camp!"

"Oh, that. Of course they'll go to camp."

"The money?"

"Folks will donate. There's a dozen members who would be glad to sponsor one of those girls so they could go."

"I don't think Charlotte will accept a cash gift like that," said Jock.

"Probably not," agreed Kerilynn. "Have to figure out a way to get it to them and her not know where the money came from." She got up to check on something in the kitchen. When she came back she had an idea. "I'll hire those girls to come work for me. After school and a couple of Saturdays. I'll pay 'em a wage. They'll get tips. They can use what money they make for their camp fees."

"Great idea," said Jock.

"Better let her know soon. Why don't you go on over to her house and give her the news?"

"You're the one hiring them—why don't you give her a call?" said Jock.

"Too busy." Kerilynn began counting money in the register. "My lunch crowd will be here soon. Go on now. Run on over and give Charlotte the news. She'll be glad to see you."

Pastor Jock gave her a look, but Kerilynn didn't let on that she saw. He pulled out a dollar to pay for his tea.

"On the house. Go on now," said Kerilynn. "See how things are going over there. Call me if she's heard any news about Beth. What's it been—a little over a week she's been gone?"

Ten days. And no news at all.

Chapter Twenty

Kim Beeson, file folders in hand, sat on the ticking-striped sofa in Charlotte's living room. Except for the sound of Treasure running the vacuum cleaner upstairs, the house was quiet. "So, this woman—she's a friend of yours?" Kim asked.

"Yes. Treasure Evans. Staying for a few weeks."

"To help out a bit?"

"Sort of. She came because she thought I needed some help, but honestly there's not a lot for her to do," said Charlotte. "Still, I'm enjoying having her here. Nice to have the company."

"Right," said Kim. "In general, how would you say things are going?"

"Better," said Charlotte, in what had to be the understatement of the year. "Nikki and Vikki went back to school two days ago. They're over the chicken pox.

So far, no one else has come down with it."

Please, God. Keep the others free of spots for at least a few more days.

Refusing Treasure's offer to take a shift, she'd been up and down with the twins for most of a week's worth of nights. They'd run fevers and itched terribly. Oatmeal baths and calamine lotion had helped. She'd used both repeatedly, evidenced by the pink under her fingernails and the slow-draining, rather breakfast-smelling bathtub upstairs.

"How're the girls doing in school?" Kim chewed the end of her pen.

Charlotte felt a wave of unease. She'd gotten the day wrong and missed her afternoon block of parent-teacher conferences last week—not exactly endearing Tanglewood to the school administrator in charge of scheduling. She'd been terribly embarrassed when Ben Jackson, whom she'd sat behind at Lighted Way the Sunday before, had called from his office to remind her of how important the meetings were. Politely but firmly, he'd told her that in the future she needed to do her best not to miss.

Charlotte still wasn't sure exactly how it had happened. There it was. One o'clock. Wednesday. Marked on the calendar. All she could figure was that since she was sleep deprived, she'd managed to lose a day and think it Tuesday two days in a row. Luckily, the girls' teachers had been required to send written reports home to those students whose parents weren't concerned enough about their children to come for their conferences.

Kim waited.

"School. Yes. They're doing okay." Charlotte concentrated, stalling to recall what she'd read in the reports. Hoping Kim wouldn't guess the truth, she filled in on her own those spots where her brain came up blank.

"Maggie's struggling in math—says she hates the subject but, thankfully, loves her teacher. Donna had all Bs on her report card, made the honor roll for the first time in her life. Sharita's biggest problem is that she's what her teacher calls 'an extremely social person.' She gets in trouble for talking too much in class. She manages to listen some of the time, though. Making the best grades of all the girls even though she never brings home a book. Nikki and Vikki have after-school tutoring three afternoons a week. They're still reading below grade level, but the teacher says they're coming along."

"Good." Kim scribbled as Charlotte talked. "I also need to update the girls' medical files today. Can you give me the dates they've been for their doctor and dentist visits?"

"Got them right here." Charlotte was grateful to Treasure for suggesting she buy folders with pockets, one for each of the girls. That one small thing had helped tremendously with keeping up with details. Except that she couldn't find Donna's. Where was it? She was sure she'd had it right here. Maybe she'd left it in the van. She hoped that was where it was.

"That's okay. I'll get her records on my next visit," said Kim. "Fire drills?"

"Did one last week. Form's right here." At least she'd managed to do one thing right.

Peaches traipsed through.

"New dog?"

"She belongs to Treasure."

"Had her shots?"

"I'm sure."

"How about the rest of the pets? You have their shot records? We talked about that last time I was here."

Charlotte didn't remember that.

"Any pets in your home must have records that they've been vaccinated. Do you have those?"

"Not where I can locate them this minute. Can it wait until next week? I'll have them for you then." Charlotte wondered where in the house any of the animals' records might be.

"I'll need them for sure by then."

"What if I can't find them?"

"If you can't get a copy from your vet, they'll have to be vaccinated again."

Charlotte imagined hauling the whole menagerie in to Dr. Ross. How much would that cost?

Kim closed her file. "There's something else I want to talk to you about."

"Something about Beth?" Charlotte had been struggling not to ask ever since Kim's arrival. Every day she called. Every day Kim had nothing to report. Perhaps Kim did have news—good news—and was saving it for last.

Please, please, let it be so.

"No. I'm sorry. I don't know anything new."

Charlotte's hands lay limp in her lap. "It's been almost two weeks. I can't stand not knowing where she is—if she's all right. Sometimes my mind runs away with me. I think about all the things that could be happening to her. I worry that she's cold or hungry. I know you don't know for sure, but based on your experience, how much longer do you think it'll be before she's back?"

Kim waited a moment before she spoke. "The truth is, Charlotte, the longer Beth is gone, the less likely it is that she'll come back. By now she's probably left the state."

Charlotte's eyes widened. "You don't believe she's coming back?"

"She's been in foster care for years. Lived all over. This is a hard thing to say, but, honestly, I'll be surprised if she's found—which is what we need to talk about. Beth being gone leaves you with an empty bed. Are you ready to think about filling it?"

"You mean you've given up? Are you still looking?"

"Of course, we're still looking. I only thought that until she's found—"

"Tanglewood is full. I don't have an empty place for another girl," said Charlotte. How would it make Beth feel to come back and find another girl's clothes in her closet, maybe even asleep in her bed?

"Of course. I understand." Kim gathered her things.

"Charlotte, these things happen. Kids run away. Some come back. Some never do. It's awful, but it's part of it. Even if we find Beth, and it's looking more doubtful every day that we will, it may be decided that Tanglewood's not the best place for her. The fact that she ran away indicates Beth may have been more troubled than we realized."

When Kim was out the front door, Charlotte stood for a moment in the entry hall. She watched through the window as Kim walked down the sidewalk, got into her car, and drove down the street. She hesitated at the bottom of the stairs. Studied, for the hundredth time, the photo of J.D. hanging there. She reached out and touched the frame, then turned and went up the stairs.

"What you doing?" asked Treasure from the doorway of Beth's room.

"Changing the sheets," said Charlotte, struggling with a corner. "They need to be fresh when Beth comes home."

Treasure didn't answer, just moved to the opposite side of the bed.

For once, Charlotte accepted her help. Together, they got the job done.

"Morning. Good to see you," said Pastor Jock. Was Charlotte's unexpected appearance in his office this morning because she had news? He tried to read her face.

"Is this a good time?" asked Charlotte.

"Great time. Just finishing my morning research." Slightly embarrassed that she'd caught him reading the *Dallas Morning News* instead of the second letter to the Corinthians or at least one of the psalms, Pastor Jock motioned to the nearly completed crossword puzzle on his desk. "Coffee?"

"Thank you. No." She sat down, didn't meet his eyes.

Pastor Jock turned his back to Charlotte, poured himself a third cup, prayed a quick plea for wisdom and discernment, and willed himself to wait for her to speak.

"Beth's social worker, Kim, came by yesterday."

"And?"

"Not what you think. She wants me to take another girl. Since it"—she swallowed—"doesn't look like Beth's coming back."

Pastor Jock cupped his mug in both hands. Not coming back? He wasn't ready to give up. Nor were Kerilynn or Les and Ginger or Gabe or Dr. Ross or any number of other good folks. Every day since she'd disappeared, someone had gone out on an organized, mapped-out-by-Kerilynn search. Flyers with Beth's picture on them were posted all over the county. Best he could tell, no one in Ruby Prairie was ready to toss in the towel.

But was Charlotte?

"What'd you tell her?"

"I told her Tanglewood was full, that six girls were all I could take."

"Nikki, Vikki, Maggie, Sharita, and Donna. Beth makes six," said Pastor Jock. "I agree. Sounds to me like Tanglewood is full."

"Did I tell her the right thing?"

"I think that you did."

"Am I in denial—believing she'll be back?"

"No. I don't think so."

Charlotte began to cry silently.

Pastor Jock handed a tissue across his desk, then waited, still and quiet. Finally he spoke. "Charlotte, no one knows. I suppose it's true that Beth may not be found. But it hasn't been that long. I don't see how any harm can come in keeping up hope, waiting a while longer."

"Kim says runaway girls are par for the course, that I need to get used to the idea."

"Can you do that?"

"I'm not sure." More tears.

"It's a hard thing."

She nodded. "There are lots of hard things."

"Like?"

"Everything." Charlotte raised her head and stared past Pastor Jock, fixing her eyes on some fuzzy point outside the window of his office. "I thought I could do this. Today I'm not sure."

"You're a blessing to those girls."

"A sorry one."

"That's all any of us are, really. Sorry blessings—compared to the magnificence of Christ. Charlotte, you've been a Christian almost all your life. You already know this. God doesn't call us to be perfect, only to use the gifts He's given us to the best of our abilities."

"That's a good thing." Charlotte blew her nose. "Because perfect is one thing I'm not."

Charlotte left Lighted Way, eased only a bit by Pastor Jock's words. She had a busy day ahead, a bunch of things to check off her to-do list. First there were groceries to buy, then prescriptions to pick up at the drugstore, a package to mail at the post office, and heartworm medicine to get at Four Paws Pet Clinic. If she made good time, she'd be able to put things away, do a load or two of laundry, and start something for supper before the girls arrived home. One of them had some kind of an activity after school. Who was it? Was this choir night for Sharita? No. Brownies for Nikki and Vikki. Charlotte tried to remember as she climbed up the kitchen steps.

Treasure met her at the door, wearing gloves and her heavy coat with the collar turned up.

"Going out?"

"No, and you best keep your coat on too. Sugar, your heater's quit."

"Oh, no." Charlotte set bags of groceries on the counter. "When?"

"Not sure. Felt a chill about two hours ago. Cranked the thermostat up a notch, but nothing happened. Turned it up a little higher, still nothing. Compressor hasn't cut on since. I've done checked the breaker box. Fuses too. Ever' one of them's fine. Must be your unit." Treasure rubbed her hands together. "I built us a fire in the fireplace, but it's not doing much good. Don't believe your firebox is vented right. Built mainly for looks."

"I'll call a repairman." Charlotte kept her coat on. "It's freezing in here."

"They's a number on the unit. Folks that put it in. We best hope they can come right on. Troy, that weather man what's on channel eight, says a blue northern's gonna blow in this afternoon."

"Maybe it's just bad wiring or something," said Charlotte.

"I got you the number right here."

Charlotte dialed but got a recording saying the number was no longer in service.

"Sounds like they closed down," said Treasure.

"I guess so." Charlotte looked in the yellow pages for someone else to call.

She tried Juan's, the only place listed in Ruby Prairie. The man who answered the phone was nice but unable to help. Two of his three servicemen were out with the flu. Tanglewood could sure be put on the list, but it would be two, maybe three days, before they could come.

Charlotte thanked the man but told him no. She'd find someone else. There was a second company listed in the book. Treasure put another log on the fire.

Snowball and Visa, fur fluffed for warmth, snuggled on the couch.

"Sorry, ma'am, but I'm fifty miles south of you," said the man on the phone. "We don't come up that far. Only person I can tell you to try is Pete's Heating and Air over in Ella Louise. He's an old man what works out of his house, but I've heard tell he's pretty good."

Charlotte tried Pete. His wife answered the phone and told Charlotte that her husband had retired, but she sold Watkins products in case she ever was in need of such.

Charlotte hung up the phone. "No one can come until the day after tomorrow. Maybe not even then."

"What are you going to do?"

Two days without heat. Maybe three. Should they all go to a hotel? The closest was a good half hour away. Getting the girls to and from school would be difficult. How many rooms would they need? They could get two adjoining. Charlotte couldn't remember how much credit she had left on her Visa. Imagine loading up the girls and driving thirty minutes only to have her card declined. Then what would she do?

The phone rang before she had time to come up with an alternate plan.

"Mrs. Carter? This is Nurse Medford at the school. We need you to pick up Donna."

"What's wrong? Is she hurt?"

"No. Looks to me like she's picked up that virus that's going around. She's thrown up twice since lunch, and she's got a temp of 100.8 degrees. Oops. There she goes again. Can you come right now?"

"Of course."

"Donna's sick," Charlotte told Treasure. "Throwing up. I've got to go get her."

"What you going do with her once you get her? This cold house is no place for a sick one. No place for any of us, less we planning on being sick too."

"There's a little electric heater on the top shelf in the storeroom. Would you get it down while I'm gone?"

"Electric heater? Honey, that's not going to do enough good. It's already too cold to stay here, and it's going to get lots colder as the afternoon wears on. We've got to get these children someplace warm. Why don't you give me the number of some of those nice people from the church? I can call them while you're gone to get Donna."

"We'll be fine. I've got electric blankets for all of the beds." Charlotte grabbed her keys. "I'll be right back."

The van wouldn't start. Charlotte went back to the house.

"Take mine," said Treasure. "It used to be a delivery van, so they's only the two seats in the front, but that's all you'll need."

Charlotte got into the van. It had a standard transmission. J.D. had wanted to teach her. Why hadn't she learned?

Sleet began to fall. Not only did Donna need to be picked up, but school would be out in two hours. The girls couldn't walk home in weather like this.

"I'll go," said Treasure, when Charlotte came back

in a second time. "Where's me a trash can to take? You got a Wal-Mart sack we can put in it? Child may be sick between there and here. Bless her heart, I'd rather her not do it on the floor of my van. You have any peppermint tea? I've known that to settle a child's stomach. Don't want to be putting sugar in it, though. Use Karo Syrup instead."

Charlotte ran water in the kettle as Treasure went out the door. No heat. Sick girl. Van wouldn't start. What else?

God, please help me to get through this. I know that with Your help—

Charlotte didn't finish her prayer. She was interrupted by someone banging insistently on the front door—loud enough to cause Visa and Snowball to run under the couch and prompt Peaches to wet on the floor.

Who would be pounding like that? Instead of flinging open the door as she usually did, Charlotte went to the window and looked around the curtain to see who was there. Was that Kerilynn's brother?

She opened the door. "Mr. Martin?"

"Name's Catfish. I need to have a word with you."

Chapter Twenty-one

Treasure? What're you doing here?" asked Pastor Jock. He was coming out of the door of the school library as she was heading down the hall.

"Charlotte's van won't start, and Donna's sick. I've come to carry her home." She turned and looked back the way she'd come in. "I didn't know you was a teacher on the side."

"I'm not. Just a volunteer. Couple of hours a week."

"That's nice of you." She stopped. "I'm turned around. Which way's the nurse's office?"

"I'll walk you there," said Pastor Jock. "What's the matter with Charlotte's van?"

"Don't know. Needs to get it looked at, but that's the least of her troubles."

"Why, what else is wrong?"

"Heat's gone out in the house. Probably the compressor. Can't get no one out to fix it for at least two days. And now we've got us a sick one to take care of."

"Where're y'all staying till it's repaired?" he asked.

"Lands if I know. Girl wouldn't call nobody. Thinks we can stay there in this kind of cold with her little 'lectric heater and 'lectric blankets for the beds."

"In that big place? That's crazy. You'll freeze."

"Don't I know it. But I can't tell her nothing. You know how she is.

Pastor Jock rubbed his chin. "How about I follow you home? See what I can do."

"Suit yourself," said Treasure. "Maybe you can talk some sense into her head. I've 'bout given up trying."

Charlotte opened up the door. "How can I help you?"

Maybe Catfish did heater repair on the side. How

did he know her unit was out? Didn't matter. God sometimes had funny ways of answering prayers. Cold as it was in the house, whoever or however He chose was fine by her.

"Come on in." She smiled at him.

He didn't smile back.

"No. No need of that." Catfish didn't move from his spot on the porch, only took off his hat. "You still aiming to find that girl you lost? If you are, I can tell you where she's at. Fact, you can go get her right now."

Charlotte's heart raced. "You mean Beth? You've seen her? Where is she? Is she all right?"

"Looks to be, but I can't tell for sure. All I know is where she is right now. You want to follow me?"

"Of course." Charlotte's mind spun. Where were her keys? Her purse. Then she remembered. "No. I can't. My van won't start."

Catfish hesitated. "Guess I can carry you in my truck," he said.

"Just a minute. No one'll know where I've gone. I've got to leave Treasure a note."

"I'll wait on you," said Catfish. He turned and headed down the steps.

"Can you move it?" asked Kirby. "If you can, that means it's not broke."

What did he think he was, a doctor? Beth wriggled her ankle a tiny bit. "A little." She winced. Her foot was starting to swell. "I think it needs ice."

The cabin had only one room, but luckily, the electricity was on and cold water ran in the sink. Kirby got up from the bed. Beth stayed there, wrapped in three quilts, with her back against the wall. He went to the refrigerator and, with effort, opened up the freezer section at the top. The one ice tray was empty.

They'd found no frozen food to speak of when they'd first arrived. Beth wondered what exactly he thought might be there now.

"This thing needs to be thawed out," he said. "There's so much frost, I can't tell what anything is." With a wooden spoon he beat on the ice until he was able to pry out a frost-covered, bloodstained package from the back wall. "Chicken livers," he read. "Whoever owns this place probably used 'em for bait. Put it on your foot."

"Okay." Package was pretty yucky, actually.

"How'd you fall?"

"I tripped coming up the steps." The cabin had no bathroom. She'd been to the woods.

"Does it hurt?"

Beth nodded. Hurt a lot. But that wasn't all. All of the sudden, she'd had enough. Way more than enough.

Two weeks of enough.

She and Kirby had stumbled upon the empty hunter's cabin the night they left Ruby Prairie. Were they lucky or what? The cabin was the perfect place to be together. If they had each other, nothing else mattered.

At least, that's how it had started out.

But the cabin was cold. And there wasn't any TV or indoor toilet. And Kirby always had to have things his own way.

Still, it was better than being on the side of the road. Was it better than Tanglewood?

Beth would never let herself say.

That night when Kirby's motorcycle had quit, she'd prayed for help. Since then, almost every day she'd thought about God. But she hadn't prayed.

Doing so now wouldn't be right.

Still. God must have been watching out for them. He'd led them through the woods to this shack. No way they should have been able to find it themselves on such a dark night.

God moves in mysterious ways. At least that's what people said in church.

The chicken liver package started to sweat. "Don't get chicken blood on the covers," said Kirby.

Beth held her foot off the bed. That made it hurt worse.

They'd almost cleaned out the cabin's stock of canned foods. There were still a couple of days' worth left, but nothing much good. The peaches and fruit cocktail they'd eaten in the first three days. The corn played out soon after, leaving canned beans, canned chili, and canned Dinty Moore Beef Stew. A person could only eat so much of that sort of stuff.

"We're going to have to figure something else out," she said.

"I know," said Kirby. They'd spoken the same

words every day for a week.

"Any ideas?"

"We could hitchhike to Mexico," he said.

This was a new plan. "I don't know," said Beth. "We better think about it before we decide."

Gone to get Beth. That's all the scribbled-on-a-napkin note said. "What could she mean?" asked Pastor Jock.

"I haven't been gone more than twenty minutes. Don't know how something could have come up that fast," said Treasure.

"How did she go if the van won't start?" He looked out the window to make sure. "It's still here."

Donna, pale, clammy, and forgotten, sat slumped in her coat in a kitchen chair. She laid her head down on the table.

"Honey, I forgot about you. You all right?" Treasure rested a hand on Donna's shoulder. "Pastor, this child's got a fever. We've got to get her to bed, someplace warm. And the others'll be home 'fore you know it. Lands! The weather. They've all got to be picked up, and I can't get 'em in my van. Only got two seats, and no safety belts in the back. What we going to do?"

Pastor Jock called Kerilynn.

Who rallied the troops.

Chapter Twenty-two

Gotta slam it hard or it won't catch," said Catfish. Charlotte did as she was told. "Where is she?"

"At my hunting cabin. Hour from here. Must've jimmied the lock to get in. I spotted them round noon," said Catfish. "Don't know how long they've been there."

"Them? They? Who's with her?" asked Charlotte.

"Some boy. Same one was driving the motorcycle night they left."

Charlotte's mouth flew open. "You saw Beth leave with a boy? On a motorcycle? When?"

"Yeah, I saw them. Spotted 'em 'bout the time the festival was closing down. Little bit later, they was in my store, stealing something to eat. I was so mad at them—mad at myself for letting them get away with it—that I kept what I knew to myself. Figured they was long gone by the time they was missed and that whatever happened to them they more'n likely deserved."

Charlotte's voice was thin. "I don't understand—if you knew something, then why—?"

"I can't answer that," said Catfish.

Charlotte could hardly think.

"Any other year I'd 'a been out to the cabin way 'fore now. Gout's kept me from it. Gets better, then flares up again."

What did the man's gout have to do with anything? Charlotte took a deep breath. "Wh-what made you decide to come get me today?"

"Coming up on them. It was either turn 'em in or run 'em off," said Catfish. "I'm a man that believes right is right and wrong is wrong. What I done, not telling nobody, has been eating on me some. Here I am sitting up in my recliner of a Sunday afternoon, knowing all along they wasn't going to find that girl in town, while the whole community's out looking." Catfish wiped at his mouth. "I should've told the law right off, but I didn't. Figured a couple of days and people would forget about it and go on with their business. But they didn't. 'Stead of getting less concerned, they got more. Longer I let it go on, worse I figured it'd be if I told."

"I can see that."

Catfish looked straight ahead.

"Miz Carter, I'm glad your girl's all right. I made a mistake. Can't go back. Wish I could. Word'll get out what I done, and I'll pay. Folks'll talk. Kerilynn won't never let me forget it. Whatever she dishes out, I figure I got coming."

They rode along in silence.

"I'm still not sure I understand what happened today," Charlotte finally said. "You say you saw Beth. Did you speak to her?"

"Naw. Don't believe they even saw me. The place is back in the woods. Muddy as it is right now, can't get a vehicle up to it. Have to park a-ways away, then walk. This morning I felt good enough to go up and check on things. Thought I might get a half day's hunting in. I was about fifty yards from the front door when I seen your girl. She was sitting on the steps, crying."

"Crying?"

"She was holding her foot like it was hurt. I was so surprised to see her I stayed quiet for a minute. Then that boy came out."

"Do you know the boy, Catfish?"

"Never seen him before. Don't believe he's from around here." *Kirby,* thought Charlotte. "I wonder how long they've been there."

"No telling. The place ain't fancy, but I kept it stocked up with food. Got running water at the sink. Wood-burning stove to keep warm by. Used to be, I got up there couple of times a month to hunt and to fish. Gabe and Chilly'd go with me. Kerilynn thinks I ought to sell the place, but I tell her times we're living in, government going crazy and all, one of these days a person might be needing someplace safe to go."

Catfish turned onto a dirt road.

" 'Bout another two miles. Reckon what she'll do when she sees you? You think she'll try and run off?"

Tanglewood's driveway filled up with cars. And Charlotte's kitchen filled up with worried folks, all of whom kept on their coats. Nomie poured coffee for everybody. Sassy answered the phone.

"I don't have no idea." Treasure answered the same

questions every time someone new arrived. "Left only long enough to get to the school. She was already gone when I got back."

"You sure this is her writing?" Kerilynn studied the note on the napkin. She'd left her glasses at home.

"I think it is," said Treasure.

"I hope she's okay," said Lester.

"I hope Beth's all right," said Kerilynn. "It's wonderful news if she really has been found."

"Just odd that Charlotte would leave so quickly," said Treasure, growing more concerned all the time.

"Her van's still here," said Gabe for the second time.

"Van won't start," reminded Pastor Jock. "Someone had to have come and got her."

"Maybe it was that social worker," said Ginger.

"What's the matter with the van?" asked Chilly.

"Don't know," said Kerilynn.

"I'll go take a look," said Chilly. "Ought to be under warranty."

"How long has the heat been out?" asked Dr. Ross.

"Quit this morning."

"Serviceman coming?"

"Day after tomorrow. Couldn't get no one out before then."

"Weather like this, they're probably backed up with calls," said Dr. Ross.

"Who y'all staying with tonight?" asked Kerilynn.

"No one I know of," Treasure answered.

"Nonsense," said Kerilynn. "Y'all have got to go someplace till it's fixed."

"You're not hearing no argument from me," said Treasure. Without Charlotte around, somebody had best take charge. "I've got a sick one—Donna—in Charlotte's bed right now, covered up in blankets, still freezing to death."

"Lester, let's you and me take her home with us," said Ginger right off.

"She's got the virus, maybe stomach flu," warned Treasure.

"I used to be a nurse's aide," said Ginger. "I know what to do."

"What about the others?" asked Kerilynn.

"I need some way to get 'em home from school," said Treasure. "Van's running," said Chilly, back in the house. "Battery was down. Just needed a boost. Looks like the dome light got left on."

"Can you go get the girls from school?" Kerilynn asked Treasure. "I'll call Ben Jackson. Tell him why it's you instead of Charlotte," said. Pastor Jock.

"What we going to do with them when we get them from school?" asked Treasure.

"I've got two extra beds," said Nomie.

"I've got a place for one," said Sassy.

"Nomie, you take the twins," decided Kerilynn. "Sharita can go home with me. Sassy, can Maggie go with you? Treasure, get some things together for yourself. I've got room for you too."

"I'm not leaving. Somebody needs to be here when Charlotte gets back with that child."

"You can't stay in this cold house," said Kerilynn.

"I'll build up the fire, close off the doors, and be fine," Treasure said.

"I'll stay with you," said Pastor Jock.

"We forgot one thing," said Lester. "The animals. What's Charlotte got—two cats?"

"And three dogs," said Dr. Ross, who had given the whole menagerie repeat shots earlier in the week. "No problem. I'll board them at the clinic."

Within an hour, the house was empty except for Treasure and Pastor Jock, who huddled under afghans in the living room. For a while the two of them made conversation. Pastor Jock prayed. After his "amen," neither of them spoke. Instead they sat staring at the flames. Every few minutes, one or the other would look at the clock on the wall.

Not a word from Charlotte. Not even a call.

Chapter Twenty-three

Catfish and Charlotte were stuck. No cell phone. No way to let Treasure know what was going on. Charlotte had been so stunned at Catfish's news she'd left without thinking. Since the van wouldn't start, how would the girls get home from school? The house was so cold—they'd be miserable. And Donna? Charlotte hoped Treasure got her home okay. What if she needed to see a doctor? Who would take her? She tried to remember if there was any Tylenol in the house.

She fidgeted in her seat, sneaked a look at her watch. She thought about the shepherd who left the ninety-nine at home to go out and reclaim the lost one. God, *look after the ninety-nine while I'm gone.*

Beads of sweat broke out on Catfish's upper lip. He put the truck in reverse, then back into drive. It shimmied a bit, flung red mud up onto the windows, then acted like it might move, before settling itself back into its ruts like a foot into a shoe.

Catfish got out to look. He walked from one side around to the other, then began dragging up limbs.

After watching for a moment, Charlotte got out. "I'll help you."

"Watch your step. Mud's slick. Need to wedge these limbs up against the back tires; give them something other than clay to grab onto. Once we get enough, I'll get behind and push while you try to ease us out."

Together, they scoured for suitable fallen timber.

"That should do it," said Catfish. He was breathing hard. "If this works, drive right over to that patch of higher ground and put her in park. Wet as it is, we'll have to walk the rest of the way."

"Beth, wake up," said Kirby. "You all right?"

Her face was red, and quilt marks creased her cheek. She'd been asleep all afternoon.

"No." She started to cry. "My foot hurts really bad."

"Bet you need an X-ray," said Kirby. "Can you walk on it?"

"No. I can't even stand. What are we going to do?"

Kirby realized he was somehow supposed to know. "Maybe my uncle could come and get us, take us to the emergency room." *If he isn't high, drunk, or in jail.* "I could walk to the road. Maybe somebody'd give me a ride to where I could call him."

Kirby hated the thought of all that. He tried to stall. "Why don't we wait one more day? Your foot might be feeling better tomorrow. It doesn't look broke. Might be just a strain."

"Kirby, no," said Beth. "That's not going to work. I need help now."

Beth had been sounding like a cranky little kid on and off for the past few days. Wanting her way about everything. Not just since she hurt her foot either. What was up with that? Whatever it was, it was getting pretty old.

"You have to go now. I'm not joking. My foot's killing me. We don't even have any aspirin. I can't stay here anymore."

She wouldn't look at him.

"So what are you saying? You know that once people find out we're here, we won't be together anymore. Is that what you want?"

"I don't know what I want." Beth was crying.

Two weeks together in a twenty-by-twenty-foot shack. Food supply dwindling. No place to take a bath. Cold. Bored. No sign of a happy ending in sight.

Something that was already cracked finally snapped. Kirby put on his jacket. "I don't need this."

"Kirby, I didn't mean—"

He stood looking at her, resting his hand on the doorknob for the longest time. Finally he said, "I'm out of here," and was gone.

The ringing of the phone broke the silence in the living room of Tanglewood. Pastor Jock jumped. Treasure picked it up.

"Any word?" asked Kerilynn. She was only an hour gone.

"Not a one," said Treasure. "I'm trying not to worry, but my mind keeps running away with me. Charlotte taking off so quick—disappearing into thin air. No thought to what she was leaving behind. That's not like her. Not like her at all. Think we ought to call the law?"

Pastor Jock nodded his head.

"I'm worried too," said Kerilynn. "We'll need to get Mark in on this if we don't hear something soon. Still, she did leave a note. Let's give it a little while longer."

"All the children settled?"

"They're fine. Joe Fazoli's invited all of us who're keeping the girls to come down for the lasagna special, compliments of the house."

"Not Donna, I hope," said Treasure.

"All but her."

"Ginger say if she's been sick anymore?"

"Not since she got her to her house. She's got her drinking 7 Up."

"Good. Might be just one of those twenty-four-hour bugs."

"You and the pastor doing okay? Staying warm?" asked Kerilynn.

"We're fine. Don't worry about us."

"Call me if you hear anything," said Kerilynn.

"You do the same."

Kirby heard them coming, saw them picking their way through the overgrown path to the cabin. In the two weeks he and Beth had been staying in the woods, no one had shown up. Why today?

When they got closer, he recognized the old man as the one from the store. He didn't know who the woman was. She looked too young and too nice to be the old man's wife. Maybe she was a policewoman. Undercover. According to his uncle, they picked good-looking women to be policewomen so as to throw people off. He bet they'd come to arrest him and Beth for breaking into the old man's store. Shoot. All they took were a couple of sodas and some stupid cheese crackers.

How did they find them? Kirby couldn't figure that one out. But one thing he knew. No way was he going to let himself get caught. Soon as the old man and the lady passed the place where he was hidden, he sprinted.

Toward the road.

And away from Beth.

Chapter Twenty-four

"There's no guns in the place. Just some extra shells," said Catfish. Guns! Charlotte hadn't even thought of guns till Catfish mentioned them.

They walked a quarter mile before the cabin came in sight. It was more like a shack, really. Weathered gray wood. Tin roof. Brush grown up all around. Empty cans tossed out near the front door.

Beth ran from Tanglewood to this?

Charlotte and Catfish spoke in low voices. The clearing where the cabin sat was so quiet and so still it was hard to imagine anyone was inside. What if Beth had left? What if they'd come this close and she'd somehow run away?

"Best let me go in first," said Catfish.

"I'm not afraid," said Charlotte. "Is there a back door?"

"There is. You go round there. Case they try and run."

Charlotte stood on the back step. She pressed her ear against the rough wood. When she heard crying she forgot Catfish's instruction to wait for a signal, and shoved open the heavy, warped door.

Catfish came in the front.

But instead of a pair trying to escape, they found Beth alone, pale and red-eyed, trembling and sobbing, hunkered as far back in the bed as she could get.

"It's me, honey," said Charlotte. "Are you all right?"

Beth couldn't speak for crying.

That was okay. She didn't have to say a word. She was safe. And she didn't pull away when Charlotte moved close.

A child lost.

Now found.

Beth could take all the time she needed.

Except that Catfish would not wait. "No," he said. "She's not all right. Look there." He motioned to the end of the bed.

Beth's foot jutted to the left at an unnatural, stomach-turning angle.

"That foot's broke," he said. "This child's nearly in shock. We've got to get her to a doctor—and quick."

Treasure got the first call from Charlotte to Ruby Prairie, Kerilynn the one after that.

Beth was in the hospital, receiving IV fluids, scheduled for surgery in the morning. Charlotte was dialing from a pay phone. What would they have done without Catfish and his surprise emergency training? Charlotte didn't know.

She'd already called Kim Beeson, told her of the situation. Since she couldn't leave Beth to take care of the others and since the heat was out at Tanglewood and since her van wouldn't start, Kim was arranging for the girls to be transferred somewhere else. Charlotte feared they might have to be put in a shelter. Kim said she'd do what she could, but she admitted that emergency placements at this hour would be hard to come by.

"Nonsense," said Treasure. "You can't be sending these girls off in the night."

"I have no choice," said Charlotte. "I'm two and a half hours away. I can't be two places at once."

"Give me Kim's number," said Kerilynn. "I need to talk to her before she leaves."

"Which hospital?" asked Pastor Jock. "I'm on my way."

Beth was in the hospital for four days. Charlotte stayed the whole time. Catfish came every evening, smuggled in food from the 'Round the Clock. He stood in a corner, holding his hat, unsure what to say.

"Sit down," Charlotte urged him time and time again.

"I'm fine," he said. "Just wanted to make sure you two had what you need."

They had exactly what they needed.

Time.

The first two days, on pain medication and groggy from anesthesia, Beth slept, waking for only short moments before drifting back off. Charlotte stayed in the room with her, holding her hand, stroking her hair when she opened her eyes.

On the third morning she was fully awake. She focused on Charlotte for a minute and finally spoke. "How come you came after me?"

"How come you ran away?" Charlotte countered.

"I don't know," said Beth. "Seems pretty dumb now."

"I came looking for you because I love you," said Charlotte. "I know that's hard to believe, but I really do."

Beth turned her face away. "Even if you love me, if you knew everything—everything that happened, you wouldn't have come."

"You're wrong. There's nothing you've done in the past, nothing you can do in the future that'll make me love you less. More important, God's love is the same. He loves you when you're good. He loves you when you aren't."

"God doesn't make any sense," said Beth.

"Doesn't have to," said Charlotte. "God just is."

Later that night, Charlotte sat beside Beth's bed. For a while they watched TV; then Charlotte turned the set off.

"There's something we need to talk about," she said. "Kirby, the boy from the shelter. I'd like to know more about him. He's the one who came and got you at the festival?"

"Yes." Beth wouldn't meet her eyes.

"He took you to the cabin?"

Beth nodded. "We found it when his motorcycle broke down."

"Did he stay there with you?"

"Yes."

"But you were alone when we found you."

"He left." Beth hedged. "I don't remember exactly when."

"How old is Kirby, honey?"

"Sixteen."

"Goodness," said Charlotte. "His family's probably looking for him. They must be worried. Do you know where he might have gone?"

"He has an uncle or something. I don't know where he lives."

"If he was your friend, I guess you're worried about him too," said Charlotte.

"We sort of had a fight. I don't think we're friends anymore." Beth covered her face with her hands.

"It's okay, Beth." Charlotte wrapped her arms around Beth.

"No. It's not okay. It never will be okay."

"What do you mean?"

"It just won't."

And that's all she would say.

Kerilynn had called Kim Beeson and convinced her that Ruby Prairie folks could take care of the Tanglewood girls while Charlotte stayed at the hospital with Beth. There was no need of her coming after them, carrying them off to some strange place.

Soon as she and Kim hung up, Kerilynn phoned Treasure to let her in on the approved plan. "Everything's set. Kim says the girls can stay right where they are."

"She give you any trouble?"

"None to speak of. Said she was bending some rules by letting the girls stay with folks that weren't certified, but since it was sort of an emergency and for only a few days she maybe wouldn't get in too much hot water."

"You tell Kim we don't want Charlotte to know? That we want it to be a surprise that the girls didn't have to go off somewhere?"

"Yes. She didn't really understand why, but she said it wouldn't be any problem. Fact is, she's going out of town to a conference or something for the next week. Charlotte won't be able to reach her by phone."

"Too bad I don't got no way of keeping her from reaching me by phone," said Treasure. "You know she's going to be calling me day and night checking on things. Especially she'll be expecting me to tell her where Kim carried those girls."

"Not only that," agreed Kerilynn, "but she'll be wanting to know about everything that's going on—the heat, her van, all of it."

"I know it."

"You still not planning on telling her?"

"Not if I can help it."

"Treasure?" Sure enough, Charlotte called the first day. "I can't get hold of Kim. Did she come and get the girls?"

"What? Can't hear you. Must be a bad connection. Hang up and call me back."

When the phone rang ten minutes later, Treasure let it ring.

Finally she had to answer Charlotte's calls. She resorted to half fibs. "Girls? Yes, they're gone . . . since yesterday . . . I know it. . . . Now don't be blaming yourself. You did the best you could. Like you said, honey, they's no way one person can be two places at once. . . . Honey, I'm sure they'll be fine."

"She was trying not to cry," Treasure later told Kerilynn. "I feel real bad."

"She'll be thrilled when she comes home and finds the girls safe and sound right here in Ruby Prairie," said Kerilynn. "When do you think they'll be home?"

"Day after tomorrow's what Charlotte told me."

"Good. Heat's back on?"

"Toasty warm."

"Van running okay?"

"Fine as can be."

"Sounds like everything's set."

"Sure will be good when Charlotte gets back and all the girls are under this roof again," said Treasure. "I'm about to go crazy stirring around in this big old house by myself."

Charlotte called Pastor Jock the evening before Beth's scheduled discharge. "I hate to impose, but could you come get us?"

"Of course. Be there bright and early. Beth feeling all right?"

"I think so. She's in a wheelchair for now. Doctor says she'll be able to use crutches in four more weeks.

She'll need physical therapy later. Oh, I just remembered. You've got a truck. There won't be room for all three of us."

"Don't worry, I'll borrow Kerilynn's station wagon. I'm sure she won't mind."

Beth was quiet when Charlotte got off the phone.

"You okay?"

"What's it going to be like when I'm back? Is everybody mad at me?"

"No," said Charlotte. "They've all been worried about you. We prayed every day that you'd be safe and that you'd be back soon."

"I hope it's not weird," said Beth.

"It won't be for sure when we first get home. It'll be just you and me."

"Where's everybody else?"

"They had to go stay somewhere else while I was gone," said Charlotte.

"Where?"

"I'm not sure. Treasure said Kim came and got them. She didn't know any details. Soon as we're home we'll call Kim and let her know."

"I hope she didn't put them in a shelter," said Beth.

"Me too," said Charlotte.

"When will they be back?"

"I don't know."

Would they ever be back? How long would she have Beth? Charlotte didn't know. All those hours in the hospital, she'd had time to think. Perhaps she wasn't the woman for this job. Facts were facts. She'd tried her best, yet when a crisis came, she wasn't there for the girls. How awful it must have been for them to have to leave Tanglewood without any warning. Without her even telling them goodbye.

The morning of Beth's discharge, Charlotte's stomach was in knots over all she'd need to do when she got home. She made a list, then lost the list, then started another one.

Treasure had called every day to check on Beth. Charlotte asked her how things were, but she didn't learn much. Of the generation not believing in unnecessary long-distance calls, Treasure had not been inclined to talk long.

Once home there would be groceries to buy, her van to get fixed.

But first—how would they get Beth and her chair up the steps? How would they maneuver her wheelchair through the narrow doorway into the bathroom?

And what about the heat?

Charlotte's anxiety grew.

Pastor Jock was on time. The discharge doctor was early. A half hour before they'd expected, the three of them were loaded and on their way.

Charlotte was eager to get home, but Pastor Jock took his time. They got lost once, took a detour to see the outside of an old friend's new city church, and stopped at Dairy Queen for cherry Cokes.

Finally the Ruby Prairie city limits sign came into view. They turned the corner on Main Street and headed straight for Tanglewood.

Something was different in the front of the house. There was a ramp, built right beside the steps.

"What? Who? How?" Charlotte asked.

Pastor Jock turned in.

Her van, freshly washed and waxed, had been moved from the spot where it had died.

"Is it running again?"

Pastor Jock smiled.

Charlotte didn't see Treasure's van.

"I thought Treasure would be here. The heat must still be off," she said, remembering she'd never asked. Had she left a check to pay for the repairs? How could it have slipped her mind? For today anyway, she and Beth could bundle up.

Tanglewood appeared so still. Where were the cats? Charlotte hoped Treasure had at least remembered to come by and put food out.

Pastor Jock parked. Charlotte turned around to look at Beth. "We're home. Probably feels funny. You okay?"

When she turned back around, everything had changed.

Folks were streaming out the front door. Treasure and Kerilynn, Les and Ginger, Dr. Ross, Ben Jackson, Nomie and Sassy, Gabe and Chilly, and more. Charlotte was stunned.

"They hid their cars at the Collinses' house," said Pastor Jock. "Everyone wanted to give you a surprise welcome home."

Charlotte's eyes welled up. Knowing these folks,

there'd be food inside. No telling what else. She stepped out of the car and opened Beth's door. "That's so nice—" Then she saw the best surprise of all.

From around the side of the house appeared the girls. As soon as they saw Charlotte, they all began to run.

Nikki and Vikki flew into her arms first. "We missed you! You were gone so long."

Then Donna. "We're so glad you're home."

"We thought maybe you weren't never coming back," said Maggie. And Sharita chimed in, "I hope you don't have to leave again."

"When did you get here?" asked Charlotte, hugging all five of them at once, kissing them, laughing and crying all at the same time.

"What do you mean?" asked Maggie.

"We didn't go anywhere," said Nikki.

"Yes, we did," said Vikki. "Remember, the night we ate lasagna we did."

"Just that one night," said Maggie.

"Then we came home," said Donna.

Charlotte caught Pastor Jock's twinkling brown eyes. "Let's get Beth inside; then everyone can explain."

"Hope that paint's dry," said Gabe as they got ready to roll Beth up the just-built ramp.

"When did you do this?" asked Charlotte.

"Last night," said Gabe. "Didn't know you'd be needing it till late yesterday. None of us knew Beth would be in a wheelchair."

"Took us till two this morning," added Chilly with a grin.

"But we got it done. You feeling okay, sugar?" asked Gabe.

But Charlotte was speechless.

Chapter Twenty-five

Sure enough. Food to feed an army. The smell of lemon oil and Mr. Clean. Flowers. Balloons. A fluffy white teddy bear sitting next to the hearth.

Ruby Prairie had been at it again.

"The girls didn't even leave town?" Charlotte couldn't believe all her friends had done.

Fixed her van.

Repaired her heat.

Taken care of her girls.

No telling what else.

Exhausted, relieved, and overwhelmed, Charlotte tried to speak. Her shoulders shook. She bit her lip. She took a deep breath. None of that stopped her tears.

The room got quiet. Sympathetic eyes bathed her with love. Ginger took the girls to the kitchen to get them some lunch. "All the way home from the hospital today, I was trying to come up with a plan," Charlotte began.

Kerilynn handed her a tissue.

"I'd decided I was going to tell the social worker that she needed to come get Beth and to keep the others where they were, since I couldn't care for them as they deserved."

"You can't mean that," said Kerilynn. "They belong here."

"You can't quit," said Pastor Jock.

"I don't want to." Charlotte rolled the tissue into a damp little ball.

"You have to let us help you," said Dr. Ross.

"You have no idea how hard that is for me," said Charlotte.

"I do," said Treasure. "Lost my mama when I was young. I'm turned the same way as you. I've just got enough years on me to know better."

"Hon, every one of us wants to feel independent," said Dr. Ross. "These girls need you. Ruby Prairie needs you," said Ginger. "And like it or not, you need us," said Pastor Jock.

Charlotte nodded. "There's no way to say thank you for all you did this past week."

"Don't you see?" said Pastor Jock. "It was our pleasure—our joy." Charlotte nodded again.

"Kerilynn's come up with a schedule," said Pastor Jock. "Different ladies are going to help you on different days of the week. The men are going to take care of your yard and the maintenance on your van. Anything in the house that needs to be repaired, we'll take care of that too."

"That sounds wonderful," said Charlotte, meaning it. She sat up straighter in her chair. "I could use the help."

"Quick! Pastor, get that in writing," said Chilly.

Everybody laughed.

Catfish Martin, until now quiet in a corner, cleared his throat. "I got something I need to get off of my chest," he said. "I reckon now's as good a time as any. I'm part to blame for a lot of this mess."

Folks' ears perked up, but Charlotte cut him off. "Catfish—" she looked him square in the eye "—it wasn't your fault that we got stuck."

"That's not what I'm talking about. I'm talking about the ni—"

"Could have happened to anyone, wet as that ground was."

"I should have told some—"

"Catfish found Beth," said Charlotte. "I'm forever grateful. Without him, we wouldn't be here right now."

Puzzled expressions all around.

Charlotte held Catfish's gaze until he sat down.

Treasure spoke up. "Long as we're talking, there's something else you need to know," she said. "I've put it to prayer, and I aim to stay on permanent in Ruby Prairie. I like it here. Climate's good for my hands."

"Really?" said Charlotte. She'd thought Treasure would have to be going home soon, which had added to her worries about managing alone. "Will you stay on at Tanglewood? There's room, and the girls love you."

"Only if I can be of help to you."

"You've always been a help."

Treasure snorted. "I can be, but you've got to start letting me do more than feed the cats."

"I will," said Charlotte. "I promise."

"Anybody hungry?" asked Kerilynn.

"Let's have prayer," said Pastor Jock.

They joined hands and bowed their heads.

"Thank You, Father, for this good day. Thank You for bringing Beth home safe. We pray for her, the continued healing of her body and her soul. Bless this house. Bless Charlotte. Help us all to love as You loved, to serve as You served. In Jesus' name. Amen."

"Amen and amen," everyone agreed before heading to the kitchen.

Charlotte blew her nose.

Pastor Jock flashed her a smile.

She flashed him one back.

"After you," he said. "Let's have some cake."

Center Point Publishing
600 Brooks Road • PO Box 1
Thorndike ME 04986-0001 USA

(207) 568-3717

US & Canada:
1 800 929-9108